UNHINGED

IVANA ALMAND

authorHOUSE®

AuthorHouse™
1663 Liberty Drive
Bloomington, IN 47403
www.authorhouse.com
Phone: 1 (800) 839-8640

Published by AuthorHouse 04/09/2018

ISBN: 978-1-5462-3724-2 (sc)
ISBN: 978-1-5462-3723-5 (e)

Library of Congress Control Number: 2018904280

Print information available on the last page.

This book is dedicated to my husband, Luther, family, and friends who have been fully supportive and loving during this dream of mine to begin writing. They've sacrificed time reading horrible drafts and offering the best insight! Thank you Stevie, S.L., A.K., L.F. & R.L!

Contents

PROLOGUE

I woke today in a panicked sweat with tears streaming down my face and hands swollen from the scorching heat of a typical Texas July coupled with a broken A/C unit. I couldn't help but feel the tightness of my wedding bands around my slightly engorged finger. I couldn't seem to shake this claustrophobic feeling --I tried, I really tried. It didn't used to hit me this way, at least not consistently.

Some days I'd get this feeling like I couldn't breathe and would want to scream. Being honest, I am completely overwhelmed by my kids, my husband, and my entire life. I wasn't even twenty-five yet and ever since the birth of our beautiful son a few months ago, I can't stop wondering "How is this my life?" "How did I get here?" "What am I doing?"

Two children under the age of three, two car payments (one of which was the ever-dreaded mom mobile that was so practical you couldn't help but love it), tons of bills, and the endless barrage of seemingly mandatory play dates. I can't believe I've turned into a suburban mom, minus the awful haircut and jeans.

I'm sure I sound like one of those ungrateful and self-pitying housewives who should have nothing to complain about because I have been blessed with a great life. One where I don't have to work because my husband is a great provider and has an income that allows me the luxury of staying home to raise our children. I have the BEST in-laws a few hours away. My family is great too, but they are admittedly dysfunctional and mostly crazy. But the truth is, I'm alone in this life Brian and I have made together.

I had such big dreams when I was finishing up my final year of college. I knew I was going to get married, to presumably and hopefully, the love of my life. Although, can you ever really be one hundred percent sure? I wanted to get my Master's degree, work for a nonprofit to help those less fortunate like I had been, and my family, and my family's family and so on. I wanted to join the Peace Corps--do something truly meaningful. I knew doing these things would be a bit difficult because I was marrying a military man, future United States Air Force pilot, but figured we would make it work somehow. Besides, I loved the idea of being able to tell people that I was a pilot's wife.

I accepted that I would live wherever the government told us my husband was needed; there would be a lot of time apart due to training and deployments. Undoubtedly, it was going to be a sacrifice on both our parts to different extents. The idea of the unknown and the ability to move every couple of years used to be exciting to me. I always loved a man in a uniform, and I especially loved MY man in uniform, so it was nothing I couldn't handle. It was nothing that our love wouldn't be able to endure.

I would surely be able to find a legitimate online Master's degree program to complete since everything can be done online these days. The Peace Corps may not have been a viable option since I wasn't fond of leaving my new husband

and children, but I could work for a nonprofit wherever we moved, right? Why not? I could plan for the unexpected.

The imagined plan to being successful would work. We'd have a great life and things would be all happily ever after! Looking back, I know this was the young, disillusioned and idealistic version of myself. This was the energetic, hopeful and naive version of myself.

Unfortunately, the vision you have for your life and what actually happens rarely align. Life, and God, have a different way of paving their way through your reality. This is that story.

1

The Encounter

I was nineteen, midway through my sophomore year at the best university ever and free as a bird. I was the typical college girl. I had a perfectly toned, stretch mark-free body I was proud to show off, partied much more than I should have and semi-regularly attended class to at least enough to make mediocre grades and keep my scholarships.

I wanted to go to school far, far away from my crazy family but the cost of out-of-state tuition was insane. I didn't want to graduate with so much debt that I would have been chained to it for longer than it took to earn my degree. Thankfully, Texas is so massive, I could just move to the other side of the state and still be a full day's drive away.

I desperately wanted my freedom. I wanted to figure out who I was, independent of my loud and nosey family.

Freshman year went off without a hitch. It was great! I loved my major (International Affairs), kept my grades up, and was even awarded some extra scholarship money. I met my best friends, Mia and April. From the moment we met at orientation, we were inseparable. It's sad to admit now though that we're not even remotely as close as we once were. It's odd to think how things can change so drastically when actual adult responsibilities are thrown into the mix.

Despite our drastically different backgrounds, our personalities complimented one another so well you'd have thought we'd known each other all our lives. Mia had grown up in a large and wealthy Lutheran family. They went on mission trips every summer to places like Mexico, China and even New York. Mia hated every minute of it. She had a wild spirit and was utterly opposed to anything that would put her into a mold of what she was expected to be. April, on the other hand, was from a small, conservative and very Mormon family. They ate meals together whenever they were all home, attended church as a family and hated confrontation of any kind. Then there was me. The oldest in a large family raised by a single-mother, even larger and crazy extended family, substance abuse issues with almost every member and proud recipient of all kinds of government aid to ensure we had a fair shot at making it out of the ghetto.

I think our diverse upbringings were what drew us all together. We were all carefree. Loved to dance. Loved to party. Loved to laugh and make ridiculously inappropriate jokes. Mia, April, and I had our favorite go-to spots on Northgate where we'd always drink for free and were guaranteed a great night out.

They were like my sisters. We'd raid each other's closets, do each other's make-up and planned on moving to a big city together after we graduated. We had nothing but fun together. We'd make bets on who'd be the first to get a guy's number. It was almost a competition to see who could look the hottest and sexiest to pull the most numbers by the end of the night. Most of the time, we never went home with anyone but each other, but one-night stands were known to happen with Mia being the biggest offender. She had no problem strutting for her walk of shame.

We all loved one bar in particular-- *Gatsby's.* We knew the manager well so it was an ace-in-the-hole for fun. There was a raised platform along the back mirror lined wall that we'd often dance on which allowed us direct access to the DJ since his booth was connected to it. It was an extremely popular bar, and I'm sure it was in large part due to that platform that seemed to always be teaming with girls wanting to show off all their moves, whether they had any or not. Fortunately, I had plenty of moves. I'm not even ashamed to tell you now that if they offered frequent flier miles for how many times I had a guy hoist me onto that platform, I could probably fly around the world twice for free.

That warm night in March, for some reason, we decided to hit up a new bar called *Caliente.* It was the best little salsa bar! They offered mini lessons before eleven so everyone could learn a little something before the actual dancing began. I'd only been a handful of times but loved it for the simple reason that they played Spanish music. I didn't speak Spanish but had grown up listening to salsa music at my late grandmother's house. It always put me in a good mood and made me smile.

"I really want a change in scenery tonight," said Mia after taking a large sip of her drink while putting on her pumps.

"You up for some salsa and reggaetón tonight? You know, my kind of music," I replied while trying to make sure my panties wouldn't be seen if I bent over too far. As great of a place as *Caliente* was, we had to drive to get there so it was only once in a blue moon that we ventured that far away from the bars across the street from campus.

"That sounds fun. Maybe I'll meet a tall, dark, handsome, and hung Mexican guy!" said April while giving us her 'come to me' sexy face. At least she thought it was sexy. We always thought it made her look like a creepy, angry stalker.

I laughed and Mia rolled her eyes. "If you want hung, you don't want to go the Mexican route! You want to go Cuban or Columbian or something. At least that's what I've heard. I wouldn't know from personal experience," Mia said.

"Mia, as much personal experience as you do have, I would be completely stunned if you hadn't had a south of the border encounter yet!"

She tried to give me a dirty look but failed. We all had had our fair share of 'experiences' but Mia's level of expertise took the cake and we all knew it. It was part of the reason I was drawn to her. She was so open and honest about absolutely everything from sex to family to exactly how bad she was failing a class. We didn't keep any secrets from one another. There was never judgement or scolding for any of the bad decisions we'd made.

April, the designated conservative (I say this with every bit of love), would have to hide her shock and embarrassment at some of our stories, so we sometimes watered down the truth or just omitted certain details to spare her semi-pure conscience. Nonetheless, she was always there for either one of us when we needed her. We were family away from family and probably closer to each other than to our actual sisters.

Mia wasn't quite sold yet on *Caliente* but luckily April chimed in. "Well, how about if I drive, we stay for a little, come back, and then walk to the *Saloon* or *Halo* and then really finish off the night strong? I haven't been yet and I've heard it's fun! I'll even limit my drinks to two while we're there," said April.

She knew how much we both liked to loosen up a bit with the help of some kind spirited substance, preferably free, so when she volunteered to be the DD for the first part of the night, Mia and I were relieved.

"Sounds perfect to me. Mia???"

"Ok, that works. Let's only stay until about midnight though. Things will be in full swing at *Halo* or *Gatsby's* if that's where we go by then. Plus, there's this new guy I kind of want to meet up with later," said Mia as she gave us both a sly smile.

In Mia's language, that meant not to stand in the way of Mia and her latest phase. Her attention span with men was short and she tired easily. This made it difficult to keep track of her newest 'boyfriend' if you could even call them that. As a result, we made little effort to remember their names. By the time we did, she was off to find someone more exciting.

We all took one last shot of tequila to get into the festive move since we were going a bit ethnic to start the night off. We ran through our checklist of things we could not leave behind: phones, fake ID, debit card, lip-gloss and a hair band.

As we pulled into the bare parking lot, we immediately regretted driving there.

"This place looks deserted," Mia said, blatantly irritated.

"Well, we took the time to drive out here so we may as well go in. It's free cover for ladies, and besides, it's not even eleven yet. Most people are probably pre-gaming, and then it'll start to get busy. It'll be fine," I said. I was not leaving until I had at least gotten one or two really good salsa dances in with a great partner.

April seconded my motion so we got out and made our way towards the bouncer checking ID's outside the doors. Sure enough, it was empty but the music was going as though it was a packed house. They had already started the salsa lesson, and there were just enough guys there that we could have a slightly decent time before our designated departure time of twelve. We chose a table that faced the center of the dance floor and ordered three Long Islands.

We sat there talking and joking around about how some of the white guys looked. It was like they had two left feet or were already drunk since they couldn't seem to even bounce to the rhythm of the Elvis Crespo song, "Suavemente", that was blaring.

The salsa instructors, a very heavy set Hispanic man who wore large wide legged black slacks (almost like the kind Steve Harvey wears), a cheap button up silk shirt (also black) and a very petite and beautiful young Hispanic woman wearing extremely high heels and a tight dress that hugged all of her curves, seemed to think they had done enough instructing and opened up the dance floor for everyone else. Some of the patrons though, mostly men, could have used an extra few minutes or even thirty more seconds of instruction. They were off beat with most of their steps and looked more like robots in their jarred movements.

A couple of the guys walked over to our table and asked us to dance. I had seen their unimpressive moves during the lesson and politely declined. April and Mia weren't discouraged by their dismal attempts. They weren't the salsa dancing 'aficionado' that I was and couldn't tell if their dancing attempts had been awful or just cute. I looked to Mia and April and gave them a smile and mouthed "Have fun".

Mia whispered to me, "Are you sure you don't want to at least do one dance and get a drink out of it? They're not bad to look at."

"I'll pass for now. As awful as they were out there, no thanks. I don't want to be someone's teacher. Plus, a guy who can't dance even a little is a big turn off. Go have fun! You know me, I'll be fine. I make friends wherever I go."

"If you say so. Be back soon," Mia said as she gave me a flirty wave.

They both scurried off to the half empty dance floor with their partners. Mia went for the tall and super skinny, brunette guy that had a semi large nose that worked oddly with his face. This left April with no choice but to dance with the other, an average looking guy. So average in fact, I wouldn't have been able to pick him out of a line up. The last one decided to hang around kind of sweetly since he thought I could use the company. He was cute- much taller than me, auburn hair, brown eyes, lightly tanned skin. He just wasn't my type. He was also extremely odd and awkward.

When he first spoke, he thought it appropriate to lead with "I saw you guys walk in and your ass looks amazing! So... do you and your friends come here a lot? Sorry, by the way, I'm Drew."

Drew had zero social awareness. He kept trying to rub my hand and arm. Every time I moved, he moved to get closer. He sat in my personal space and kept leaning in to talk straight at my face rather than just yell over the music or lean in to talk into my ear. Each time he opened his mouth, a smell that could only be described as a combination of bad fish, Fritos and rotten eggs seeped out. He drew out all his *h* and *o* sounds, further intensifying the onslaught of mouth sewage. Everything about him was just creepy.

"Um, ok. Thanks, I guess. No, we don't really come here often. It's kind of far from the dorms. We prefer not to have to drive when we go out." I tried to scoot my chair over, but Drew was oblivious to my discomfort and continued to slide his chair right over.

"That's cool. I could always be your DD or back up to call. I'm on probation right now for doing a bunch of stupid shit so I'm not supposed to drink. I'm always the DD for my friends," he smiled like this was a remarkably endearing fact.

I gave him an awkward smile and scanned the dance floor for Mia and April. April spotted me first so I gave her my best crazy eyes look that screamed "Help". She whispered something in her dance partner's ear and then pointed towards the bar. He walked in that direction and she made a beeline to the table.

She smiled and said, "Whew, your friend is a really good dancer. I was so out of breath I had to ask for a drink break." I could tell she was trying to get Drew to offer to go to the bar for me, but he either didn't pick up on it or simply figured if I wasn't going to dance or grind on him during the next song it wasn't worth the money. Either way, he stayed put and April's dance partner, Mike, was already headed back to our table with her drink.

Before Mike could reach our table I half coughed and half cleared my throat and said, "I should probably go grab a drink or something. My throat's a little scratchy and my current glass is empty. We'll be right back. April, can you come with real quick?" We both smiled. I grabbed her hand and we walked to the bar quickly.

"That guy is super weird. You may like him though. He's on probation for something so he could be your DD whenever you need one! Boom, built-in chauffer," I said as I flagged the bartender down. "Please don't leave me alone with him! He seems a little off."

April threw her head back and started laughing hysterically. "You sure know how to attract some winners. Let's get your drink, and I won't leave the table unless it's to dance with you!"

I ordered my drink and told her it was a deal. We went back to the table and to my luck, our suitors had disappeared, and Mia was sitting alone wondering what happened. We got back, sat down and briefed her. Unlike April, she didn't think my creepy encounter was nearly as hysterical and told us the guys had decided to hit up some pool bar, and they hoped we'd meet up later. It wasn't in the cards.

The traffic in the club started to pick up and the dance floor started filling up. There was a big group pushing tables together and it looked like they were settling in for a night at *Caliente*. On the outskirts of the group I saw HIM.

He was more than hot, he was drop-dead handsome—young Clint Eastwood handsome. Tall with nicely styled brown hair that was shorter on the sides and long enough on the top that he could style it a little like Brad Pitt. I could even see his piercing blue eyes from the dance floor. He had rolled the sleeves of his shirt slightly so you could see his impressive forearms which was further accentuated by a nice tan. He was definitely my type. I instantly had butterflies in my stomach when I saw him. The simple act of potentially speaking to him made my stomach lurch and cause beads of sweat to form under my arms. I couldn't tell if it was love or lust at first sight, but there was something about him that instantly drew me to him. We briefly locked eyes, and I gave him a small smile and turned to dance with my friends. When it was over, we sat down at our table and I told them about the guy in the big group to our left.

"Which one are you talking about?" asked Mia as she took a big sip of my drink. She stared blatantly, looking and pointing asking, "Him? Him? That one?"

"Stop it! I don't want him to know we're talking about him. That would be so embarrassing. He's the one to the far left sitting down," I said feeling the heat in my face rise.

"Oooooh! He IS gorgeous!" shouted April.

"I know! I'm all sweaty and nervous. I want to talk to him, but I want him to talk to me first," I said wiping my palms on my shirt.

"Just grow some balls and go over and ask him to dance," said Mia as she took another long sip of my drink.

Just then, one of the guys from my crush's group came over and sat down next to me.

"Hey! I'm Ryan. My friend over there thinks you're cute but is too shy to ask you to dance. He doesn't know that I'm asking you to ask him so don't say anything if you do decide to go over and ask him," he winked and left.

I could feel my cheeks starting to get red again. He had noticed me or at least noticed I had stared at him earlier. Mia nudged my leg from under the table. She found Ryan and asked him to dance. April and I casually walked over to the group to introduce ourselves. I found the most direct route to the gorgeous man in the group.

It had started to get loud by that point, so I had to yell into his ear to talk. "Hi," was apparently all I could muster to say. Smooth, right?

"Hi. I'm Brian. Nice to meet you." He gave me the warmest smile. He had perfect teeth and a magnificent mouth. His bottom lip was slightly full and his top lip was just slightly thinner than his bottom. When he smiled, the corners of his mouth turned up, just a touch, and his eyes brightened with it. I couldn't help but want to kiss him.

His smile made my heart stop. It was that feeling you get when you're at the top of a roller coaster and you're about to drop. You know you're about to drop, but you're still anxious and excited. Then the coaster starts going down the highest part of the track and your stomach feels like it's in your throat for a second. You feel weightless for an instant. It was fear, happiness, and wonder all at once. It was pure adrenaline running through my body, unlike anything I had ever experienced and instantly, I knew he was "the one".

As cliché as it sounds, my love or lust instantly clarified itself for me, and he was IT. I didn't know him from Adam (yet) but there was an instant connection. In those brief seconds of introduction, we both could feel it. I hadn't experienced anything even close to that before. He put his hand on my lower back and leaned in close to yell into my ear to see if I wanted to dance. I smiled and just shook my head yes. It was as if I had turned into a mute all of a sudden.

We were dancing and I yelled to him that he was, and I quote, "a good dancer for a white guy." He started laughing and said I was pretty good myself. It was so loud on the dance floor that holding a conversation was pointless so we just danced. It was already eleven fifty so that meant his Cinderella had to get ready to leave. We got in another dance before Mia started waving to me to hurry up. Brian and I made our way back to the table.

"Sorry but it looks like my time's up. My friends and I made a deal on how long we'd stay so I've got to head out. We're heading over to *Halo* or *Gatsby's* if you and your friends decide to go to Northgate."

"I'll see if they're up for it. We just got here not too long ago so most of them will probably want to stay for a while but why don't you give me your number, and I'll call or text you later and see where you're at."

"Sure!" I sounded overly enthusiastic, turning into one of those puppy dog type of girls in the blink of an eye. I instantly wanted to cringe at my reaction but tried to play it off. He put my number into his phone and gave me a small peck on the cheek (butterflies!). I got one last glimpse as I waved and was ushered out by Mia.

All I could think about was when Brian would call. He seemed different from every other guy I had ever talked to. He was genuinely nice and an authentic, true-blood gentleman. I leaned my head back on the passenger side headrest, closed my eyes with the biggest smile on my face.

"What's with you? Feeling ok?" Mia asked.

I looked at her like a giddy school girl. "Better than ok. I'm going to marry that guy one day." I could hear them laughing as I stared out the window thinking about Brian.

2

Whirlwind

It had been four long and excruciating days since I'd met Brian. I hadn't heard a peep from him. I had started to think I really was crazy. Maybe Brian was just a nice guy but wasn't into me the way I thought. Maybe the connection was one sided. Then he called. Thrilled was an understatement. I won't bore you with the details of that first conversation since it was rather short, but it was long enough to make our first official date.

We both had time the next evening (a Wednesday) for dinner so we settled on meeting outside my dorm at six. I wasn't a fan of a mid-week date because it meant we'd probably be on a time crunch. I had an eight am class the next day but was just happy we had finally made plans to go out. If things went well, I was sure there'd be a second date.

As soon as I got off the phone, I realized my cheeks were burning. I'd been smiling from ear to ear during and after our brief conversation. I couldn't wait to tell the girls so I picked up my cell and immediately called Mia.

"Guess who finally called?!!" I yelled into the phone.

"Whoa! Chill out for a second before I go deaf over here," whispered Mia.

I toned it down just enough so as not to blow her eardrum out. "Oops, Sorry. I forgot you were in the library studying. Brian! Brian finally called me! We are going out tomorrow which means I'll need help getting ready. Are you free in the afternoon?"

"That's great. I'm so glad he finally wised up and called because I was going to hunt him down if I had to hear you talk anymore about why he hadn't called yet." She was still whispering and I'm sure fielding off dirty looks from anyone who was sitting close by.

"I know. Sorry. I've been kind of obsessed the past few days but I really like this guy. There's something about him. Anyways, I don't want to keep you since you're studying, but seriously, are you free tomorrow late afternoon?"

"Yes I'm free, and yes I'll help you look gorgeous! I'll call you when I leave the library and am headed back to the dorms."

Mia didn't have to live in the dorms. Unlike mine, her family was well-off and could afford an off-campus apartment for her, but after we met freshman year, she told her parent's dorm living was convenient and wouldn't mind staying on campus for sophomore year. Mia, April, and I had planned on living on campus until the end of sophomore year so I could save up for an apartment. We were going to rent a three bedroom and split the costs of everything. I had a part-time job that would suffice enough to pay whatever bills we'd take on. Until then, we were perfectly content living next door to each other in Sanders Hall.

Mia and April both knew how OCD I was when it came to my personal space and cleanliness of my living area. Dorm rooms were about as big as a sardine can, so I paid a bit extra for a single room, otherwise, we'd have loved to live together.

My OCD habits probably stem from the fact that I'm the oldest of six kids and lived in a house with them, my two cousins, my aunt, my mother and my mother's loser boyfriend. It was a packed house in a neighborhood where most of the homes qualified for Section eight housing.

There were a ton of little children constantly roaming unsupervised, and we seemed to always have pet roaches that we couldn't get rid of. I was always scared to use the bathroom at night because the minute I would flick a light on, you'd see a handful scurry away to some unknown place that you could never quite seem to find. Between the people and roaches, there was always someone watching what you were doing. Needless to say, privacy was a much-appreciated novelty that I didn't want to give up anytime soon.

I headed out for my next class but stopped at April's room and left a note on the little whiteboard on her door saying, "Future 'hubby' called. First date tomorrow! Call later. Hugs!"

I was already excited and nervous. After how dumb I sounded during our first introductions, I was glad I'd get a second chance to make a better impression. I just needed to keep my cool and act normal. Not like some high school nerd that was finally asked out by the popular star football player.

Mia and April both came to my room with several pieces of clothing so I could find something that was cute, form fitting, but not slutty. That was the key. Look gorgeous and hot, but not easy.

"Ok, what look are you going for tonight exactly? Nerdy chic, sexy stripper, plain Jane? I could keep going if you need more options," said Mia.

"Hmmm," I said while scanning the large pile of clothes the girls had brought over. "I need to keep it a little classy. I don't want him to get the wrong impression."

"Good call. Even if you are willing to put out, he doesn't need to know that right away," Mia winked at April who just smiled and nodded.

"I really like the floral blouse. It's super cute and doesn't show too much. It could work." April put a purple and blue blouse covered in a monstrous floral print that even had a silk bow you could tie at the neckline up to my chest so I could see what it would look like.

"Um, thanks, but not for tonight. It looks like something I'd wear to church or an office party, not a date. I need to impress Brian and not have him think I'm a nun, or worse, a Mormon." Mia and I always liked to give April a hard time for being Mormon. She wasn't a practicing Mormon, but her family was. We thought they were a little crazy and resembled a cult.

"Ha ha. Real funny," April said as she threw her blouse back on the bed.

"Here, this one is pretty and not grandma looking at all." Mia handed me a nice blouse from the top of the pile.

It was a beautiful semi-low-cut pink cotton candy colored sleeveless blouse that perfectly accentuated my tan and toned arms. "Perfect! Now I just need something to cover my ass."

Mia threw a pair of cute navy skinny ankle pants at me. "These should fit and will look great with that top."

I slid my shorts off and went to try the pants on.

April gasped and started laughing. "You sure you're not going to put out on the first date? You put one of your nice thongs on and shaved!"

"Hey, don't judge. You never know where the night will lead. Wouldn't want to miss out on anything," I continued to slide the pants on while smiling at the mere thought of what sex with Brian might be like. A guy that gorgeous had to be great in bed. In all honesty, I didn't want to give anything up so quickly, at least not with Brian right away.

"Well, finding the winning outfit didn't take long," said Mia.

I put on my nude sandal wedges and was pretty satisfied myself.

"What are you doing with your hair? Do you want me to curl it for you?" April asked.

"No, I'm just going to straighten it. It's easier and the flat iron is already on." I didn't have nice hair that I could just wash and go and have it dry perfectly. I didn't have curly hair, but it dried with funky kinks. Some would be straight and everything else would be all frizz. It was awful.

"Please let me do your makeup? Not that you're not naturally beautiful, but you need a little makeup and we all know you're not great at applying it." Mia always poked fun at the fact that at the old age of nineteen, I barely owned any cosmetics. The little that I did own, I barely knew how to use properly. Still, as an adult, I don't know the difference between concealer and foundation. They could be the same thing, and I would never know.

"Of course you're doing my makeup! I can't go looking like a savage, can I?" I winked.

Twenty minutes later, I was completely made over and ready to go.

"I don't look too shabby." I said while giving myself the one over in the mirror.

"You look incredible! If he doesn't want to jump your bones when he sees you, I will!" Mia said. Her sense of humor was sometimes meant as a joke but sometimes meant as a confession of some sort.

"That's probably not happening tonight. Not the first date! Maybe the second though," I said with a sly smile.

It was almost show time. Mia and April both had an exam the following day so they left to start studying. I sat at my desk going over all the topics we could discuss that was first date appropriate. I didn't want it to be boring or have that awkward first date silence so I prepped.

There's probably nothing I've ever hated more than first dates. They're so incredibly awkward most of the time, and I have always been very aware that I am out with a total stranger who could possibly kill me on a back road somewhere or be the next President. You never know.

I ran through a quick list in my head of acceptable talking points: family was an ok topic, but steer clear of the bipolar mom and drug addict absentee father which might scare him off; school was safer, major, future career wishes, etc., much more normal; hobbies, but I might come across as an old lady if I mentioned my pack rat tendencies and scrap-booking past-time. It was probably safest to avoid my love of Sudoku and stick to exercise and writing.

I let out a sigh and realized it was exactly six. I looked out my window that faced the courtyard and saw Brian standing there waiting, looking at his watch. My heart immediately starting pounding, and I could already tell my talking points would turn out disastrously. I was already nervous and beginning to sweat. I grabbed my purse, put my lip gloss on, said a quick prayer, and headed out.

I couldn't tell you what he was wearing, but I know it was perfect. I couldn't stop staring at his face. He had such gorgeous eyes and that great, mesmerizing mouth. He greeted me with a big smile and a hug.

"You look beautiful."

"Thank you. I wasn't sure where we were going so hopefully what I'm wearing is fine." I could feel my cheeks burning and was reeling that he'd called me beautiful. No one had ever used that term before except family, which didn't count. I wasn't used to such a gentlemanly type of man. Words like hot and fine were usually all some of the other guys I dated could seem to think of.

We walked to the parking lot adjacent to my dorm. He kept his hand on the small of my back so he could guide me to where we needed to go. I had butterflies in my stomach.

"It's really nice out today. Not too hot or too cold" I said. *Idiot,* I thought! Of course, it wouldn't be too hot or too cold, we had just barely started spring.

Brian was so sweet though. He smiled and said, "It is. I love spring. It's probably my favorite time of year."

"Me too," I paused. "Well actually, now that I think about, it may be a tie between spring and fall. I like watching how the leaves on the trees change color. It's so pretty." I sounded like a ditz.

We got to his car, thankfully, and he opened my door for me. He drove a well-loved (I say this as nice as possible but it really looked like a hunk of junk that was at least fifteen years old) red Chevy Tahoe that had seen better days, but it was better than what I had, which was nothing yet. As he shut the door, I took a deep breath, and tried to pull myself together so I could talk about something and not sound like a total flake.

"Do you want to eat anything in particular or have a place in mind?"

"No. Surprise me." I wanted to come across as a laid back and go with the flow type of person, which I wasn't and still am not. I've always been a planner. Very particular about everything, except when it comes to my type of guy. If they were smart and could make me laugh, that was my type. If they were pretty to look at, that was an added bonus.

"Ok. Do you like barbeque?" he asked.

"Of course. How can you be a Texan and not like barbeque? That's like sacrilege." I was proud of myself for that comment. I wanted to show him I was funny and smart, though I couldn't tell if I was succeeding.

He let out a small laugh and agreed. "Very true. Does Dickey's sound alright?"

"I actually haven't been there yet. It'll be nice to branch out."

As he pulled into the parking lot, I have to admit I was disappointed and regretted not picking a place myself. It wasn't the kind of atmosphere you think of when you're on a first date. Barbeque doesn't exactly scream romantic.

The smell of charcoal and fire was in the air from their smokers out back and the 'restaurant' (I use the term loosely) looked more like an old warehouse outside. As we walked in, it didn't get much better.

The seating options consisted of numerous picnic tables (no tablecloths) lined up in rows and the menu was a large board behind a big counter where you had to wait in line to place your order. Definitely not ideal but hey, maybe the conversation would get better, and maybe we'd even end the night with a nice first kiss.

Unfortunately, the conversation was terribly awkward. I would have preferred getting a tooth or two pulled sans anesthesia if that meant skipping the whole thing.

"So, uh, what do you like to do for fun?" I asked sounding lame.

"You know, the usual," he replied, followed by a silent pause.

I waited for more of a response. When there wasn't one, I fought to keep the conversation alive. Though all I could come up with was, "Cool, like what?"

"Um, I don't know. I've gone skiing a few times in Colorado. I really liked that. I also run."

"Wow, skiing? Must be nice." Another silent pause, this time from me.

"What about you?" We both took turns like this. Our eyes darting either across the room or down at our paper baskets filled with barbeque to avoid eye contact. The whole thing was like some terrible Diane Sawyer interview. Though there were a few bright spots.

"What do you plan on doing after you graduate?" I asked.

"I have a contract with the Air Force so I'll commission as an officer. I really want to fly, preferably fighter jets, but those spots are really hard to come by." The way his face lit up when he talked about flying was the cutest thing.

"Fly? That's pretty awesome. So, are they helping with school then?"

"No, I'm actually on a full track scholarship. I've been running since I was four or five so I'm pretty good at it." While some guys could have said this and sounded like a total stuck up asshole, Brian sounded modest. I think he realized how I may have interpreted it because he quickly added, "I'm definitely not the best on the team though. Not by a long shot. What about you? Any big plans after you graduate?"

"Well, I'd love to join the Peace Corps or find some organization where I could work abroad somehow, but I need to sit down and talk to my academic advisor and really see what my viable options are. I just want to do something meaningful. Make a difference somehow. I don't want to sound cheesy, but I really do want to make the world a better place." I looked down at my food.

"That's great. There aren't a lot of people who'd be willing to give up a comfortable life here to go to some third-world country."

"Thanks. I appreciate that. My friends, Mia and April, you met them at the club, anyways, they think I'm setting my goals a little too high and should be a bit more realistic about how I can 'save the world'. That's all too deep for a first date though…. What's your family like?"

"They're pretty normal people. My parents have been married for over twenty years. They both taught in the one and only high school in my town but are retired now. I have a twin sister who goes to school here, but we're not real close. She likes to do her own thing. And we have one dog and one cat, Pete and Daisy. All normal."

It all was so cookie cutter to me and almost foreign that a family could be so small and perfect. When he asked me about my family, I kept it very vague.

"Oh, I'm Hispanic so you can correctly assume that I come from a pretty loud and large family. I'm the oldest of six. My mom's a little crazy but she raised us pretty much by herself. I don't really talk to my dad. We're a pretty normal large family." The term normal is relative right? He didn't need to know every detail right away.

In total, our first date only lasted about an hour and a half and that included travel time to and from the dorms. The drive back was right in line with the rest of the date--slightly awkward and silent.

He walked me back to my dorm. "I had a great time tonight."

"Me too. Thanks for dinner." To say I was disappointed in how the overall date went was an understatement.

He leaned in and gave me a peck on the cheek. "I'll call you soon. I'd really like to see you again," he said politely.

"Yeah, same here." I thought he was nice for lying. As much as I'd hoped there'd be a second date, I wasn't going to hold my breath.

To my surprise, around midnight I got a text from Brian to come outside for a minute but he didn't say why. I hurried out without even checking myself in the mirror--big mistake. As I walked out I saw he had set up the most adorable mini picnic under a large tree in the courtyard of my dorm. He even had a single rose for me.

I was shocked. Not only had I not expected to hear from him again, I certainly didn't expect to see him so soon and looking disheveled in my overly large sweats, mismatched shirt, flip flops, and no make-up. I'm pretty sure I looked like a hobo.

The evening had cooled a bit making it perfect for a midnight picnic. There were clear skies but it smelled like rain. The breeze was just light enough that a few wisps of my hair were gently moving across my face. Like I said, perfect. He had laid a large grey and plaid sleeping bag down and pulled out some snacks from a plastic bag from the C-store--two packs of cheese filled crackers, some Twix bars, one individually wrapped banana nut muffin, one blueberry muffin, some water, and cokes. Not everything could be perfect. I mean, what male college sophomore brings a picnic basket to school? It was the thought and effort that struck me most.

"I didn't know what you liked to eat, so I just got a little of everything," he said nervously. There was that smile again. For the first time, his confidence waivered. It was endearing and made me fall for him even more.

I gave him a big smile back and looked down at all the loot before me and went straight for the Twix. "This is perfect. What are you doing here? I mean, this is so incredibly sweet but earlier was a bit… awkward. Don't you think?"

He looked down at his hands and then back up at me with those gorgeous eyes that seemed to be even bluer in the evening light than they did during the day. He let out a small laugh, "Um, yeah. It was, but most first dates are, right? I figure now that we got the awkwardness out of the way we could have a real date. I know it's late and we both have an early class, but I figured the sooner, the better."

"That sounds good to me. Sorry about earlier, like you said, first dates are uncomfortable, but this is really, really nice."

We sat there picking at all the junk food and talked for the next four hours. It was perfect. I know I've said that word a lot but you get few moments in life where it's actually true, and this was one of them. We talked about anything and everything from our favorite sports teams (Cowboys for both of us), to favorite classes (history for me and management for him) and even our family. I felt myself telling him things I'd never even told Mia and April. It wasn't that I didn't trust them inherently, but there was such a sense of comfort with Brian that I couldn't explain. He didn't even flinch. In fact, he seemed to think it was extremely interesting.

"So what's a typical day at home like? I know you said you have a big family but what was it like growing up with so much family? There's only a handful of my family so I couldn't imagine. It must have been so much fun."

"Well, since you asked… I'll be one hundred percent honest, just brace yourself for crazy. Someone is always yelling at someone else, especially my sister and me. We don't get along very well. I remember this one time, we got into a knock down drag out fist fight in the living room. Instead of my mother breaking us up, she locked us in our room to fight it out or talk it out. Of course, we chose to continue fighting it out. I ended up with claw marks on my arms and neck and she ended up with a busted lip and chunk of hair missing." I started laughing just thinking about how crazy that fight was. I couldn't even remember why we had started fighting.

"Man. That bad? All siblings fight like that though, right? I only have my sister, and I'm sure my parents would have killed me if I'd had hit her," he said with a chuckle and smile in his voice.

"Oh we didn't fight like that all the time, but there's a lot of us so it's bound to happen. I do love my family, I really do. It's just that I'm very different than the rest of them. I've never had that desire to stay close so I can help out and keep up with crazy. I always knew once I got to college, I was gone. I visit but don't think I'll ever actually move back."

"I understand that. I won't ever move back home either. Different reasons though. It's just too small of a town. I don't know what I'd do for work there. After the Air Force anyways. I have to go where they send me.... What about your dad? Do you talk to him at all?"

"No. He's always been on and off drugs and really wasn't around after I turned about five or six. I don't want a relationship with him anymore. He's never been around to begin with so what's the point now? To be honest, I don't even know where he is anyways." I shrugged and changed the subject. It always made me a little sad and angry at how easy it was for my dad to just walk away and not even look back. I didn't want to spend my time talking or thinking about him.

"Sorry. I didn't mean to upset you or anything. I didn't realize..."

"It's ok. It is what it is. Anyways, how's your family? Any black sheep?"

"Nope. We're extremely boring people. Trust me. I'm assuming you have a few in your family?" He smiled at me.

I started laughing. "How'd you know? Oh! I have to tell you this story. You'll either find it hilarious or run for the hills. I happen to think it's hilarious. So, over winter break, one of my crazy uncles broke into my other nut job uncle's house to steal a TV. It had been snowing and my burglar uncle literally left a trail of footprints from my uncle's house to his house around the corner. When my uncle called the police to report it, my cousin, a 9-1-1 dispatcher just happened to answer the call to an 'Oh Shit! That you Dre?!' Obviously, my uncle was arrested for breaking and entering and theft. They're all a little out there. I've asked my mom many times if she isn't sure that I wasn't secretly adopted."

Brian hadn't taken off full sprint away from me yet so we kept talking about our families. Any story he thought was crazy or odd for his family was easily beat by mine. Living in a place where the most scandalous thing to happen is a slightly out of hand party by teens in the middle of a farmer's field doesn't lend itself to great storytelling. At least not in my opinion. Brian kept laughing hysterically, which made me laugh. I'm sure we woke up half the dorm, but we had such a great time. We were so at ease with one another. It was as though everything just fell into place and nothing was difficult. Nothing was off limits.

When I looked at my phone hours later and realized it was almost four-thirty in the morning, I slightly panicked.

"Oh my god. I can't believe what time it is. I have class in less than four hours."

"Is it really that late?" asked Brian.

"Yeah. Guess I better head in and at least get a nap before I have to get up. This was really nice. I'm glad our second date was infinitely better than the first," I said beaming.

"Me too. I have classes all day tomorrow. I guess we're in tomorrow already, so today. Then I have a group meeting for a project in one of my classes but if you're free Friday, want to do something?"

"I'd like that. Just call me."

He walked me to the door so he could open it after I swiped my ID to get in--such a gentleman. He held the door open and as I started to pass in front of him to get inside, he gently grabbed my right hand so that our fingers interlocked, pulled me in, hesitated a moment looking into my eyes, and gently kissed my lips.

His lips were as soft as rose petals. There were more than sparks going off—it was like fireworks. It only lasted about fifteen seconds but was just enough to give me those gigantic flutters in the pit of my stomach. We both smiled at each other and reluctantly said good night.

As I got to my room, I was walking on air. It was the best second date I'd ever had and the best first kiss I'd ever had. If I was being really honest, it was the best date and best kiss period. All I could do was count the minutes and seconds until Friday evening when we'd see each other again. I was so happy I was sure I'd dream of sunshine and unicorns that shit out rainbows and all that other magical stuff. But I was utterly exhausted and I slept hard and straight through my first and second class of the day. It was worth it.

The next few weeks were incredible. It was a whirlwind romance. After that second date, Brian and I were either texting constantly or just together—I'd practically moved in to his tiny apartment that he shared with one other guy. Mia and April were starting to get a little upset with me because I had pretty much dropped off the grid since Brian entered the picture. If I wasn't in my dorm, I was at Brian's.

April and Mia walked into my room with sullen, nervous looks on their faces.

"What gives?" I asked hesitantly. "You guys ok?"

After a minute of silence, it was Mia that broke it. "Actually, no. You've been virtually MIA since Brian came around. We don't see you, we don't hear back from you. We're worried you're going to back out on us at the end of the year when it's time to move into our apartment." She hadn't taken a breath during her outburst.

April interrupted, "Look, I get it. Mia does too. You're really into Brian, but you've kind of left us out to dry. We want you to be happy, just don't forget about us. We love you."

I sighed. I felt utterly guilty. "I'm sorry. I know I haven't been around, but I am still moving in with y'all! Don't worry. Things are just… different with Brian. He's so, so… I just can't explain it."

"He's lucky he's gorgeous and we like him or else I'd be way more upset," Mia said, "But you need to make more of an effort with us. Our little trifecta is all thrown off now. I feel like we don't ever see you anymore."

"I know. I'm really sorry. How about we schedule girls' nights or something. We can go out, eat, whatever. And there will be minimal talk about how dreamy Brian is," I said half-jokingly. Talk revolving around Brian would probably be difficult to avoid.

"Geez. If you can pencil us in, that'd be great!" Mia said sarcastically.

April interjected, "I think what she meant to say was thank you, but let's let our girl time be organic. If we all have time, great. Bottom line is, just make an effort to be a little more present for us. We miss you!"

"Ok, fine.... How's the sex? I've got to know. With a body like that, man! He's tall too so is he packing?" asked Mia with a big overly, enthusiastic smile at the thought of the details of his package. I ignored her.

"Well, we actually haven't yet," I said a little embarrassed.

"WHAT! All these weeks you've spent ditching us and y'all aren't even doing it? What kind of crap is that?" Typical, fast Mia.

"Just chill out Mia. It's not that big of a deal, and it's kind of nice. Refreshing. But really, why haven't you?" asked April with a sheepish curiousity.

"We just haven't." I confessed with embarrassment.

"But why haven't you? Is he a closet gay? You can tell us." Mia said probingly.

"Honestly, if it were up to me, we'd have done the deed two or three weeks ago but Brian wants to wait a little. He's not a virgin or anything like that, but he thinks what we have is really special and wants to wait a little longer."

"Wow," said Mia, she was floored. "That is probably the cheesiest thing I've ever heard! Are you sure he's not gay?"

"Mia! Don't be rude. I think that's great. Honestly, I do. It'll mean so much more when you two finally do 'do it'." April was fully supportive of Brian's reasoning.

"Thank you. I really did think something was up when he first stopped me from trying to rip his clothes off, but now I think it's a good idea. We're still getting to know each other better and I really am falling for him. I don't mind waiting. It's not that we haven't done stuff, just not the full sha-bang stuff. Trust me, when it happens, you two will be the first I tell."

"I guess that makes sense but jeez, you two have been with each other nonstop for what, two months now," said Mia, resigned to the fact that I didn't have any juicy details for her. "Well, to each their own I suppose.

"In other news," I said changing the subject, "he wants me to meet his parents soon. Fingers crossed, it'll go well."

3

Meet the Parents: Round 1

Finals for the semester wound down which meant doing nothing but light studying and a relaxing by the pool at the rec center on campus with Brian. Mia, April, and I began our apartment hunt.

It looked like I was going to finish off the semester with decent grades, even with all the slacking off I'd been doing by spending so much time with Brian. It was hard to study when we were together because it was so easy to just lay in bed and do nothing. And no, we still hadn't gone all the way. By then we were both so nervous that it was almost too scary a thought to pop the cherry. We, or at least I had anyways, built up how great it would be in my head that it would be too much to bear if the entire thing was a disappointment.

There were two weeks of a break between the end of finals and the start of the first summer session, so Brian and I decided that one of those weekends would be a great time to meet his parents. Seeing as how I still didn't have a car, and I had no desire to go home in between semesters, we decided Brian was going to drive us to his parents' house for an entire weekend. I would've been fine with just a quick one day and back visit, but he wanted me to see his hometown and introduce me to some of his friends.

"I really think this weekend will be fun. I'm sure my parents will love you and so will my friends. You have nothing to worry about. Just trust me," Brian said with reassurance.

"It's not that I don't want to meet your parents, I just don't know if ramming me down their throats for an entire weekend is the best way to gradually introduce me to them. There is the chance that they won't like me and the whole trip will be a nightmare." I really didn't want to be stuck for two full days if I didn't hit it off with them, especially his mom.

"It's not that long and we'll do things during the day so it's not like we'll be in my parent's house the whole time. It'll be fine. Please, just come, and don't stress out," he pleaded.

He'd finally worn me down and I'd hesitantly agreed. "Fine, we'll go and plan to stay the weekend, but if the trip turns out to be a total disaster and your parents end up hating me, we are out of there. We'll tell them Mia and April ate some bad sushi and need some help recovering. Ok?"

He just laughed at me. "Ok. I think you're being ridiculous, but ok."

It was a few days before we were set to head to Brian's house and school was finally done! Mia, April, and I had just signed our six-month lease on a great three-bedroom, three bath apartment that included our utilities, internet, and furniture. It was on the bus route to campus and had a pool. We were beyond excited to move in and feel more like adults. All we had to do was move our belongings from our perspective dorm rooms. The added bonus, it was in the same apartment complex as Brian's.

Since we wanted to get settled as quickly as possible, Brian generously offered to volunteer himself and a few friends with trucks to helps us so we could get it done in one trip and then spend the rest of the day lounging and drinking by the pool.

"I cannot believe we are finally out of the dorms! Free at last, free at last, thank God almighty, we are free at last!" yelled Mia like a crazy person as we moved our last box of junk into the living room of our apartment.

"Yes! Thank goodness! Now, who wants a beer?" I asked.

Before anyone could answer, I was already passing beers around the room. Brian and his friend had picked up a case of beer for us since they were the only ones of legal age. The girls and I ordered some pizzas as a big 'thank you' for moving all our stuff in.

While we waited for the delivery guy, we unpacked just enough to find our pool stuff and get ready. Our apartment looked like a bomb had gone off in every room. It made my skin crawl slightly, but I was too exhausted and just wanted to relax so I fought every urge to tidy up, even a little.

We walked down the two flights of stairs, a short pathway, past the volleyball court, and entered the gate to the very large shamrock shaped pool. It was already scorching hot out so we jumped into the deep end before laying in our lounge chairs to continue working on our tans. Brian and I were the first to get out and claim our spots.

"Thank you so much for helping us out today." I said squinting while adjusting the back of my lounge chair slightly upwards.

"You don't have to thank me. I did offer. Besides, you know I would do anything for you," he said as he sat down next to me on my chair and kissed me gently. Even after being together constantly for over two months, I still had that giddy butterfly feeling whenever he touched me or smiled at me. I thought I was the luckiest girl in the world to have someone as sweet and kind and gorgeous as Brian.

We locked eyes for a minute and as he held my hand, he asked, "Want to get out of here and go for a walk?"

All I could do was nod with a giant lump in my throat.

"Hey y'all. We're going for a walk. Be back soon. Watch our stuff ok?" I yelled to April. She gave me a thumbs up and Mia lifted one eyebrow at me and smiled. I just smiled back and tightly held onto Brian's hand, following his every step.

We walked out of the gate, not saying a word to one another but somehow knowing something incredible was about to happen. We walked hand in hand straight to his apartment on the other side of the complex.

As soon as we got into his apartment, he slammed the door shut and made sure it was locked. He pressed me against the wall and kissed me hard and passionately. The light switches jammed into my back but it was a small price to pay for such a lust filled kiss. He looked me in the eyes and asked, "Are you sure?"

"I've been sure since we met," I whispered into the bend of his neck, kissing him lightly. We practically ran into his room. Before you could blink an eye, I had already untied my bright green bikini top. He stopped and looked at me full of love.

He ran his hands through my wet, chlorine smelling hair and in a low breathy voice said, "I love you".

My heart pounded so hard I could feel blood in my ears.

Another kiss. "I love you too," I replied. I meant it with all of my being.

I had loved him for weeks but was too afraid to be the first to say it. Fear of rejection is a strong emotion, even stronger than confessing something that holds such magnitude. Those three little words carry so much weight and have the power to change your life, for better or worse. And he loved me back! I was glad that we had waited to actually make love, not just have sex. The moment was indescribabe. I had had sex many times before, but never 'made love'. My entire body felt like it was on pins and needles.

He guided me down to the bed and slowly got on top of me. He looked into my eyes with a sense of longing before he bent down to kiss me again. I could feel my heart pounding in my fingertips, my ears, my eyes. This was it. This is what I'd waited months for. My entire body was awake and could sense every little thing. I'm going to keep the rest of the intimate details to myself. They're just too sacred to share, but let me see if I can find the adjectives to describe that moment, our first time: intense, magical (better than Disney, the place of magic, magical), an out of body experience with explosions and fireworks. He was gentle but still always in charge. Everything about it was beautiful.

We laid there entwined, full of sweat in his frigidly chilled room. Brian looked down, kissed my forehead, and said, "I really do love you. I wasn't just saying it to say it."

I looked up at him and smiled, "I know you did. I meant it too. I'm glad we waited for this moment. It was… really, really good and totally worth the wait."

He just smiled back and we fell asleep in the afternoon light with our wet clothes still laying at the foot of the bed.

If we were inseparable before, we were even more so after. All we wanted to do was explore each other's bodies more. It's like we had to make up for lost time, and we had lots of it since neither of us had school for the next two weeks. I had even cut my hours a little at my call center job.

Mia finally had to ask, "So, when you and Brian disappeared at the pool the other day, did you finally fuck?"

"Oh my God, Mia! Don't be so vulgar about it." April said with shock.

"Thanks, April. We actually made love, not what you want to call it." I shrugged and kept flipping through the TV channels.

"Ugh, gag me. Is that what you're calling it now? 'Made love'? You kind of sound like an old lady using that term."

"It is when you actually love the person, Mia. It was really sweet and everything about it was perfect and romantic. We waited a long time, and it was worth the wait. I know that's a little difficult for your nympho appetite, but it was worth it."

"Well, I think it's sweet. And I'm proud of you both for waiting that long. I know you didn't want to, but all good things…," April trailed off because both Mia and I were already rolling our eyes and nodding. I was pretty sure it was her favorite saying because she used any opportunity to let us know the importance of patience.

"Ok, *Mother Teresa*. We know already. I'm just glad you finally did it and it didn't suck…. Seriously though, I am happy for you. If you really love him and he loves you back, then I guess I'm glad you waited and had that 'special' moment," Mia said using air quotes.

"Thank you. That means a lot." I knew she was going to ask so I gave them all the details of our first time. I won't share them with you, but I had to share them with my girl. We shared everything.

A few days later, it was the highly anticipated trip to meet Brian's parents. I had never been taken home to meet anyone's parents, other than friends, so my nerves were at an all-time high. I wanted to make a great first impression. Even though we had never talked about it, I felt like Brian was my last boyfriend. If we didn't get married, I'd probably be devastated. I did keep this to myself though. I didn't want to seem crazy. Yes, we had declared our love for one another, but we still had only been together just shy of three months. I was sure his parents and my mom would protest, even if we did say we were ready.

We left midafternoon on Friday. It was a pretty short drive, clocking in at just over an hour and a half from school so we'd get there in time for dinner. Brian had already made plans for us to go to a party at a high school friend's house later.

"You excited?" Brian asked. He certainly looked excited, but I didn't know if it was because he was introducing his girlfriend to his parents, was excited to see them or excited to party with his friends.

"I guess. A little nervous. I've never actually met any of the parents of the guys I've dated before. I mean, I still haven't even met your sister, and she goes to the same school as us." Truth be told, I had never dated anyone long enough or let it get serious enough to be introduced to the parents.

"Just relax. It'll be fine. My parents are pretty laid back. I'm sure they'll love you. And my sister doesn't really count. She's always busy anyways. I rarely even see her." He squeezed my knee and turned the radio up.

I had dozed off at some point during the drive and awoke startled to find that my body was bouncing up and down in the car. We had left civilization behind and were on an all dirt and rock country road that was windy and hilly. I yawned, stretched as much as Brian's old Tahoe would allow and admired how gorgeous the landscape was.

I'd grown up in a large city where the skyline consisted of a ton of apartment buildings, some rather run-down houses, and large skyscrapers in our downtown area where all the best shopping and restaurants were located. The change of scenery was refreshing. The sky looked vast but close enough you thought you could touch a perfect marshmallow shaped cloud. There were a few houses you could see on their little plateaus that were each surrounded by acres and acres of corn and cows.

Everything was so picturesque it looked like it could have been on a postcard. That's what I've always loved about Texas. There is beauty and grandiosity everywhere. I'm sure the same could be said about a lot of states, but if anyone knows how proud Texans are of their state, they'll tell you that Texans are their own breed and would never willingly chose to live anywhere but Texas. It's perfect in every way. I marveled at how Brian could have grown up in a place as peaceful and charming as this strip of countryside.

He slowed down and turned right onto a tiny dirt road framed in by chicken fencing. There was a wide, rusted metal gate with a sign that read 'NO TRESPASSING' and massive bales of hay next to it so that it would be impossible to close the gate at all. All that stood between me and a great impression was a two-minute drive down this dusty road.

As he pulled up, a large lab came running from behind the house and stopped right at the end of the paved flower lined pathway that led from the grass to the front steps of the wide wrap around porch. It was fitted with the quintessential swing and matching white rocking chairs. There were four very large and mature trees that seemed to hug the home and create a private getaway. The house appeared camouflaged under the shade of the trees. Several large white framed windows peered out of the yellow facade of the house as though they were watching our every move.

To the side of the house was a big makeshift garage and shed area that housed tools, old bikes, and other essential items I assumed people who lived in the country needed or couldn't bear to part with-- a few wheelbarrows, ladders, a big fancy riding mower, garden tools I had never seen before in my life, and other items that looked like junk. I thought how great it must have been living there as a kid with a ton of places to hide outside and no nosey neighbors to harass you. Their property sat on several acres of land but still seemed quaint and cozy. There were a few patches of land they used to grow some vegetables and fruit but the rest of the land was used for pure enjoyment.

As we got out of the car, Brian's mother, Nancy, came out and stood on the top step of the porch with a big smile—Brian's smile. She was about my height, five foot four, but that's where the similarities ended. She had strawberry blonde hair, pale blue eyes, and lightly tanned skin. She had aged well and was the kind of woman you could tell was a bombshell back in her day. She started to walk down the steps to help us with our tiny bags.

"I'm so glad you made it safely. How was the drive?" Nancy said as she briefly hugged Brian and then moved on to me before he could respond.

She placed her hands on my arms, gave them a gentle squeeze, and gave me a big bear hug that caught me a bit off guard. "I'm so glad to finally meet you! Brian is finally bringing a girl home after all this time away at school. How exciting!"

I gave an awkward laugh, hugged back, and said, "It's nice to meet you too. You have a beautiful home. The drive here was wonderful."

"Isn't it lovely? You certainly can't beat the views. Now let's get in the house before we melt out here," she said as she grabbed my overnight bag and started walking up the porch stairs. "I made a pot roast with vegetables for dinner, salad, biscuits, and a peach cobbler so I hope you two are hungry!" she yelled as she opened the front door.

Brian and I made our way towards the front door. "She seems really nice. I like her already," I whispered to him.

"See. I told you. Nothing to worry about." He put his arm around my shoulders and kissed my head as we got to the front door.

The house smelled like home. The pot roast permeated the house but there were also hints of lavender and lemon in the air. It was just as pretty inside as it was outside. Everything was open but still cozy. Every wall was covered in family photos, kids' artwork that had been framed as if they were prized treasures, miscellaneous maps, and paintings. It was a hodgepodge of things, but they were all exquisite and made the house feel so country chic. The hardwood floors gleamed as though they had just been polished and there were a few brightly colored area rugs that made the white stucco looking walls pop. It was a far cry from the houses I had grown up in where the closest thing to decor was hanging a few rather old photos, and maybe a printed piece of cheap artwork that my mom had found at a garage sale or picked out of someone's trash.

Brian went out back to find his dad so I made my way to the wall of pictures. I spotted a picture of a seven-year-old toothless Brian. He was adorable. Next to it was an awkward picture of him looking rather gangly. You could tell he was on the cusp of puberty and would eventually grow into his looks. We all have those awful pictures we'd wish would vanish, but our parents wouldn't think of getting rid of or hiding to spare our embarrassment.

I was so focused on the pictures I never heard Nancy walk up behind me. "Wasn't he so cute as a kid?" She proceeded to give me a brief history of each of the pictures, spending more time on the ones of Brian. My responses to most of them, "Oh", "Wow", "Really?"

As she spoke, I tried to imagine what it must have been like to grow up in such a picture-perfect setting with two parents and just one sister. It must have been glorious! I snapped out of it just in time to hear the tail end of her description about a picture of Brian bursting through the finish line at a high school track meet and her question, "So did you play any sports growing up?"

"Me? Oh, not really. I tried volleyball and was awful so that only lasted one year, and then I ran track senior year but hated it at first. I had wanted to quit but that's not really in me to just quit things so I stuck it out. It wasn't too bad by the end of the year though when I was actually in better shape and could run more than five minutes without wanting to pass out."

"I'm not a big runner either and never have been so don't feel bad. In fact, I'm not a big workout person in general. Gardening is about the extent of my physical activity. It's good you didn't quit though. You never know if you'll like something or be good at it unless you really try at it," she said encouragingly.

I smiled at her and before I even thought about what I was about to say, I just blurted out, "You know, I really like you already. You're so nice and we literally just met ten minutes ago. I was really nervous about meeting you and your husband but I'm glad I came and didn't chicken out last minute." As soon as the words left my mouth, I felt my face get red and hot. I had just embarrassed myself to the hundredth degree.

She smiled back, gave me another hug, and said, "That's really sweet of you. I want you to feel comfortable in our home. I said it earlier, but Brian's never brought a girl home from school so I know you must mean a lot to him."

Just then Brian and his dad walked in through the French doors that led to the back patio and headed towards Nancy and me.

"This is my dad, Henry."

"How do you do?" his dad said as he offered his hand for a good solid handshake.

I gave him my best shake and smiled. "Hi! So nice to meet you."

There were some more pleasantries before Nancy politely interrupted, "Let me show you two where you'll be sleeping. I'm not naive and am sure things go on at school so you're welcome to stay in Brian's room with him or one of you can stay in the study. It's a sofa bed so it's not all that comfortable in which case, Brian will stay there and he can be the one to get a crick in the neck."

I looked to Brian with a 'what do I say? is this a test from your mom?' kind of face. Rather than understanding the look I was giving him he said, "Thanks mom. We'll stay in my room."

"I can stay in the study, really. I don't mind," I said. I wanted to at least try and look more like the model virginal girlfriend.

"Nonsense. Brian's bed is practically new and comfortable. Besides, you two are technically adults. Just no hanky panky in there," said Henry with a little laugh in his voice. He winked at Brian and I wasn't sure if that was to mean 'go for it, just don't be loud' or 'seriously, no hanky panky in there'. Either way, nothing was going to be going on until we got back to my apartment or his.

The rest of the evening turned out well, and thankfully, uneventful. There was the standard line of questioning: how many brothers and sisters do you have (three brothers, two sisters), where'd you grow up (a place not nearly as nice as this), what's your major (International Affairs), what do you do for fun, and so on and so on.

They told me stories about Brian as a kid and the kind of trouble he'd gotten into, which wasn't much. He was a model son who'd always made the honor roll, participated in several extracurricular activities, and was voted most popular in his senior class. His sister, Sarah, on the other hand, was apparently more of a handful.

"Oh, Brian's always been a sweet boy. Just so thoughtful and not much of a rule breaker. But his sister definitely gave us a run for our money. I think the worst thing Brian ever did was cut class but Sarah… I had to start dying my hair to cover the grays early on," Nancy said, rubbing her temples as though the memories were enough to make more aged hair appear magically.

I looked at Brian and smiled. Even when we'd first met, he never struck me as a bad boy. "Oh really. She was that bad?"

"Oh, yes! Sarah was brought home more than once in the back of a cop car for cutting class with her boyfriend. Which, I guess wasn't that bad, but she also liked to play the 'find Sarah' game. She'd tell us she was spending the night at a girlfriend's house but actually sneak off to a college party a few towns away." Nancy looked upset just talking about it.

"That's kind of scary. I think my mom would have killed me." I actually had no clue if my mom would be upset or not. She wasn't ever home too much to know my whereabouts unless it required me being present to babysit all my siblings.

"She's lucky nothing terrible ever happened. We thought about sending her to some kind of boot camp but didn't want to push her away. On the bright side, I think she got a lot out of her system before moving away to school. At least here, we were just a quick phone call away to bail her out of her messes."

"I think that's enough talk about Sarah. We don't need to get into every bad thing she did in high school. She's straightened out a lot, Mom. She's been keeping out of trouble at school," Brian said reassuringly.

Dinner was delicious, the conversation was great, and I was thoroughly enjoying myself when Brian interjected that we had to get ready to meet his friends. It was already going on nine thirty and everyone was meeting up at his best friend, Scott's house for a little reunion. Before leaving, I insisted on helping clear the dishes and at least help load the dishwasher so Nancy wouldn't be left with a big mess. Once that was finished, I freshened up and was ready to go and, hopefully, make another great first impression.

We drove about fifteen minutes down yet another dusty dirt and rocky road until we reached a massive estate in the middle of nowhere. There was a sprawling house and about ten cars parked in the middle of a field. Not far from there was a big bonfire in front of an ancient looking barn. We were the last to arrive and a few of the guests were already three sheets to the wind. Brian found Scott after saying some polite 'hello's' and 'what's up's' to a few people that he didn't seem to care enough about to stay and make meaningful conversation with.

Scott and Brian greeted each other with a big high five and hug combination as though they hadn't seen each other in years. They started talking about the drive home, how nice it was to be back visiting at the same time finally so they could hang out, and a few other pleasantries before Brian remembered I was standing there uncomfortably waiting to be introduced.

"Oh! Sorry man. This is my girlfriend. We're here until tomorrow sometime or maybe Sunday--not sure yet. Wanted her to meet the folks and show her around the town."

I gave an embarrassed smile and shook Scott's hand. "Hi. Nice to meet you. Brian's told me a lot about you."

"Really? He hasn't mentioned you at all," Scott said in an asshole-ish type of tone. I just stared at him not sure if he was joking or serious.

"Dude, don't be a dick already," said Brian. "Just ignore him. He's lacking in the manners department and suffers from a low IQ at times."

"Um... ok. Can we get a drink?" I was already irritated. I could tell Scott and I wouldn't be the best of friends. He seemed like a standoffish kind of guy, and I had little tolerance for rude people.

"Yeah. Let's go inside and grab something." Brian took my hand and led me into the barn that was surprisingly updated and looked like something out of a magazine.

"Wow! I wouldn't have expected it to look like this in here," I said astonished. Everything was ultra-modern and done impeccably tastefully.

"Oh, yeah, Scott's parents are pretty well off. This property was passed down to his mom and they run a cattle farm and own an oil well or two. Seriously, ignore Scott. I know he can be an asshole at times, but he's a cool guy."

"If you say so. Let's get a drink."

Brian grabbed two beers from the enormous stainless-steel refrigerator that was completely stocked with Coronas and Coors and a few random imported beers I'd never heard of. We headed back out to stake our claim on a pair of empty Adirondack chairs near the bonfire even though it was hot and muggy out.

We pretty much kept to ourselves the rest of the night. Brian said he only knew a couple of the people that were there, and he'd never been particularly close to any of them. Our seclusion, I'm sure, didn't help Scott's feelings of growing animosity towards me.

He was used to being the center of attention. Only child to parents, who were when they were home, doted on him like he was made of glass. Whatever he wanted, he got. I think they were trying to compensate for their lack of parental guidance. His parents spent a lot of time traveling, and not always together. It was rumored that they had an arrangement and were 'openly' adulterous. He'd been raised by a string of nannies. When one got tired of dealing with his wild antics, they'd give their notice and another would take her place.

Scott walked over, even his walk was cocky, and stood with his back to me so I couldn't see Brian clearly. "So, how's school going man? The parties any good?"

"Um, school's good. I haven't had much time to go out though. I'm trying to keep my grades up. You know I'm on scholarship, and I've got to stay competitive to get that flight spot."

"Oh shit. Forgot about that. So, you're still actually planning on being all that you can be?" He was the only one who laughed.

"You know that's the Army's slogan right, not Air Force," I said. He didn't even look at me. He acted like a spoiled child that had had his favorite toy taken away. He seemed to already hate me, and yet hadn't bothered to talk to me for more than thirty seconds. Oh well, I thought, no loss to me.

Brian finally got up and walked around Scott to sit with me on the arm of my chair. "Yes. I'm still planning on commissioning with the Air Force. That's been the plan for three years now or have too many of your brain cells been destroyed to remember that long ago?" I thought I sensed a hint of anger in his voice towards Scott but wasn't sure.

"Ha ha. I remember man. Just didn't think you were still going through with it. I'll leave you with her. Have fun. I'll catch up with you later." Scott wandered back off to talk to his more important guests.

We stayed until about one just drinking and talking and had a great time, just us.

I yawned. "I think I'm about ready to head out. What about you?"

"Same here. Let's go say bye to Scotty boy," he said.

Brian and I walked over to a drunk Scott. Brian slapped Scott on his back. "Hey, man, we're going to head out. We're both tired from the drive. Thanks for the beer and opening your house, like always."

"Are you leaving already?" Scott slurred. "Don't go yet, it's still early."

"Thanks for having us, Scott. Your parent's house is beautiful," I said trying to reinforce the point we were leaving.

Scott looked at Brian and said, "Shit, man. You get a girlfriend, and she turns you into an anti-social douche."

"He's just keeping better company these days, Scott," I replied and turned to Brian, "I'll wait for you in the car. Thanks again for the invite, Scott." I walked off fuming at how rude Scott had been all evening.

A couple minutes later, Brian hopped in the car and immediately apologized for Scott's behavior.

"You don't have to apologize for him being an asshole. I just don't get why he was such a jerk. He doesn't even know me."

"Scott is just Scott. We were really close in high school and still are so he can get a little jealous. He's normally not that bad. He's just always had that high school mentality of 'bros before hoes'," said Brian.

"Whatever. That's just stupid. You guys aren't in high school anymore, and it's not like he wants to date you so I don't see what the big deal is. He should be happy if you're happy. Anyways, don't defend him. He's a big boy and responsible for his own stupidity." I knew if we kept on the topic of Scott, we'd get into our first fight, and it would probably be a big one.

"I know, but you just don't know Scott like I do. He'll be fine. Once you get to know him, I'm sure you both will get along just fine." Brian's voice was starting to get irritated but I had to get the last word in.

"I really don't care if he likes me or not. I'm not a big fan of his already and I don't plan on spending a lot of quality time with him anyways. Just tell him to at least be a grown up and cordial. Surely all his mommy and daddy's money can buy some manners." I knew that comment was probably crossing the line. I really knew nothing about this guy or his family, but he was the stereotypical rich kid that threw a fit whenever he didn't get his way or didn't like something. He probably never had to work for anything a day in his life so he could stay in his lane, and I'd stay in mine. There was no need for us to be friends, ever! Even if that meant Brian would have to pick and choose who he'd spend his time with if I ever came back to his hometown.

Brian glared at me and looked like he wanted to say something but instead just said, "I'll talk to him," and went quiet. The rest of the drive back was silent. If Brian wanted to defend Scott until he turned blue, fine. I wasn't going to be treated poorly for some spoiled brat, regardless of if his best friend was my boyfriend.

We pulled up to his parents' house and to both our surprises, they were still awake and sitting together on the swing on the front porch. It was sweet to see a couple still so in love after almost thirty years of marriage. Something that seems increasingly rare now.

"How was your little get together?" Nancy asked with a kind smile on her face.

Brian gave a 'don't ask' look and headed inside so I responded, "It was ok. I don't think Scott was a big fan of me tagging along though."

"Oh, Scott," Nancy whispered under her breath. "Just pay him no mind. He's always been a little territorial over Brian. He is a sweet boy after the initial brashness wears off." She gave Henry a look that I couldn't interpret and offered me a small smile.

"I'll keep that in mind. I'm beat. I'm going to head to bed. Good night."

I headed to Brian's room, and he was already lying in bed with his back towards me so I didn't bother to say anything. I got into my sweats and slid into bed beside him.

He rolled over, put his arm around me, and said, "Sorry. I didn't want Scott to ruin the night. He was an ass so you had every right to be angry. I just would like it if you two could get along. He's my best friend, and you're my girlfriend. Ok?"

"Ok….," I begrudgingly added, "I'm sorry too. I shouldn't have made that last comment about him. It was uncalled for." Apologies have never been my strong suit.

He kissed me, and we fell asleep listening to the hum of the window air conditioning unit.

I told Brian I wouldn't mind staying Saturday and just heading back on Sunday morning if he wanted more time to spend at home. His parents were so sweet and generous. It was nice to be surrounded by nature and quiet. He said it was my call so we stayed.

The rest of the weekend was so relaxing and peaceful. I genuinely had a great time getting to talk to his parents and learn more about their family, their family history and hear about Brian as a kid. I had correctly assumed that I made a good first impression because that Sunday after we had given our hugs and said our goodbyes, we got into the car, Brian looked at me and said, "My mom loves you!"

"Well, I love her! She was so nice! Your dad was nice too but a little quiet."

"That's my dad. He liked you too, though. Now all we have to do is take me to meet your family."

I was already dreading Brian meeting my family, especially after now having met his mom and dad and seeing how normal, low key, and laid back they were. I knew it was inevitable though. If we were serious, which we were, he'd have to meet my mom and all the other people living in my house.

4

Meet the Parents: Round 2

We spent a week back at our apartment complex to unwind and fully unpack before heading into the lion's den known as my mother's house.

At Brian's request, I had called my mom.

"Hey, girl! You do remember you have a mother?" she screamed into the phone. I was sure she had lost some or all her hearing since her volume levels were loud and louder.

"Hi, mom. Of course, I remember. I've just been busy," I said with slight irritation.

"Yeah, yeah, yeah. You've been busy. Miss fancy pants off at college. To what do I owe the pleasure of your call, my lady?" she said and let out a large cackle.

I smiled to myself at the thought of my mom with her head back laughing hysterically at her joke. "Ha ha, mom. Look, I don't have a ton of time. I just..." she cut me off before I could finish.

"My first born hasn't called me in days and now you want to rush me off the phone already. What do you need?"

I sighed, "You know it goes both ways, right? You have fingers to dial my number if you really want to talk to me so badly. Look, I didn't call you for this crap. I just wanted to let you know that Brian and I are heading up there this

Thursday for a very short visit. And I mean short." I could feel my blood pressure slowly rising.

"Brian? Who's Brian? Oh! That guy you've been dating? Or am I thinking about someone else?" I wasn't sure if she was talking to me or herself.

"Yes, Brian, the guy I've been dating for a while now. It's gotten kind of serious and he wants to meet you so we're going to drive up. Please, please, please, just be normal for once. Don't do anything embarrassing," I pleaded.

"What the hell do you mean? I AM normal. I'll be myself like always. He'll love me." She didn't quite get that her being herself was what I wanted to avoid.

"Look mom, I'm sure he will. Just don't overwhelm him or be too… overbearing," I said as politely as possible.

I hung up and took a few deep breaths. Conversations with my mom led to adverse health reactions. I looked up from my phone and gave a tired smile to Mia and April who were sitting in the living room.

"Wow, so you guys are doing the whole 'meet the parents' bit?" Mia said with sarcasm in her voice.

I'd been spending less and less time at my apartment and with my roomies than Mia would have liked. I wasn't sure if she was jealous or disgusted by the head over heels in love scene she was becoming accustomed to. They'd party, and I'd pass for a movie night in with Brian.

"Yeah, you know it's serious. Has been for a while."

"I'm still in shock that you're willing to let him stay at your mom's house. Did you warn him about how she can be a little, you know, out there sometimes?" April loved my mom but knew how she was and made a small crazy face.

"I've warned him a little, but really, there's no describing my mom. She's a class all on her own. We're not staying long so hopefully it won't scare him off."

Wednesday night rolled around and I asked Brian, "Are you 100% sure you want to go meet my family? It's not just going to be my mom and brothers and sisters, you have to meet. Everyone will want to meet you. We're coming back Saturday no matter what! It'll be exhausting."

"Yes! I'm sure already. I don't know what the big deal is."

"If you're sure, then ok, but just be warned half my family is legit crazy."

He laughed at me and said, "I really think you're overreacting."

People always thought I was over exaggerating about how insane my family was until they met them. I never understood why they couldn't take my word for it considering how little I went home and why I picked a school almost eight hours away from my family.

We loaded Brian's car Thursday morning, I said a prayer, and we hit the road. I'd already given him the game plan: as soon as we got into town he'd meet my mom and siblings first, and then my aunt and cousins who had just moved out to a small apartment down the street. Friday afternoon we'd go to my uncle's house since he hosted big family gatherings on Fridays. It'd be a one stop shop kind of deal. And we'd be out of there first thing Saturday morning. The whole trip would be quick and painless (fingers crossed).

We pulled up to my mom's neighborhood and the differences between my hometown and Brian's were beyond noticeable, like night and day. There was nothing but identical looking run-down townhomes, trash cans toppled over in some of the front yards, and kids running around outside in diapers through sprinklers. There was a patrol car that would sporadically drive through to make sure no one was causing trouble. And it was loud, very loud. A stark contrast to the oasis and serenity of Brian's country-cottage upbringing.

My mom saw us get out of the car and came running towards us like a bull who'd just seen a gigantic bright red cape. I'll pause here to describe my mother so you can get the full visual of how utterly ridiculous her entrance looked (not that someone running at you isn't ridiculous anyways, but hear me out).

My mother was very beautiful when she was young. You could still see hints of beauty at times, but the birthing of six children, all the stress of being a single parent, and working tons of odd jobs to still never be able to make ends meet had taken a toll on her aging body.

My tiny mother of only five feet two inches was slightly heavy weighing in at one hundred and fifty pounds, and I swear that half of that was cleavage. She was always so top heavy that I marveled at the fact that she didn't topple over every time she stood up to walk. She had an awful dye job that she claimed was supposed to be a 'radiant auburn' but somehow looked like a reddish magenta color that made her naturally curly hair frizz out even more. Even if auburn was the color she was going for, it would not have worked with her pale skin tone. She was the Hispanic version of a really bad Carrot Top. So, imagine having this fifty-two-year-old, heavy set, Hispanic Carrot Top running out with boobs flapping up to her chin all to say hello. I didn't know if I should laugh hysterically at the comedic scene unfolding in front of me or die of embarrassment.

"Whew.... I'm out of breath... so excited you're home, and with a boyfriend!" my sweaty mother panted after her ten-yard dash.

I gave her a small hug. "Jeez mom. You training for the Olympics or something? We made it."

She didn't get the joke or chose to ignore me and introduced herself to Brian with a big boob on chest hug where she kind of shimmied back and forth to really emphasize her excitement of him being there.

"I'm Adoracion. Everyone calls me D or Dora... but I'm no explorer!" she said as she made a bada boom sound with hand movements before she let out her extremely loud signature laugh you could really call a cackle.

Brian let out a loud laugh but I just felt my face getting flushed with embarrassment. "Please mom. Let's save the stand up for later. Can we just go inside?"

"Yes, yes, yes," she said quickly and dismissively. "I'm melting out here."

I looked to Brian and rolled my eyes and quietly said, "Probably had something to do with her fifty-yard sprint."

"Ssshhh! Leave your mom alone." Brian said in a protective tone.

We walked up the three-stepped stoop and went inside. It wasn't much cooler in the house than it was outside. The central A/C didn't work very well and my mom hated having outrageously expensive electric bills. She kept it set to seventy-eight no matter how hot it was outside and relied on sporadically placed standing fans in rooms that were used the most. The blinds were always kept drawn. You felt as though you'd stepped into a bear's den.

The house was eerily quiet.

"Where is everyone, mom?"

"Your brother went to hang out with his girlfriend's family today. He got a white girl from a rich family and is all of a sudden too good to spend time with his own momma. Your other brother is floating the river with JJ and his family. He's another one. Barely fourteen and thinks he's grown!"

"Why'd you let him go then? The river is full of drunk college kids. Bad idea, mom."

"Honey, when you have kids, talk to me. Until then, no input needed or wanted!" she said with a humph.

"Fine, but I brought Brian home to meet everyone and no one is here. What about Ana?" I asked.

"She's at basketball camp for the day. At least one of my teens is being productive and thinking about her future!"

Ana was thirteen and breathed basketball. It was assumed that was her ticket out of the ghetto and onto college.

My other brother and sister who were just eleven and eight had gone to spend the next few days with their dad so it looked like Brian would only meet two of my five siblings. I was kind of relieved but slightly annoyed. He could slowly be introduced to the entire family, but we'd driven all that way for him to meet everyone, and my mom had let them all leave. Brian didn't seem to be too disappointed which annoyed me further since he had insisted on the trip and wouldn't even get the full experience that is my family because that's what it is, an experience.

My family was like the fun house at a circus except we didn't charge admission. The ride was always free. There were twists and turns at every corner, and things weren't always what they appeared to be. One of my uncles, for example, was a true genius, and not in the sense that he was an artist or had great ideas. He was extremely intelligent and very eloquent, but he couldn't hold a job to save his life. You'd never know by looking or talking to him but he'd spent more than half his life in jail for petty crimes.

My grandparents, who barely spoke proper English, lived in the worst part of town but were great business people. They owned several little corner convenience stores in the ghetto neighborhoods where young kids always seemed to get away with buying anything from cigarettes to cheap 40s. We were all convinced they had a secret stash of cash somewhere since my grandfather was always handing five-dollar bills out to the grandkids like candy, but we couldn't figure out where. My grandfather was also pretty bat shit crazy. He walked around with no pants on but wore nice button up shirts that he never actually buttoned, and flip flops with tall socks. He only got dressed when he had to leave the house. Even if company stopped by, that was his attire. He saw no need to impress anyone, especially in his own home. My grandmother, on the other hand, was one of the more normal members of my family. Although, I've always wondered how normal she could really be after having put up with my grandfather for over sixty years.

Anyways, Brian would meet them the following day along with my aunts and uncles. It was extremely rare that I spoke to my father. The last time we spoke was two or three years prior, and he was probably too high to realize who I was. I had no intention of introducing him to Brian, ever. Until the get together at my uncle's house, Brian and I decided to lay low at my mom's for the rest of the day. It was already midafternoon, and we were exhausted from the drive.

Unlike Brian's parents, my mom was not having us share a room. You'd think a woman that had children with three different men would be a little less uptight about things like that, but she was surprisingly traditional when it came to her kids. She always said she didn't want us to end up like her. She raised us in the church and preached the no sex before marriage thing. It was near impossible to take her seriously considering her track record of baby daddy's and loser boyfriends that tended to move in rather quickly.

We set our bags in our respective rooms and no sooner than we'd sat down did my mom call out from the kitchen, "Can y'all two go to the grocery store? I need a few things."

"Ugh, and so it begins." I sighed.

"What?" Brian was confused.

"I am now officially the bitch around here. She'll consider herself off duty from grown up responsibilities since I'm home."

"Oh," was all Brian could say. I'm sure he instantly regretted his insistence on coming.

"What do you need, Mom?" I walked to the kitchen and it wasn't just a few things she needed. It was an entire list of things. She had not prepared for us coming.

"Goodness Mom. Why couldn't you have done this before we got here? We just spent all day in the car," I said with a large attitude.

"Well, if you two want to eat, run to the store. I've been busy all week cleaning and working. I picked up some extra shifts at the diner and have been too tired to do anything else. Just go."

"Fine. Money?"

"Take thirty out of my wallet. Can you cover the rest? I need to use the rest of that money for bills and my food stamps are out," she said lighting a cigarette.

I felt my blood boiling. That was why I rarely went home. I was never a kid there. Even at almost twenty, I wasn't technically a kid, but you get my drift. Whenever I went home, I was another parent. I had always been cast in that role. I was the oldest so that meant, no childhood for me. I had to help watch all the little ones while my mom worked, cleaned while she slept after a double shift or cleaning someone's house after getting out of a shift. I'd even gotten a small job myself at the fast food place a few blocks down, not for my own spending money or college fund, but to pitch in around the house for things we needed like toilet paper and essentials, like food.

I loved my family and loved my mother because I understood things were tough and she was trying, but I still couldn't be around them for long. My mom always threw all these responsibilities on me without asking if I wanted them or minded doing things. I was just always expected to do things and not say a word about it.

"Fine. I'll cover as much as I can but I have my own bills now too, Mom. The money I make from my call center job at school is supposed to go towards those."

"Ok miss money bags. Get what you can. I'll see you two in a little."

I turned, desperately hoping Brian didn't hear any of that short conversation. Where he came from and where I came from were such different places it was almost comedic. I couldn't even imagine what was going through his head about my family and me.

"Do you mind if we take your car and run to the store? Sorry about all this," I said sheepishly.

"Yeah, no problem. Let's go. Just tell me where to go." I swore I heard pity in his voice.

We went to the closest HEB and started on our list, shopping in silence. When we got to check out, I prayed that between my mom's money and mine I would have just enough. Of course, as luck would have it, I did not. Before I could say anything to pay, Brian handed the cashier his card. My heart melted. I really loved him. He was so generous on top of all his other great qualities.

"Brian, you don't have to do that. I can pay for it." I lied.

"I want to though. Have to make a good impression, right?" he smiled at me and kissed the palm of my hand.

If he wanted to make a good impression, he was on the right track. A handsome white guy that paid for things and was kind, funny, and smart. My mom would be all over him. She'd be so excited that I'd picked a 'good one'.

We got back and I gave my mom her money back. "What's this for?" she asked.

"Thank Brian. He paid for everything."

My mother was ecstatic. Just as I'd expected she said, "Don't let that one go. He seems like a good man. And to put up with you! Keep him!"

Late in the evening, my mom made a big traditional dinner of red rice and beans with pork shoulder and potato salad. My brother and sister had come back and seemed to take a liking to Brian. My sister thought it was cool that he wanted to be a pilot, and my brother was excited to have a man around to talk sports with. Everything was surprisingly normal and calm. About two hours after dinner though, Brian got an upset stomach from something he ate because he spent the rest of the evening in the bathroom.

I gently knocked on the bathroom door. "Brian? Are you ok? Need me to bring you anything?"

"No. Thank you, though. I think I'm feeling a little better. Be out soon."

I could hear him puking and had to cover my ears. My stomach has never tolerated vomit well. "Do you want to head back home tomorrow? Or just stay here and rest before we leave? We don't have to go to my uncle's." If I were lucky, we'd cut the entire trip short and just go home.

I heard him turn the water on before he opened the door. His face was pale and he looked exhausted. "No. I should be ok tomorrow. I feel much better now. I just need to go to bed."

"Ok. Get some rest. I love you." I kissed his cheek and went downstairs.

I stayed up watching a movie with my mom and sister before heading to bed. I checked on Brian. He was passed out but looked better with color returning to his beautiful skin. Thankfully, he woke up the next morning feeling back to normal, which was a relief, but the downside meant he'd be introduced to everyone after all.

We spent the day at the local park laying under a tree just holding hands and talking.

"I really like your mom. She's not crazy the way you make her out to be."

I laughed. "Brian, you've been here less than twenty-four hours. Give it time, I'm sure you'll change your mind."

"No, really. She's nice. Definitely a character and very different than my mom, but I like her. I'm looking forward to meeting the rest of your family later today." He sounded so genuine.

"Ok, if you say so. If you love them that much by the end of this trip, you should probably consider getting your head checked."

By the time we got back to my mom's house, she'd already left early to help my uncle set up and take over a big batch of rice. She also left a note telling us not to be late and to pick up a case of beer and bottle of rum. I hoped she wasn't already beginning to use Brian. She knew he'd have to get it and pay since I wasn't even allowed into the liquor store. I hid the note and later told my mom I never saw it when she saw us arrive empty handed.

We got to my Uncle Johnny's house around five with the party in full swing. There was a giant pig turning in the front yard over a fire, a sprinkler out back for all the little kids to run through, coolers of beer, two huge tables filled with food, and a group of old men that had their own little band (family friends of my grandfather) set up on the front porch. They had brought out their guitars, congas, and maracas and were already playing and singing some great salsa music.

"Wow! This is every Friday?" Brian was amazed.

"Just about. More like every other, but it's the summertime so this is bigger than usual. Kind of like a kick off to summer. Ready to meet everyone?"

I grabbed his hand and led him to the back of a group of folding chairs where my uncles and aunts were already sitting and having a heated discussion about how much my fat uncle actually weighed! Before I could say anything, my uncle ran into the house and reappeared with a scale.

"Get on it, Hector!" yelled my Uncle Johnny. Everyone started laughing. My family could be beyond ridiculous. They had music playing, great food, and wanted to weigh my uncle for entertainment. My uncle started asking people how much they thought the scale would say and how much they wanted to bet. The highest bidder, my Aunt Valia shouted out "I say three-fifty! I'll put a dollar on it!"

My Uncle Hector looked over his shoulder and said, "Shit. You're crazy. I'm not that much. Why don't you bet some real money too you damn cheap skate?"

There were a few other bidders and then he got on the scale. "Three hundred and ten pounds! Looks like Valia was closer than anyone else. Give the woman her money!" yelled Uncle Johnny.

She won a whopping nine dollars and put the money in her back pocket. She stuck her tongue out at my Uncle Hector, and they continued drinking and shit talking to one another. I finally stepped into the group to give everyone hugs and kisses and introduce Brian. If you've ever seen the movie 'My Big Fat Greek Wedding', that's kind of what my family's get togethers were like— super loud, lots of alcohol, tons of unsolicited advice and opinions being thrown around. They're loving and crazy.

Despite the ludicrousness of the scene unfolding before him, Brian seemed naturally at ease and took a seat next to my Uncle Johnny and Aunt Valia's longtime boyfriend,

Dom. Beers were passed around and everyone kept talking. I was told several times by my grandmother to eat something, even though I had already started on a big plate of food in front of me. I was always too skinny. Too skinny or too fat (when I gained the freshman fifteen). It was always something. Even when I was "too fat", everyone was quick to offer me heaping spoonful's of rice and beans to fatten me up even more.

Suddenly there was a big commotion and my grandfather came running out of the front door yelling with a broom in his hand. He was swinging it at my Uncle Al (his full name was Alonso but no one ever used it).

"Ah.... Piece of shit! You don't come back here you little thief...." he yelled in broken English. "And don't try talking to your mother. I won't have it!"

My Uncle Al jumped off the front porch and turned around, "Pop. Relax. I didn't take anything. I just asked Ma if I could have some money. She said she didn't have any so she gave me the necklace to sell it." He looked to my grandmother hoping she'd back him up, whether it was true or not, who knew. She kept quiet. Everyone knew to just go along with my grandfather whenever he went on his little rampages.

"See. You no ask. You just take, take, take. Get a job! You're a bum. Just get the hell out of here." He swung the broom at him again and looked like he was going to fall over from all the momentum.

My grandfather had shrunk significantly with age but still had some strong bones and was like a little pit-bull. He got angry quick but calmed down just as fast. He'd be over it the next day but he'd never apologize, even if he was wrong. The funny thing was, he was only ever mean to his own kids and wife. With friends and his grandkids, he was the kindest, most gentle creature you'd ever imagine. He'd sneak the kids little pieces of Mary Jane candies before dinner, give them small sips of beer when the parents weren't looking, and always had money ready to hand out to anyone that needed it, except his children.

With my grandfather's outburst over, the party resumed, and my Uncle Al threw up a peace sign and hopped on his bike.

I looked to Brian and once again, found myself apologizing.

"Why do you keep apologizing? I'm having a great time. Your uncle asked if I wanted to go to some bar later. *Freddy's,* I think."

I let out a big sigh. "I really want to leave first thing tomorrow."

"Yeah. We'll still leave tomorrow. I think it'd be fun to go out. He said your aunt's husband or boyfriend, or whoever he is, is going too and your Uncle Al, and one or two other guys."

"Ok. If you really want to go. Just call me, and I'll pick you up so you don't have to worry about driving," I resigned. If my uncle and the rest of the crew were inviting him out already, he was a shoe in with the family. All I cared about was getting back to my own apartment as soon as possible.

Brian was hurting the next day. He called at four am to pick him up, and he was beyond drunk. I let him sleep until ten and then forced him to get up and shower so we could hit the road. He loved my family. They absolutely loved him. Things were looking up.

5

Oops...

The next few weeks went by in a flash. Things had been smoothed over with Mia. April was happy as usual. And Brian was... my everything. I saw everything in a new light now that I was in love. When I got a mediocre grade, Brian was there to be my cheerleader. When he was hungry, I played house and would whip up the fanciest recipe I could find. Brian's waistline never suffered since he was still running a lot, but I had gained a few pounds which was not good. We were in prime bathing suit season. It didn't look horrible but I had a small muffin top developing. Brian didn't seem to care especially since my ass was a little plumper, but I was uncomfortable.

By the end of June, after my twentieth birthday, I decided to start my diet and do the lemon and pepper cleanse to lose those pesky five pounds. Not a lot, but five pounds is still five pounds. I had always worked out so I asked Brian if I could tag along on a run, just as long as it wasn't more than three miles. We headed out and everything was fine. I felt good, just understandably hot.

The sun was blaring and it was ninety degrees out with virtually no wind. About ten minutes into our run, I yelled to Brian who'd taken a bit of a lead, "Hey... Hold on... I don't feel too well..."

Then everything went black.

"Oh my God! Are you ok? Can you hear me?" Brian yelled trying to stay calm but I could sense a slightly frantic tone in his voice.

I tried to snap myself out of it but was still so hot and had a blaring headache, probably from bashing it on the concrete running path. I let myself just lay there and waved my hand to Brian so he knew I could hear him.

I managed a, "Yeah… can I have some water." He poured some onto my head and then put his bottle to my mouth while he held my head in his lap. I took a small sip and felt a thousand percent better which wasn't saying much considering I still felt like I'd been hit by a bus.

I slowly sat up on my arms. "Shit. Must be dehydrated. And I don't think I ate enough breakfast this morning." I was squinting to keep the sun from blinding me further. "Can you help me up so I can get out of the middle of the path?" I was mortified. Who passes out in the middle of a walkway? Half the people ignored my little scene and the other half gawked like I had two heads.

"Are you OK? What happened? Do I need to take you to the ER?"

"I'm fine. Like I said, probably didn't drink enough water or eat enough. It probably doesn't help we came out at the hottest part of the day. I'm fine. Let's just walk back. I want to lay down." I was exhausted and my headache was worsening.

"I really think I should take you to the ER and make sure you don't have a concussion or anything." Brian was insistent but I didn't have health insurance. I certainly wasn't in a position to foot the bill for anything beyond what I had already taken on with the apartment bills.

"No! I just want to go home. If I start to feel funny, we'll go. I swear."

Brian reluctantly agreed, and we slowly made our way back to my apartment. When we got in Mia said, "Well that didn't take long."

"Probably because I collapsed a few minutes in," I said nonchalantly.

Mia laughed and then she looked at me. My hair was a mess, I was bright red, and I looked like I'd been thrown into a tornado and spit out. "Wait, are you serious? You ok?" She sounded just as worried as Brian.

"I'm fine. I'm going to take some Tylenol and lay down. Come check on me in an hour and if I'm unconscious or laying in vomit, you'll know it's serious." I kept walking and collapsed on to my bed. All I wanted to do was sleep. I heard Brian and Mia arguing through loud whispers.

"You're a great boyfriend, Brian. Take her out running, let her collapse, and then bring her home instead of taking her straight to the ER. What the hell were you thinking?"

"I tried to get her to go. She refused. I'm not going to force her," he said with frustration.

"It's just irresponsible of you. Get her to go."

A few minutes later I heard my door open and Brian was standing there with a large glass of water and the Tylenol I never grabbed.

"Mia really thinks she or I should take you to the doctor. Even if it's just the one at the campus clinic. Will you please just go and make sure your head is fine?"

He looked so handsome, even with sweat dripping from his face. "Just let me get an hour or two of rest and then I'll see how I'm feeling. Even if it's a concussion, what are they going to do? Tell me to be careful, not fall down a flight of stairs, and get some rest which I'm already trying to do."

"Ok. Well I'll come check on you in an hour." He handed me my pills and water and gave me a long, tender kiss before heading back to his place to shower.

After several checks and only two hours, I felt like my old self again. I didn't bother addressing the doctor issue. I went about the rest of my day. Brian had an exam the following day so I told him to stop worrying and just go back to his apartment so he could study.

Mia, April, and I lounged around the rest of the evening talking and watching trash TV.

"You really need to take better care of yourself. I know you're trying to lose a few pounds but eat more," April scolded.

"Yes, mother," I said giving Mia a wink. "I really don't see the big deal other than how embarrassing the whole thing was. I'll eat better and just avoid running in the middle of the day. No biggie."

"Ugh, if it makes you feel better, I feel pretty fat right now. These cramps are killing me and I'm so bloated!" groaned Mia. April said something that I tuned out and my heart started racing. I broke out into a sweat. I must have had a deer in the headlights look because they started laughing. They both asked, "Hey! What's wrong? You feeling ok?"

"Oh my God… I don't remember the last time I got my period." I was in a panic. I really couldn't remember. All the trips to Brian's parent's house, seeing my family, summer classes, work, all the time I'd been enjoying with Brian, I never thought to think about why I hadn't gotten my period. I'd been so caught up enjoying my new love and new place that it didn't occur to me to wonder about where lady flow was.

"Are you pregnant?" Mia asked rather excitedly.

"Are you?" April said with concern.

"No! I mean I don't think so. No! There's no way. I mean, there's a way but we're careful almost all the time."

"Almost doesn't count," said Mia singing. Her amusement at the potentially catastrophic situation was upsetting.

"God, shut it for a second Mia! Let me think for a minute… I got it right before we moved in here so that was, what, early May? So, I'm only… oh God… almost three weeks late… can that be right?" I said panicked.

"We need to get a test. That's a long time to be late," the voice of reason, April added.

I knew she was right but didn't want to. I was scared about what it would say. I didn't want my future determined by peeing on a stick. Couldn't I just use a Magic 8 ball and take that for its word? *Magic 8 ball, am I with child?* Shake, shake, shake and roll the ball over: *Not today. Ask again in a few years* would be the appropriate response. If only life were that simple.

"I'm not getting a test today. I need to talk to Brian first. I'm pretty sure I'm not, but if I am, I want to give him a warning shot that I might be knocked up before just springing it on him." I was also hoping that I would magically get my period that night and not have to mention it at all to him.

It was the worst night of sleep in my life. I tossed and turned wondering with fear. What if I was pregnant? What would I do? I still had at least another year of school if I really busted my ass getting classes done. What would his parents say and do? What would my mom do? She'd be devastated to think she'd be a grandmother already, I knew that much. What would Brian DO?

We loved each other but springing a baby on him… What would he say? How would he react? He had his own plans. He was leaving in a few weeks to start a one-month officer training course, and the following summer, he was commissioning into the Air Force. He wanted to fly. How would a baby and I fit into that picture?

I was so overwhelmed, I went to the kitchen and took a shot of vodka. I immediately felt guilty. If I was pregnant, I was already a horrible mother. Could I even keep the baby? There were so many thoughts and questions buzzing through my mind. I actually thought, "Why don't I just throw myself down the stairs outside? That should take care of any potential problem?" Then I snapped back to reality. I would have to just be as calm as possible and wait to talk to Brian after his test.

I had that constant feeling of nausea. I assumed it was from being on edge about all the 'what-ifs'. The constant panic made me even more nervous, which in turn made me even more nauseous since I thought it was from being knocked up. I was on a merry-go-round until I eventually fell asleep just after the sun came up. As the first in my family to go to college, I didn't want to fail. I could disappoint my family or myself. My education was something I cherished like I would from winning the lottery.

I woke up to my cell ringing. It was Brian. I thought about not even answering but figured I'd better put my big girl panties on and talk to him.

"Hey." I wanted to vomit.

"Hey. I'm done with my test. Think I passed. What are you doing?" Brian asked so innocently. Not the tone of a guy who was just about to have his world rocked.

"Um… I actually just woke up. I didn't sleep well."

"You ok? Are you still feeling bad from your little spill yesterday?" He tried to make a joke but I couldn't bring myself to laugh or even say anything. I was just silent. "Hey. What's wrong?"

"We need to talk, and I'd rather not do it over the phone." I had knots in my stomach. It probably sounded like I was going to dump him, or tell him his dog died, or worse, his girlfriend was pregnant. I'm sure he was anxious the entire way to my apartment but this really was a conversation we had to have in person.

He got to my place in record time. Seven minutes flat. There was a hesitant knock on the front door. I knew his mind must have been racing for him to knock rather than use the key I'd given him.

I yelled for him to come in and motioned for him to come to my room.

"So. What's up?" He was more than hesitant, almost sheepish and timid as he walked in.

"Ok. I'm not sure how to say this and if I even really need to say anything at all, but I wanted to let you know so I could give you a heads up just in case…" He cut me off.

"Stop rambling. Just say it please." I could see little beads of sweat on his forehead. "What's going on?"

"I might be pregnant." It was like a bomb had gone off. Things were deadly silent. I could feel ringing in my ears and my body was buzzing from the adrenaline and heat. He sat down on the bed and put his head down for a second before looking at me.

"You might be pregnant? You're not sure?"

"I'm almost three weeks late. Could be from my diet or I could be late because we've been so busy the past couple of weeks travelling and school. Stress can do wonders to a girl's body. I could also be late because I'm pregnant. I haven't taken a test or even bought one yet because I wanted to talk to you about it first." He didn't say anything. I stood at the foot of the bed for what felt like an eternity before I finally spoke again.

"Please say something. I've been freaking out all night thinking about it." I was wringing my hands together and started to feel sick again. He was going to walk out and never come back.

"Well, let's go get a test. That's the only way we'll know for sure, right?" He said it so calmly. I wasn't sure if he'd heard me correctly.

"Yes. But those things can be wrong sometimes." I was being delusionally optimistic.

We walked to his car like we were on a death march. He drove to the closest drug store and parked. I was mortified just knowing why we were there. I couldn't bring myself to go in and buy the test. I'd feel like everyone would be staring at me, casting judgmental looks at the irresponsible Puerto Rican girl who was already becoming a statistic. Pregnant, unwed, and not even out of college yet.

"I can't go in. It's too embarrassing." I said, my voice wavering.

"I'll go. Just any test?" Brian was being extremely calm about the whole thing.

"Any test should be fine I guess. I don't know. I've never had to buy one before." He nodded and got out of the car. I desperately wanted him to put his arms around me for comfort, or at least tell me things would be fine, but so far, he'd been quiet, collected, and distant.

I knew it was a lot to take in with no warning, but I wanted him to be sympathetic and affectionate like he always was. Looking back, it was selfish of me to expect him to be this big hero to the damsel in distress because in reality, this was happening to him too. It wasn't just my feelings that were involved but, I was only concerned with wanting to be comforted rather than offering him any comfort as well.

I sat in the car bouncing my knee and fighting back tears until he got in the car. He handed me the bag and drove off.

When he parked in front of my building, I turned to him and blurted out, "I'm sorry. I didn't want for this to happen." I burst into tears. I was doing the ugly cry. The one when your mouth opens and turns down at the same time. You can't keep your eyes open and snot starts running all over the place. I looked like a hysterical woman.

He leaned over and hugged me for a long time. He was back. Tender and loving. He just held me while I cried and soaked his shoulder in tears. After a few minutes I pulled myself together as much as I could and checked my face in the mirror. My eyes were already red and puffy and my cheeks were red from me wiping them dry. I looked awful.

"No matter what the test says, we'll figure it out. I love you." He brushed my hair back and got out of the car.

Waiting those three minutes to see what the little line on the pregnancy test was excruciating. I paced back and forth in my room while Brian sat there watching me. I had no idea what was going through his mind but I at least knew he wasn't going to totally abandon me, at least not yet. He looked at his watch and said we could look at it. There was a lump in my throat and my heart was pounding. I looked down and let out a deep sigh.

"It's positive." I started crying again. Brian sat motionless.

"What do you want to do?" he asked.

"I don't know…. I don't know," was all I could manage through my, now, silent tears.

6

Adult Decisions

The next few days were terrible. I see-sawed back and forth between hysterical crying and smiling like a nut job at the thought of having a baby. One minute I was happy thinking of this little, innocent, perfect being that was part of Brian and me. The next I was so terrified I wanted to scream. As much as I loved Brian, I HAD to finish school. I was the first person in my family to make it to college. I didn't want to be a pregnant failure, a dropout, a statistic.

Brian was as supportive as possible but understandably freaked out. He had become slightly distant and quiet. We tried to act normal but there was this big cloud hanging over us. To make matters worse, I already extremely sick. I felt alone. I hadn't told Mia or April yet, and hadn't even thought about seeing a doctor. After a week in limbo Brian finally sat me down for a serious talk.

"Listen, we have to actually talk about this. The longer we wait, the harder....," he stopped in the hopes I'd intervene. When I didn't, he continued, "The harder certain options become. If we don't go certain routes, you have to start going to the doctor. We don't even know if it's ok or in the right spot or whatever they check for," he said hesitantly.

I was in shock. I couldn't believe he'd actually brought up "certain" options. He couldn't even bring himself to call a spade a spade—abortion. I had to admit, I had seriously considered it for a brief second, but to hear him say it aloud, hurt. I felt like he'd be totally ok with killing this child, our child. He also sounded like he'd done some research, at the least, while I'd barely done more than vomit or sleep since having my fate determined by that little stick.

"How could you even propose the idea?! I'm not getting an abortion! If you don't want to have this baby, FINE. I can figure things out alone, but I am not doing that. I will raise the baby myself or give it up! Jesus! How could you even say that…," I yelled.

"Relax and keep your voice down," he said looking around his room like we were being watched. "I'm not saying I want that, but we have to talk about everything. You're just all over the place lately and haven't said anything to me about what you really want to do." He looked at me like I was the only one at fault.

"I feel alone here. You haven't said much of anything either which doesn't help. What if I did want to keep the baby? You've given me no sign that you'd be ok with that." I could feel myself starting to slip away into a hysterical woman again.

He looked at me with a resigned smile, "You're right. I haven't said anything. Honestly, I am completely freaked out. What would we do with a baby? I'm leaving in a few weeks for training and graduate in a year before I commission. I think I'd be ok raising a baby, but I don't know that for sure. It'd be easy for me to finish school. I already have a job lined up, but what about you? You still have two years left. Not to mention you have to actually push this thing out. I've done some research and that shit looks awful! Plus, you're already sick. Do you think you could finish school like this?"

I slumped down onto the bed, closed my eyes, and said, "I don't know. I haven't thought that far ahead, but I know I am absolutely not having an abortion. Not gonna happen. End of story. So don't even bring it up again." I had sincerely hoped I'd closed the door permanently on that talk.

"Ok. I won't mention it again. So that leaves having the baby to keep or giving it up."

Without even thinking I said, "Keep."

I opened my eyes and sat up to look at Brian. He was so handsome, even with massive bags under his eyes. I knew that was the only decision I could ever had made. I loved Brian so much that it actually hurt sometimes, and I knew he loved me the same. I gave in to my pregnancy hormones and started crying again. I was so overwhelmed by everything—being pregnant, sick, thinking about school, and love. I already felt so much love for Brian and this little alien creature inside me that I didn't know what to do but cry. I had just made the most difficult decision of my life and knew with every ounce of my body that it was the right one.

Brian sat down next to me and grabbed my hand. He leaned over and kissed my cheek. "Keep." He repeated it in a definitive way and sounded a little happy about the idea, although this may have all been in my head. I was probably trying to be too optimistic about his feelings in the matter. "Ok. We're keeping it." Then with no notice, he slid off the bed, down onto one knee and said, "Let's get married. I love you. I will love this baby. Will you marry me?"

I started to cry even harder. I don't know what I expected from him—run screaming, try to make it work only to leave when things got tough, try and convince me to give the baby away. I did not expect this. Brian was perplexed. He got back on to the bed next to me.

"What? What's wrong? This is the best thing for us," he said, his voice disappointed or relieved by my reaction. I was unsure of which in my tear-filled stupor.

"We don't need to be married to have this baby. I don't want you to think you have to marry me. I'm not trying to trap you."

"I know. I'm asking because I want to. We both know it was going to happen sooner or later so why not sooner?"

I had assumed we'd get married but we had never actually talked about it. For the first time in my life, I was speechless.

"Well… are you going to answer or just sit there?" He squeezed my hand and brushed my hair back.

I smiled. I knew he was right. We'd have gotten married, and though the situation wasn't ideal, a baby just helped move things along in the right direction for us, right?

"Yes. Let's get married." I practically jumped on top of him to kiss him. Things felt like they had clicked back into place. We had a multiple orgasmic sex session that afternoon and laid there with my head on his chest until I fell asleep for my second nap of the day.

I woke up to rush to the bathroom for an unexpected date with the toilet, again. Pregnancy had become a pain in the ass quickly. I was sick, a couple pounds heavier despite the lack of appetite and vomiting, and I was constantly tired. That evening I dozed off thinking how shitty I felt physically but being beyond happy with Brian and the thought of our life together. How naïve I was to ignore the long-term reality of our choices.

I woke up around midnight. Brian was staring up at the ceiling. I looked up at him so he knew I was awake.

"Hey," I smiled at him but he kept staring off into nothing. "What's wrong?"

He hesitated for a minute. "Fuck. We have to tell our parents."

My stomach felt queasy again. We had just made two of the biggest decisions in our lives –keep the baby and get hitched. The thought of discussing it with our parents had never crossed our minds. I knew telling my mom would be easy, or at least easier than telling his parents. She didn't help me financially and had no room to judge considering her past, but Brian's family, would probably be devastated and embarrassed.

They were paying for his apartment, books, and car. The school's track program and Air Force were both taking care of various school tabs. He would be the prodigious son tarnished by yours truly. He was their golden child. He never did any wrong, not even during high school. Add on top of that, they were pillars of their small community and would suffer awful embarrassment.

Then I thought about how I would disappoint them. I wasn't even their kid, and I didn't want to disappoint them. I couldn't even fathom how much more difficult it was for Brian. His parents seemed to love me, especially his mom, but once we told her the news, she'd hate me. I'd be cast into the role of the slut who seduced her one and only perfect son who managed to trap him by not only getting pregnant, but by forcing him to marry me.

"Well, I can just call my mom. I'm not driving all the way home to tell her. I already know what will happen. She'll either go all hysterical and make it about herself and how 'young' she is to be a grandmother, or she'll be delusional and get excited by the idea. Either way, I'm not up for her shenanigans. I have enough to deal with it."

"Ok, fine. But what about MY parents? They're going to flip out. How am I supposed to the tell them? *Oh, I got my girlfriend pregnant, and we're getting married ASAP.* I don't think so." His voice sounded both irritated and scared.

"No. You obviously can't tell your parents like that. Should we go together? Would that make it easier?" I thought the gesture of offering to go was nice but didn't actually mean it. I was terrified of having to sit down with his parents and have the conversation.

"Yeah. That would make it easier. I don't think they'll go all ape shit if you're with me."

Damn it! I thought. I was going to have to have this awkward and terrible conversation with them. "Ok. Why don't we go this weekend? Get it over and done with. Like ripping the Band-Aid off."

He rubbed my hair and said he'd call them and let them know we were coming up for the weekend.

We made a game plan before we left Friday evening on how we'd tell them. We'd get in and have a nice dinner, kind of like the last supper before we dropped the bombshell the next day. I didn't want to spend the whole weekend feeling uncomfortable. If they took the news horribly, we could get out of there early enough on Saturday to get back to our life—the one we still had to work all the kinks out of. If they took it well, we'd stay to see if they could help us figure things out realistically. I knew the likelihood of them being happy about the whole thing was almost at zero but I was still hoping they'd be ok and supportive with the news.

Nancy was happy to see us, like always. I rolled my eyes in my head thinking, "Lady, if you only knew what we were about to tell you. You'd wish Brian had never met me."

"You look wonderful! You're almost glowing! What are you doing differently?" She was so genuine it made me want to cry. I would have hated me if I were her.

"Oh, nothing really. It's probably just all the sun I've been getting lately." In reality, that wonderful glow people talk about is just the constant sweat you have from throwing up half the day. Wonderful glow my ass. I gave Brian a look, and he thankfully intervened.

"Mom, it's been a long day. I think we'll just eat dinner and head to bed."

"Well ok. No plans tonight to see Scott or anyone else?" She seemed surprised. She was onto us. My paranoia and guilty conscious was setting in.

"No, not tonight. We may meet up with him tomorrow." He headed into the kitchen to start gathering plates to set the table. I inhaled and immediately wanted to vomit. It was Nancy's delicious pot roast. My hormones destroyed everything from my waist line to my taste buds. How was I going to get through dinner? I'd have to suck it up, eat, and then rush to the bathroom to vomit quietly, if that was even possible.

Henry joined us and was his normal, quiet, polite self. We said grace and I ate slowly, trying my best to avoid the meat and not smell anything.

"You ok, sweetheart?" Nancy asked.

"Oh, fine. I think I got a little carsick from the drive up and am still not feeling too well." I gave a small smile.

"You poor thing. Well, I won't be offended if you want to excuse yourself."

"Are you sure? I'm so sorry. Brian drove a little too fast on all those bumpy roads today, and it's really messed my stomach up. I'm so sorry." I got up slowly from the table and headed straight to the bathroom. I splashed some cold water on my face, took a small sip, and then ran for the toilet. I had turned the bathroom fan on and desperately hoped no one heard anything. After a few minutes regaining my composure and a few swishes of mouthwash, I headed out and waved goodnight to everyone and went straight to bed. I slept for more than twelve hours before waking up at nine.

When I woke up the next morning, I knew it was going to be an awful day. It was already thundering and dark out. The wind was blowing, and I could hear the tree branches knocking against the roof of the house. All that was missing was the torrential down pour that was headed our way. *Great,* I thought. Even if we wanted to leave immediately after telling them, I'm sure Brian's parents would insist we wait until the rain cleared to be safe. I slowly got out of bed and ate a saltine cracker that Brian had thoughtfully placed next to the bed during the night.

As I was getting dressed, Brian came in. He looked like he hadn't slept at all.

"Hey, you're awake."

"Yeah, the thunder woke me up. Your parents already up?"

"They are. Ok, now don't be mad." He was gearing up for something. Whenever someone says, "Don't be mad" the first thing you do is to get mad!

"What did you do?" I was angry and my growling stomach wasn't helping.

"Well, I told my parents everything last night after you went to bed." He exhaled deeply as though he'd been holding his breath the entire time.

"Why would you do that? I came here to be with you to do it. If you were just going to blab it out alone, why'd I even come? I could have just stayed home!"

"Sshhh. Keep your voice down. I told them because my mom already had a feeling you were. I mean, you didn't eat last night, we heard you throw up, you went to bed early, and please, please don't take offense but your ass and tits are huge! It doesn't take much to put two and two together."

I was offended. But I liked my bigger assets, and I knew he was right. I was also relieved that I didn't have to see their look of disappointment when we told them.

"Still, you should have waited or at least given me the heads up last night sometime that you were going to tell them alone."

"I should have, but I didn't want to wake you up. Sorry."

"Well are you going to tell me what they said? How'd they react? Should I jump out the window and hitchhike home?" My stomach was in knots. I was so nervous about how they'd react and how'd they see. It almost felt like we'd been caught in the actual act. I mean, I'm sure they knew we were having sex at school but were careful. Plus, it's not one of those things you really openly talk to your parents about, but admitting that not only had we been having sex, we were stupid and irresponsible about it was a double whammy.

"Um... they're not happy about it but what can they do. They said we're technically adults and they can't make our choices for us, but they're going to be supportive and do what they can." I felt like he was holding back information and just giving me the nicest recap of the conversation.

"What does supportive mean? I mean, are they going to cut you off financially?" I sounded like a gold digger and knew it as soon as I said. We both knew, though, that if his parents didn't keep paying for his apartment, we'd be homeless. We really hadn't thought our plan through very well.

"I don't know. I don't think so. At least they didn't mention it. I think there's a lot we need to figure out so we can actually sit down with them and see how much they're willing to help until I commission next year and have a full salary. We haven't thought about much of anything."

I'm sure his parents had asked a ton of questions because Brian was starting to look overwhelmed. "No, but we can figure out as we go. Right?" I knew that was a horrible idea. I've always been a planner and having so many unknowns is a big stressor. We needed an actual outline of where we wanted our life to go. I couldn't be in limbo with everything.

"I mean, we could but that's probably not a good idea. Where are we even going to live? We're going to have a baby. Do you really think Mia and April would be ok with me crashing at your place all the time and a baby screaming half the night?" We needed to figure it all out but I couldn't help but feel like many of the questions were coming from his parents.

"Look, Brian, I've already told you, we don't have to get married, and you don't even have to deal with any of this if you want to walk away. I'm having this baby and that's about all I can figure out for right this minute. Having this conversation, here, in your old bedroom at your parent's house really isn't the place I wanted to have this conversation. I thought we were just here to tell your parents I'm pregnant and are getting married, not hash out every single freakin' detail."

"I'm not saying I'm changing my mind on anything. I love you. I want to marry you. And I want to have this baby with you, but my parents brought up a lot of stuff that I had no answers to. You still haven't even gone to the doctor yet. My mom made a really big deal about it and said that should be the first priority to make sure the baby is ok."

I resigned. We were making adult decisions but still acting like teenagers. After a long stretch of silence, I said, "You're completely right. I need to go to the doctor. I will go to the campus clinic first thing Monday morning. Then I'll ask them about insurance or if I can just be seen there."

"Good. Should we go out and have some breakfast now?"

"I don't even want to face your parents. They must think I'm awful."

"They don't. Trust me. My mom has actually already blamed me for everything and my dad is, well, you know my dad. He's going along with my mom. He seems to be pretty ok with it though or dealing ok, you know."

I let out a deep breath. "Ok. Let's go."

I very reluctantly stepped out of Brian's room and headed to the living room. I could smell bacon and realized how starving I was. As soon as I saw Nancy, she burst into tears and walked over with her arms open.

"I wish you two would have told us sooner. We could have helped you two figure things out much quicker." The woman was a saint. I couldn't have been that kind if I were her.

"I'm so sorry. I, we, didn't mean for any of this to happen. It just did. I'm sorry." I started crying.

She pulled away and looked at me. "Sit down. Now, I know things like this happen and I don't want to blame anyone. You both are equally at fault." She was wiping her face and blowing her nose. "I just want you to know, we are here for you. You two have a lot to sort out and we are going to help you however we can. Right Henry?" He looked at me blankly and just nodded. He looked like a shock casualty.

"Thank you. You both are so kind and generous, and I don't deserve it. I can't say anything more than I'm sorry. It's a big shock to me, and Brian too. We really didn't want for this to happen. It's not ideal in any way but I'm sure Brian told you, I'm going to have the baby." I looked down at my hands the whole time like a child. I couldn't even bring myself to look at Nancy or Henry for more than half a second.

Henry finally spoke and sounded indifferent about the whole thing, "There's no use in apologizing and the what-ifs now. What's done is done."

Nancy gave a quick look towards Henry, and he went back to staring at the blank TV. "Here's what we're going to do, first, you have got to see a doctor. We have to make sure the baby is growing well and see exactly how far along you are. Then we can think about marriage, living arrangements, and school. Have you spoken to your mom yet?" She was like a machine. She was being gentle but firm and taking charge of everything. It was not at all what I had expected.

I just nodded no.

"Well, then I guess you better tell her. It's not something a mother wants to be kept in the dark about." She glared at Brian.

"Ok. I can call her today." I quickly added, "The drive is too long to actually tell her in person, and I'd rather tell her sooner than later."

"As long as you tell her." That seemed to wrap up the conversation for the time being. We ate breakfast in silence with the occasional, "Feeling ok?" aimed at me every so often since I'd been outed. I ate small bites and just nodded my head. Not only did I feel sick, I felt like I'd killed their dog and they were still being civil and decent towards me. I just wanted to get out of there.

We left as soon as we were done. There wasn't the normal happy goodbye we, or at least I, had become accustomed to. There was the standard big hug but this time a small, sad smile from Nancy and a "Take care of yourself and that baby. Make sure you go to the doctor as soon as you can," she said robotically. I think they were hoping it had all been some terrible mistake and a doctor would clear it all up.

On the drive back, I made the call to my mother. And I'm so glad I called rather than waste a trip home. Here are the highlights of that splendid conversation:

Me: "Mom, I have some big news so you should probably sit down and let me talk first before you say anything."

My mom: "Shit, spit it out. Did Brian dump you? How could you mess..."

Me: "No mother. Brian didn't dump me. In fact, we're getting married very soon. I'm pregnant."

My mom: silence.... silence... silence... then wailing into the phone, "Oh my GOD! How could you be so stupid?! You can't have a baby....(sobbing then wailing)...." Oh my God!... I can't be a grandma...." I had to pull the phone away from my ear she was so loud. It was so comical I started laughing. Brian looked at me like I was the crazy one. I just pointed to the phone and shook my head still laughing. I didn't say anything for a full eight minutes. She continued to wail and rant and sob, never even realizing I had set the phone on the dashboard and shut my eyes to focus on something other than my nausea. Once it was quiet, I picked up the phone.

Me: "You done? Look, I don't have any other details for you other than what I just told you so don't ask. I'm going to the doctor first thing Monday morning to check and make sure the baby is ok. I really don't feel well and am in no mood to talk about this right now. Calm down and I'll call you tomorrow or Monday after my appointment. Ok?" I didn't even give her a chance to start up again before I hung up. Could you even imagine how this conversation would have gone in person?

Almost all the important people knew everything except two, Mia and April. I figured I would talk to them after my appointment when Brian and I could come up with a tangible plan.

Brian skipped his class so he could come with me to my appointment. We held each other's hands the entire time, letting them get sweaty from nervousness. The nurse called my name, and we headed back. I laid back on the table with my stomach exposed and answered all the questions they had for me: number of sexual partners, was Brian the father, last period, last pap if any, and other questions the nurse insisted were standard. As she was finishing up the doctor came in.

He was a short and slender little Indian man that had a lisp when he talked. He was sloppily dressed but was kind and didn't show any outward judgement towards us. He looked at the information I'd just given and got to work pouring hot jelly on my stomach and began my ultrasound. It seemed like he was searching for something that wasn't there and then we heard it. The quick swoosh, swoosh, swoosh of the baby's heartbeat. And then we saw her (at least that's what I'd hoped the baby was). She looked like a little bean. The little flicker where the heart was beating so quickly. One hundred and sixty beats per minute the doctor said. Perfect and healthy. I squeezed Brian's hand and had tears coming down my face.

I looked to Brian and he had the biggest smile on his face and kissed my hand. That was our baby. The timing may have been horrible, and being a young mother certainly wasn't something I'd ever seen happening to me, but actually seeing that little peanut on the screen next to me was something I would never be sorry for. The doctor printed out a few pictures for us to keep, referred me to an OB clinic that dealt with uninsured, or poor patients to be blunt, and told me I was nine weeks along and due mid-January.

As soon as we left the appointment, Brian turned to me and said, "Let's just get married now."

"What do you mean now?"

"I mean, now. Let's just make an appointment and go to the Justice of the Peace and do it." He was so excited about the idea.

"What about our family, your parents? Won't this just further piss everyone off?" I was starting to get excited about just getting married right then too but didn't want his parents even more upset with us than they already were.

Brian thought for a second. "I guess. Ok. Why don't we tell them we want to do it this weekend at their house? We can get the legal stuff done this week and have our church pastor come to the house whenever he's free."

I smiled and hugged Brian. "Let's do it!" Everything felt right.

We went straight to the courthouse, filled out all the paperwork, and then scheduled an appointment to legally get married on Friday. We'd have an official ceremony Saturday at his parent's house. We each called our parents and told them the plan. They were both less than excited, especially my mother if you could imagine, but Nancy said she'd have everything planned and ready for Saturday.

When we got back to my apartment, Mia and April were sitting at the kitchen table eating cereal and gave us both a quizzical look.

"You two look all giddy and cheesy! How was the visit with Brian's parents?" Mia asked.

I'd been avoiding the girls in fear of them finding out I was pregnant sooner than I was ready to tell.

"You should probably head back to your place. I'm going to talk to the girls about… everything," I whispered to Brian. I kissed him goodbye and took a seat at the table.

"We need to talk." I sounded like I was going to break up with them.

"Ok. Talk. We haven't seen you in what feels like forever. We miss you." April sounded hurt. If she was hurt, Mia was angry, and my news wasn't going to help.

"I know. I'm really sorry. Things have been kind of all over the place lately and well… you know how I had told y'all I hadn't gotten my period…." They both nodded and said yeah in unison like they knew what was coming. "Well, turns out I'm pregnant. Due January fourteenth." I pulled out the sonogram pictures.

"What? Are you serious?" April was excited and happy for me. She got up and gave me a big hug. "Why didn't you tell us?" She looked to Mia and said, "We're going to be aunts!"

Mia looked like I had betrayed her. "Why didn't you tell us?" She asked with an attitude. "We live together. We've always told each other everything. This isn't just some 'Oh I got a new bike' kind of news. This is really big. I mean, what are you going to do? We don't have room here for a baby. What about school?"

I wanted to cry and hit her at the same time. I was under so much stress and pressure as it was, having to make Mia feel better about my situation wasn't on my list of things to deal with. I understood where she was coming from, I really did. We had been pretty inseparable before Brian, and now I spent almost all my time with him. The girls and I had made all sorts of plans for junior year about throwing parties at our house, going out, having a constant sleepover type atmosphere, and I had ruined it. Our trio had dwindled to a duo of Mia and April.

"I'm really sorry, Mia. I obviously didn't plan this. It just happened…"

"You may not have planned it, but you apparently did nothing to prevent it from happening in the first place. It's so irresponsible. You probably just ruined your life." I could see April step forward to try and diffuse Mia, but I waved at her to stop.

"You know, Mia, I love you. I love you and April. You two have become my sisters. I'm sorry things are not working out the way we had all planned, but shit happens and I'm not going to keep apologizing to everyone about this baby! I have never loved something so much, and he or she isn't even here yet. I just want you to be here for me. I just want y'all to love me back, love my baby, and be supportive. That's it! If you can't do that…" I started crying, again. I had turned into the biggest cry baby.

Mia's face turned sheepish after having been such a bitch. She and April walked over and gave me a hug. "We're both here for you. I shouldn't have been so rude. I'm just surprised is all," she said rubbing my back comfortingly.

"It's ok, I guess. I know I've been a shitty friend lately. Things change but it's all been good change. I do have more news though. Brian and I are getting married at the courthouse on Friday and then having a ceremony at his parent's house on Saturday. I need you two to be my maids of honor."

They both hugged me again and said absolutely.

The next few days were a blur. I still had classes to take, work, and was in constant contact with Brian's mom to give whatever help I could for Saturday's little ceremony. Not to mention, I had to find an appropriate dress. Mia, April, and I went to the mall and found the perfect dresses. I found a beautiful white dress. Even though I didn't think a knocked-up bride was supposed to wear white, I was going for it anyways.

Mia and April both found gorgeous, matching bridesmaid's dresses. I bought an extra one for Brian's sister. Seeing as how I hadn't met her yet and wouldn't until the ceremony, I figured it would be a nice gesture. A *Hey, I'm your new sister-in-law. I'm carrying your brother's baby. Be a maid of honor with my two best friends in the whole world* kind of gesture.

Friday's courthouse ceremony came and went with little fanfare. It was an old, heavy set judge that was wearing way too much cologne to mask his B.O. in a dirty looking courthouse room. It smelled like old feet and the A/C was barely working. I wore a striped maxi skirt with sandals and a tank top. Brian wore cargo shorts and a t-shirt that said "10 things you say when you have whiskey dick". Totally inappropriate! I still have no clue why he picked that shirt to wear while we legally said vows to become husband and wife but he did. I was happy to become Mrs. Brian Roberts so I let it slide. We repeated everything the judge said, kissed, and walked out like we'd just settled a traffic ticket. We headed back to pack and got ready to leave so we could celebrate with our family and a handful of friends.

We arrived around nine that morning and Nancy had outdone herself. Everything was gorgeous! She had set up a large white tent with large fans spread out to keep things a little cooler. There were little white lights strung in their trees. The front porch banisters where we would say our vows (again) were lined in white and pale pink hydrangeas. There were a few large round tables already set for our few guests with white tablecloths and pale pink lace on top. There were candles waiting to be lit and more flowers on each table. For having less than five days' notice, everything turned out beyond perfect. Even if she'd had more time, I couldn't imagine a more beautiful wedding. Naturally, I cried.

"Oh, honey, is something wrong? We can change it. It's your day!"

"Nothing is wrong. It's just so pretty. I can't believe you did all this for us."

"Of course I did. You're my daughter now. Brian loves you and so do I. Things are happening in a different order but it doesn't change anything. I told you we were here for you and I meant it." She was an angel!

I gave her a big hug and pulled out one of the pictures from our first ultrasound. She put her hand to her mouth and started crying. "Oh my goodness! That's my grandson… or granddaughter. I can't believe it. Isn't that a little miracle?"

I smiled and agreed. "Guess I better get ready. My maids of honor should be here soon. Has Sarah made it here yet? I wanted to ask if she'd be a maid of honor too. I even got her a dress."

"Isn't that so thoughtful of you! She'll be here in about an hour. I'll make sure she comes and says hello right away. You're mother also called me and will be here around the same time. She seemed a little frantic."

"Sounds about right. Whatever she does or says, just ignore her. She can be a little erratic at times." Nancy laughed thinking I was joking.

I had just finished showering when Mia and April got in. They both looked great with their hair and makeup done. They started getting me put together as quick as possible so I could have a few pictures taken. Then we heard her, Hurricane Dora! I needed a drink to prepare and brace myself for her but had to settle for ginger ale.

"Good lord! Look at this house! Y'all must make a fortune! It's so nice. Long drive though and in the middle of bumble-fuck nowhere."

An awkward laugh from Nancy who was clearly not prepared for the woman that arrived. I looked to April, "Can you please get my mother in here, now?"

"Oh! You look gorgeous! A little puffy but gorgeous!"

"Hi Mom. You look…" I looked at her and not only had she recently dyed her hair so it was more vibrant than usual, but she was wearing a skin tight white dress that showed every nook and cranny of her beefy little body and platform red faux patent leather shoes that she couldn't walk in. "What the hell are you wearing? You look like someone tried to shove Staypuft into a sausage casing!"

"Don't be ugly! I wanted to look nice. Impress your new in-laws. Maybe meet a single guy here."

"There are so many things wrong with that statement. First, if you want to impress them, wear something age and body appropriate that isn't WHITE! Secondly, don't curse! They're not like that. And lastly, who do you think is coming? This is a small ceremony like I told you on the phone. There will not be single guys your age and we are not club hopping after this. Just please tell me you have a backup outfit?"

"I don't and even if I did, I think I look pretty damn good. I'm not changing. I'll tone it down a little though if that'll make you happy. Look at your boobs! You really are knocked up."

Why did I invite her? I thought. It was way too late to send her home. The ceremony was starting in less than an hour so kicking her out would just cause more of a scene. I told her to just sit with me nicely and help me get dressed. My hair and makeup was done so my mom helped me slip into my dress. It was a simple strapless, knee-length dress that was covered in lace and had a simple satin belt around the waist. It was the first time my mom was quiet. She just stared at me and gave me a motherly smile.

"You look like the perfect bride. I can't believe my baby is getting married and having a baby." It looked like she was going to cry but then stopped when the door opened. It was someone I hadn't met yet but knew from her pictures, Sarah, Brian's twin sister.

She was gorgeous, just like Brian, only feminine. They both had the same blue eyes and the same smile. The only difference was her hair was deep red and she had a few freckles on her cheeks. "Hi. Nice to finally meet you," she sounded cautious like she wasn't sure if she would like me or not.

"Nice to meet you too. Sorry it's taken so long and we're meeting like this but, you know. Things are a little… crazy. I got you a dress if you wanted to be a bridesmaid or maid of honor with Mia and April. Totally feel free to say no if you don't feel comfortable. I just thought with you being Brian's sister, it would be nice. Your mom told me your size."

She gave a small smile. "Thanks. If you want me to stand up there with y'all, I'd be happy to. No problem." I had a feeling she was there all together against her will but who could say no to a bride that was already emotionally unstable. For our first meeting and under the circumstances, it went relatively well.

It was time to walk down the small aisle. My mother and Nancy walked out together, then the girls. I was going to start walking when Henry stopped me. I was nervous about what he would say based off his silence after the news from our last visit. He looked at me kindly and said, "Welcome to our family. Now, let me walk you down the aisle."

"Of course." I hugged him and held back tears. I couldn't ruin my makeup just yet.

The rest of the evening was perfect despite a few hiccups, mainly from my mother, but I had already prepared myself to just ignore it and have fun. Brian looked like a movie star in his grey suit and looked at peace with everything. Mia and April looked beautiful as always dancing on the small makeshift dance floor that was just a large area rug Nancy had pulled outside from their living room. Even my mom looked like she was having fun. We ate delicious food, all cooked by Nancy, and ate a lot of cake that she'd ordered from the local bakery.

The sun started to set and the little lights in the trees came on. It became bearable to be outside so the fans were turned off. Brian and I danced most of the night as though no one else was there. It was going on nine and that meant closing time. I was exhausted. Nancy was too after all the work she'd done. My mother headed back to the hotel that Nancy and Henry had generously paid for. Everyone else got in their cars to make the drive back to where ever it was they came from.

Brian and I were about to start cleaning when Nancy and Henry walked over.

"Stop that. We'll take care of everything. Sit for a minute," said Nancy as she sat at one of the dirty tables.

We set the dishes in our hands down and sat.

"We wanted to give you two a wedding gift. We need to have our grandbaby in a safer vehicle when he or she arrives." Henry handed us the keys to their new Honda CR-V.

"Dad? Mom? Are you guys sure?" Brian was just as stunned as I was.

"Of course, we're sure. It's our gift to you and that baby. And here, another small gift." Nancy handed us a key for the honeymoon suite of the local hotel.

"Thank you. Thank you so much. You have no idea how generous this is of you and how much we appreciate it." I got up and hugged Nancy, then Henry. Brian and I were so grateful. We gave many more hugs and 'thank yous' before we left.

We got into our new car and headed for the hotel. Sadly, I was so exhausted that Brian didn't get any honeymoon suite loving. It was rather anticlimactic after the best day of our lives so far. That night I fell asleep happily in Brian's arms, having dreams of my fairytale ending that I was sure we would have. If only someone had warned me, they don't actually exist.

7

Big Changes

Summer came and went, and so did Brian. Off to his final few weeks of training before he could commission at the end of the year. I slowly got bigger and started feeling more like my old self—a big relief. I was tired of being tired, and tired of throwing up half the day. We even managed to work out most of the kinks in our new life as husband and wife. We figured out how to manage our household budget, dinner planning, and all the other mundane things included in marital bliss.

After much discussion, Mia and April were gracious enough to let Brian's roommate take my room at our place so I could move into Brian's apartment. It was our first home, and we wanted our baby to have his or her own room.

I switched my major from International Relations to Political Science since it would bump my graduation date up to Brian's graduation date. I just needed to hunker down and take an extra two classes each semester to make sure it happened. My advisor warned me it would be difficult, especially since I was due at the beginning of my final semester, but thankfully, my new mother-in-law offered to help us out the first few weeks. The hope was that I wouldn't fall behind and we would learn the ropes of parenting. Everything appeared to be falling into place.

The fall semester marked the halfway point of my pregnancy. We had a baby pool going to guess what the sex of the baby would be. Most people agreed it was a girl since my hips and ass had practically exploded. Brian couldn't make the appointment so I went alone. The doctor wrote it down and placed it in a sealed envelope so we could open it together when he got back from his training exercise. The second he walked into the apartment I tore the envelope open.

"I KNEW IT!!!!" It's a GIRL!" I showed Brian the little slip of paper with sloppy handwriting. To say I was over the moon happy was an understatement. "I get to have a little mini-me," I squealed.

Brian had the biggest smile on his face. He walked over and hugged me. "She'll be beautiful just like her momma."

Knowing what we were having made everything definitive. As if my growing belly and body parts weren't enough. We knew it was a little girl. What would she be like? Who would she look like? We daydreamed about the life we'd give her and the picture was always perfect.

Mia and April were even more excited than I was, if that was possible. Since the wedding, I had made more of an effort to make time for them like the old days. It was definitely a modified version though. No Jell-O shots for me or dancing on top of bars. A few days after we found out the baby was a 'she', the girls and I opted for a relaxed night out—just dinner and a walk since the air was finally cooler in the evening with fall being in full swing.

"So, I've been seeing someone." Mia had a shy smile and looked like she was nervous to mention it to us.

April and I both exchanged glances since this was the first we'd heard about it.

"Really? Who is he?" I was extremely interested to find out. Mia looked smitten. It looked like she was serious about her mystery man.

"Well, it's kind of a long-distance relationship but we see each other most weekends."

"I thought you've been going home to see your parents?" April said offended to have been kept in the dark.

"Well, who is he? How'd you meet him?" I was excited to hear all the details. I had never seen Mia beam at the mere thought of a guy before.

"I actually met him at your wedding..."

I racked my brain. Who was there that was single? It was mostly just family and they were either too old, too poor, or too married for Mia. Then it hit me. Shit. "Please don't tell me it's Scott."

She smiled and looked down. *Damn it* I screamed in my head.

"We hit it off, exchanged numbers, and have been talking and see each other whenever we can ever since. He's really sweet. He's a good guy."

"Bull shit. He's so rude. The guy hates me. Why didn't you say anything? The wedding was almost three months a go!" I said with genuine shock and anger. Brian knew nothing about this secret hook up either, and if he did, he was smart enough to let Mia tell me herself. April grabbed my arm gently in a 'You don't want to upset the pregnant lady' kind of way.

"He really is a good guy, and he doesn't hate you. I think you guys just got off on the wrong foot. Besides, you have no room to talk. You've been in la-la land since you met Brian. And yes, things almost feel back to the way they used to be, and April, no offense, but I still feel lonely sometimes. Scott understands me and he's funny and he's really smart and..."

"Just stop. Stop. Even if he actually is all those things, which I don't think he is, you should have said something. This is coming out of nowhere. Does Brian know?"

"No one knows, or at least no one knew. He's felt the same way as me— just kind of left out now that his best friend is married. That may have been the reason we started talking, but it's turned into something more. I really, really like him."

April spoke up and said, "Well, if you say so, then I'm happy for you. I can't lie and say I'm not upset you haven't said anything to me at least though."

I rolled my eyes. April was always way too nice and forgiving. "Fine. If you really, really like him, I guess. It's whatever, though. I'm not going to pretend I'm happy about it. I know he doesn't like me, and the feeling is mutual. Just be careful. I really think he's a fox in sheep's clothing." I was still fuming. I had been caught completely off guard with Mia's news.

When I got home later that night, I asked Brian if he knew anything and luckily for him, he was just as shocked as I was. Or he probably just valued his life enough to lie about it since pregnant women tend to be highly emotional.

Over the next few months, things with Brian were definitely more strained and Mia seemed to really be falling for Scott (barf!). Finals for the fall semester didn't help, but it was much more than that. I was the size of a house, our little girl was getting big, and that meant my due date was right around the corner.

Our sex life had pretty much dwindled to once every two or three weeks if I was lucky. I'm pretty sure my size and big belly didn't help. I wasn't graceful like I used to be. And the bickering was at an all-time high.

We fought over everything from making sure the shower curtain was closed all the way so it could dry properly to who was going to do the grocery shopping that week or making sure the toilet seat was left down. Stressed was an understatement. It was new territory for us. Things had been smooth sailing up until that point.

I felt like Brian resented me. Maybe he felt trapped, even though I gave him the option to walk away. I was starting to feel resentment towards him for the imagined resentment towards me. I had sacrificed too. I changed my major, my body was a walking disaster— no more two-piece swimsuits for me thanks to my 'tiger' marks also known as stretch marks, and I felt like I was losing my two best friends. I knew that was the life I had chosen but it was still difficult. I wanted to be a normal college junior. Going out whenever I wanted and be carefree, but that ship had sailed. I was officially an adult and was about to bring a new life into the world. I couldn't screw her up. I may have failed in certain parts of my life, but I wasn't going to fail our daughter.

I stopped 'nagging' Brian about all the little things and made sure I was the perfect housewife. I cooked, cleaned, ironed, kept my part-time job, and made sure I made it to classes. It was utterly exhausting but Brian seemed to be happier and more stress-free so I was happy to make him happy.

It was right after our uneventful New Year's celebration at his parent's house that I felt a horrible pain. My stomach went tight like a brick and I wanted to vomit it hurt so badly. I woke Brian up and told him I didn't feel right. He ignored me thinking it was just gas or more Braxton hicks contractions so he went back to sleep. A few minutes later, another sharp pain.

I shook Brian. "Please get up. I think I'm in labor." Another stabbing pain.

He rubbed his eyes. "Are you sure? It's not just gas?"

"Brian, I'm sure. Please. We need to get up and go to the hospital. I'm in pain. My back is starting to really hurt. I'm going to get your parents and let them know what's going on."

I slowly got out of bed and made my way to their room. They jumped out of bed and rushed around gathering their things like they were the ones in labor.

"Now honey, just stay calm. We will be with you two the entire time. Henry, make sure we have her bags in the car and the car seat is in there too."

"Thank you so much, Nancy. I'll go see if Brian is ready." It was nice to be made a fuss over. When I walked into Brian's old room, he was barely getting his pants on. "What the hell is taking you so long Brian? I need to get to the hospital. I'd like to get an epidural at some point. This pain is excruciating. Hurry up!"

He put his hand to his head and asked for his water on the nightstand. "I'm moving. Give me a minute."

"No! If you wouldn't have had so much champagne, you would be fine right now. Move!" I threw the bottle of water at him and bent over and took deep breaths. Brian had insisted we celebrate New Year's like normal people our age, even though I was nine months pregnant and had no interest in staying up to ring in the New Year. Scott was home and Mia had come with him. They were officially a couple. With Brian in no position to drive, his parents drove us to the hospital with a quick pit stop to get Brian some coffee.

By the time we got to the hospital, I was in so much pain I couldn't walk and couldn't focus on being angry at Brian. It was unlike anything I'd ever felt. I was sweating, my heart was racing, there was awful pain shooting from my back to my stomach, and I was throwing up. It was the worst experience of my life! The nurse looked at me and sent me straight to a room. Twenty minutes later I was fully dilated and pushing. Brian looked so scared. I was in so much agony I couldn't speak.

After a few minutes of pushing and other 'pleasantries' no one tells you about when you have a baby, I heard her tiny cry. They set her on my chest while they rubbed her little back as her cries strengthened. It was the most beautiful thing I'd ever heard in my life. I burst into uncontrollable tears. I was so overcome with love for my daughter, our daughter, Nina. Our perfect little Nina. I looked over to Brian and he was crying, overwhelmed by seeing this little being. His little girl. It was the best day of our lives.

Brian's parents came in after I was transferred to the recovery wing and cried when they saw her too. It was amazing to see how this tiny person could create such a big reaction. I called my mom to tell her the news.

She answered with a hint of a slur, clearly having celebrated New Year's like I should have been.

"Ha *(hiccup)*, Happy New *(hiccup)* Year's! What's your butt still doing up? *(hiccup)*. Ain't it late for you?"

"It is late and I'm exhausted. I just wanted to let you know I'm in the hospital…" She cut me off before I could finish.

"Hospital! Why? *(hiccup)*"

"I had the baby. Nina is here, and she's so beautiful, Mom," I said full of emotion staring at my little girl.

There were instantaneous sobs. "Oh, Lord. *(hiccup)*. Thank you, Jesus! Hey! Y'all hear that *(hiccup)*," she yelled to the people in the background. "I'm a grandma now! I wish I was there! I still can't believe I'm a grandma! I'm too young for all this old people shit," she said half laughing and half crying.

"Mom, I'm beat. Let me get off the phone so I can send you pictures."

"You better! Send me pictures of the little chubby thing. Just one thing. Have her call me Nona. Not grandma!"

"Whatever you want, Mom. I'm getting off the phone now. Love you."

I texted out pictures of Nina to everyone and they all said the same thing, "She's beautiful," "She's perfect," "Can't wait to meet her." All things a mother already knows about her child.

I spent the rest of my time in the hospital being poked, prodded, and pushed on by nurses. Brian spent the entire time holding Nina. He never put her down. It melted my heart to see how much he loved her already. Nursing was awful for me, but I powered through the pain since 'breast is best', and Nina was going to have the best from the very start, even if that meant I cried every time I nursed her.

School started a mere two weeks later, and I was still trying to recover from pushing out an eight-pound baby. Even with the help from Nancy, there was only so much she could do since I was nursing around the clock. I was too exhausted and my grades were going to suffer horribly.

"I think I'm going to have to take a semester off," I told Nancy one morning after dragging myself out of bed.

"Honey, are you sure? I know how hard you've been working."

"I just can't do everything. I'm so grateful for all your help, but I'm so tired. I can barely focus in class. I think it's what'll be best for everyone, especially Nina," I said trying to convince myself this was the right thing for us all.

"If that's what you really want. What does Brian think?"

"I haven't mentioned it yet, but I'm sure he'll be on board. Besides, I can take some online classes once I'm ready and in a good routine. It'll all work out. Plus, I don't want to keep you away from your life for too long. This is the best thing to do," I said with a smile.

Nancy decided she'd stay for another week or two to help before heading home.

It was a tough decision and my mother wasn't thrilled, but it was too much for me to jump back in to my final semester, especially since I was slated to take twenty-one hours of classes to make sure I graduated with Brian.

I think everyone was secretly relieved. Brian never had to shoulder the responsibility of doing much. He was going to be the breadwinner working for the US Air Force and I had gotten pregnant so it was an unspoken agreement that I would have to sacrifice the most, which I did without saying a word.

Brian was the perfect husband right after having Nina, but once school started up again, things got a little rocky. I understood he was tired from pulling late nights studying, keeping in shape for the Air Force, and being a new father and husband, but he was different. It was an instantaneous change; it was little things at first. He'd come home from a PT session with the AF instructors or come home from school, give me a brief hello, and head straight to Nina. Or he'd casually forget about plans we'd made to spend some quality time together. He would offer less and less to help me out with small things around the house. I kept quiet. I was the one at home without a job, so I should have been able to handle cleaning and errands and everything else. That's what I told myself. Even though I was starting to become more annoyed and hurt by Brian becoming so distant.

Nina was about seven weeks old when I just snapped. She had spent almost three hours crying thanks to colic, and Brian walked in after spending two and a half hours out doing who knows what. There was no 'hello', no 'how was your day', no 'let me have her so you can get a minute'.

Instead he said, "Jesus, she was crying when I left and she's still crying. What have you been doing the whole time?"

I lost it and turned into a crazy lady. I gently laid Nina in her swing and calmly walked over to Brian. Without saying a word, I smacked him as hard as I could across the face.

"What have *I* been doing the whole time? Where the hell have *YOU* been? How dare you imply I'm sitting around on my ass all day while our daughter screams her head off! I bust my ass around here all-day cleaning, cooking, doing laundry, raising a baby who loves to do nothing more than scream half the day, and you're off doing whatever you want."

He looked at me with watery eyes and took a step back. "What the fuck is wrong with you?! I was at class! That's where I'm always at!"

"Really?! Because it takes less than ten minutes to get to your class and it's only a forty-five-minute class. You were gone for two and a half hours today! What were you doing that extra hour and fifteen or twenty minutes when you could have been here actually helping? Actually, being a present participant in this marriage?" I screamed. I sounded like a stalker but was too angry to care.

"I stopped at the library to get some work done. I knew I wouldn't be able to concentrate enough to do it here." It was more than reasonable, but I was so angry I just kept going.

"I call bull shit. You could have let me know that at some point today. You have completely stopped communicating with me. You've stopped helping around here. You don't even act like you're attracted to me anymore. You do your training, go to class, and when you're here you act like you're in prison." I was yelling and crying at the same time.

"What are you talking about? I do help, and I didn't tell you I was going to the library because I didn't want you to nag me about it."

"You *were* helping. Notice I said that in past tense. For weeks now, you've become withdrawn and expect me to just pick up after you and do everything by myself. When's the last time you put your own clothes away or washed a dish or even loaded a single plate into the dishwasher? And another thing, I have never nagged you! I know you need to study so if you need a quiet place, fine, then tell me that. Don't just disappear and not answer my calls or text when I try to get a hold of you. This is a marriage, Brian. That means there are two of us, and we need to do things together. It's starting to seem like I'm in this by myself."

"I know this is a marriage, but I shouldn't have to check in with you all the time. You want me to do dishes, I'll do dishes. Just tell me what you want." He sounded hopeless.

"That's not the damn point. I need you to be in this with me. I need you to go back to being the helpful, sweet, and loving man you were before we had the baby. Not what you are now. I need you to see if I'm overwhelmed or exhausted from nursing half the night. Offer to help me. Kiss me or hug me. Show some kind of affection. I just don't understand what's going on with you?" I had finally calmed myself down a bit and our arguing had put Nina to sleep.

Brian sat down on the sofa and put his head back. "I'll try harder. I'm sorry. This is just… it's all overwhelming."

I sat down next to him. It was quiet except for the swishing of Nina's swing moving back and forth.

"You don't think I know that. I'm overwhelmed too, but we need to talk to each other. This is our family. I don't want to feel like I'm alone here."

He grabbed my hand. "I know. I'm sorry."

I looked at his face and it was still bright red. "I'm sorry too. I shouldn't have kept quiet for so long. And I should never have hit you. I just snapped. Let me get you an ice pack."

That had been our first real argument, and it was a big one. I walked to the kitchen and got him the ice pack to soothe his cheek. He laughed at me. "You know, that was a pretty good hit."

I felt horrible about it. "I'm really sorry. I just… I don't know. Like I said, I've felt overwhelmed too. I don't know if I'm a good mother. I can't even get my own baby to stop crying half the time. I just need you here. I need you. I should have said something weeks ago but thought I could handle things myself."

"Well, I know now. Trust me," he said rubbing his cheek before placing the ice on it. "I'll be more present and I'll help more. And for the record, I am still attracted to you. You're more beautiful now than before." He smiled at me with one side of his face squished against the ice pack. I gave him a kiss and everything seemed settled.

Things were better after our big blowout. Things with Brian felt normal again. He was compassionate and loving. We were both communicating well. I started to wean Nina from the breast so he offered to do a feeding at night every occasionally. I could finally get more than three hours of sleep. Nina's colic seemed to end which was the biggest relief because I thought I would break soon. We were one big happy family. Brian's grades were better during his final semester than they'd ever been and my advisor told me I would be able to do most of my final coursework online over the summer which was when we were set to move.

School was a few weeks from being done, and I could feel my anxiety levels creeping up. Once Brian graduated and commissioned, we'd be moving away from all our family and friends to Montgomery, Alabama for about six weeks while he completed his last round of officer training for the Air Force. Then it was all a big question mark.

We didn't know what job he'd get slated for, where we'd live, how long we'd live there. It was all a crap shoot. We had both hoped he'd get selected to be a pilot and that we'd then move to Florida for training before hopefully getting stationed in San Antonio, but there was no guarantee even one of those hopes would happen. For all we knew, they'd select him to be in charge of some chow hall at a base in Wyoming or Delaware or Timbuktu. We just didn't know. While the unknown can be exciting, when you're utterly at a loss for having a total say, the prospects can be daunting. Letting others decide your fate can make or break you.

It was finally May. The weather was gorgeous and Brian was finally free to relax and spend some time with his little family. After studying non-stop for a week, he'd taken his finals and found out he had passed so he'd be walking the graduation stage that week. We spent the next few days packing our apartment to get ready for the movers to come and spending a lot of time at the pool with Nina. Mia and April had volunteered to watch her so Brian and I could go out on an actual date, something we'd almost forgotten existed.

"So where are we going?" I was so happy to get out.

"I figured it'd be fitting we go to the place we had our first date." He leaned over in the car and gave me a kiss. I felt butterflies in my stomach again, the way I had when we first met.

I smiled thinking about my first impression of Dickey's. "Sounds perfect to me."

We ate our BBQ platters off of the cheap Styrofoam plates and plastic utensils and talked about how much things had changed and how happy we were. I was ready to head home but Brian said we couldn't go home until we had eaten dessert.

"If you really want dessert, ok. I am so full though. I don't know if I can eat another thing."

"That's ok. Let's go for a small walk and maybe you'll be a little hungry by the time we get dessert," he said playfully.

We drove back to campus and went for a stroll. He led me to my old dorm, and there it was. He had somehow managed to have a picnic set up under the big tree outside my old dorm. Under the tree was that same big sleeping bag and a bag filled with junk food--candy bars, muffins, and soda. I had a feeling April or Mia had helped. For a brief minute, I forgot about everything—it was just us.

"Oh my goodness! Brian, this is so sweet. I cannot believe you did all this. This is probably better than our first date." We walked hand in hand to the tree for our dessert picnic. It was a great way to close out our time in that place and move on to what else was in store for us.

Just a few days later, the movers came and shipped everything off to base housing. We put our last few belongings in the car. We'd planned on staying with his parents for a week before leaving to Alabama since our shipment wouldn't be delivered for at least two weeks.

It was graduation day. I had never been prouder of Brian as he walked across the stage in his uniform as a Second Lieutenant and grabbed the tube that contained his diploma. I felt a tinge of jealousy that I wouldn't be getting my diploma in the same way. It would probably just be mailed to me once I was finished with my classes. If I was lucky, I'd get a congratulatory phone call or pat on the back. There would be no fancy dress to wear underneath my maroon robe, no cheers or applause, just a tube in the mail with my diploma.

We had a small party at Mia and April's since we were officially homeless until we got to Alabama. His parents and sister were there, Brian's old roommate, and of course, the charming Scott made an appearance.

Scott and Mia admittedly looked adorable and happy which irritated me. I didn't see what she saw in him other than the fact he had money, but Mia wasn't quite that shallow.

Things were going well. We were all eating and drinking and admiring how gorgeous and big Nina had gotten when Scott decided it was appropriate to make a toast.

"To my best friend that I've known since grade school. I love you like a brother and am proud of you. You really are a good man. Even married a decent girl when she got pregnant. So, it inspired me. I didn't get Mia pregnant so don't worry, but we are getting married! To Brian… and my soon-to-be wife, Mia!"

Not only had he insulted me, but he made the toast about him and Mia. I was furious. Why didn't Mia tell me? I took one last sip of champagne and whispered to Brian that Nina needed a nap. I gave his parents a hug and told them we'd see them at their house. I thanked Mia and April for hosting while giving Mia the dirtiest look I could, and I ignored Scott altogether. It was time to hit the road.

8

Fitting In

We'd been in Alabama for three weeks. The days with Nina were largely devoid of conversation beyond the mundane chatter between Nina and I. I'd talk and she'd just smile away or cry, unamused with my attempts at filling the space with noise. Other than Nina, I was largely alone.

Brian spent long days in class, and he was one of the few married guys in his training cycle. My age didn't help much either. I was a full two or three years younger than some of the other wives. I had little in common with the few wives that were there.

Brian was loving his coursework and was at the top of his class. This boded well for him getting a pilot's slot at the end of his training a few weeks later, but that meant he spent a lot of time studying and working out to maintain his weight and max out his physical fitness test.

I was determined to be proactive in making new friends, even if we were only going to be at Maxwell for about another month before moving on. I'd come from a great support system with Mia, April and Nancy, to being totally on my own in a place I didn't really like with no friends.

I saw a Facebook post about a mommy and me workout group that met twice a week at the local park. It seemed like the perfect place to meet women who would hopefully be nice (we were in the south for goodness sakes) and Nina could find some little play friends. She was already six months old, and I could tell she needed more stimulation than what I could offer.

My first mommy and me session was horrible! I arrived ten minutes before the start of the workout so I could introduce myself and Nina to the other moms. Reasonable and smart, right? There were exactly six women already there. They looked slightly older but not too much, so no big deal. I placed my diaper bag down and set Nina down while I set up our little yoga mat. I picked precious Nina up and made my way over to the circle. The first thing that I noticed was how nice they looked for a mommy and me workout. I mean, they were wearing the tightest and nicest looking cropped yoga pants that I considered suitable for everyday wear and little tank tops with their cleavage pushed up. They all had their hair perfectly curled or straightened, and a full face of tastefully done makeup. I, on the other hand, looked like a hobo. Not even a cute, trendy, chic hobo. I had a pair of faded yoga pants that had paint on one leg and an oversized shirt that read 'No pain. No Gain'. I don't even think I brushed my hair that morning, let alone put on makeup. Even if I didn't find my new best friend in that group, I'd probably make at least one. I was determined to remain positive.

I walked over with a big smile, ready to introduce myself. The leader of the group, who surely went by the name of Candy or Fluffy or something equally absurd (I've never been good with names), gave me a fake smile and welcomed me to the group. She proceeded to introduce the other women, and when the introductions were done, they went right back to their previous conversation without even a second look at me or Nina. They had their clique, and I was not welcome.

I stayed for the entire hour session out of stubbornness. I didn't want them thinking they could run me off that quickly. That, and the fact that it was too nice a day to sulk back home with Nina. Once it was over, I gathered my things quickly and went straight to the car. Another mommy and me session wasn't in the cards. I'd have to find something else.

When I got home, Brian was curious to find out how my outing went.

"How'd it go? Were there a lot of other women there?" he asked while changing out of his uniform.

"Um, it was ok. I don't think it was really my thing though. Everyone seemed nice enough, I just didn't really click with any of them." I was too embarrassed to tell Brian how awful the women were to me.

"Oh, that's too bad. Maybe you should try it just one more time. You never know, you may grow to like it, maybe some new people will be there."

"Maybe.... I think I just want to focus on getting back into shape a little more intensely though. I've lost all the baby weight but things are still a little flabby and jiggly where they shouldn't be all flabby and jiggly. You know?"

"I think you look great," he said in a rather robotic voice that I tried not to take offense too.

I signed Nina up for the daycare at the local gym and vowed to go five days a week.

After the first few days back at the gym, I was sore but feeling better. Working out had always been therapeutic for me and reclaiming my body after all those months was almost like a high. I felt better and more at peace with everything—being away from everyone I loved, even my crazy ass family, lack of friends in a new place, and having no degree or job.

I noticed that I always ran into the same woman and her son, who looked about Nina's age, at the same time at the gym. She looked just as disheveled as I did most days and like a down to earth person. I went out on a limb to introduce myself while we dropped our kids off at the daycare.

I looked over and awkwardly smiled. She probably thought I was some psycho gym stalker. "Hi."

"Hi. How are you?" she asked.

"Good. Glad they have a daycare here. It's so nice." I hadn't even started my workout and was already sweating.

"Yeah. It is. Have you been coming here long?"

"Oh, no. My husband is in the Air Force, and we just moved here. Still trying to get my bearings. Find things for Nina and I. Nina's my little girl over there. She's a little over six months old." I smiled and pointed to the little dark haired, blue eyed baby that had drool running down her freshly cleaned dress.

"Oh. What squadron? My husband and I have been stationed here for almost a year now."

"He's not really with a squadron. He's doing his officer training course before he can get slotted for a job. He's hoping to get a pilot's slot. He has a few more weeks before we find out if he's got one and where we'll move to next."

"I'm Maggie by the way," she said as she extended her hand.

"Nice to meet you."

"Mind if I tag along with you today as a workout buddy? It's always easier for me to stay on track if I have someone else pushing me." I hoped I didn't sound like a total loner.

"Not at all! I'm the same way," she said with a kind smile.

During our workout, I found out we had a lot in common. We were both from Texas, the oldest children of our family, her son was close in age to Nina, and we liked the same kind of music and TV.

She reminded me a lot of April. Maggie was so nice, genuinely sweet, and normal! Not like the women I had met at the park the week before. Before we left the gym, we exchanged numbers and made plans to grab lunch with the kids later in the week. I was so giddy. I had finally made a friend! I know it probably sounds pathetic, at least it does to me, but finally meeting someone that was nice to me and liked me made me feel more optimistic and good. I had someone other than Nina (sometimes Brian) to listen to my ridiculous rants or stupid jokes. Another adult that understood some of the challenges of being a parent when your husband is gone a lot.

Maggie and I hung out a lot the next few weeks, she even introduced me to a few of her friends. They were all just as nice as she was and all had kids. I had found my little circle of friends. I figured hosting a little barbeque at our tiny house would be a great way for Brian to meet Maggie, her husband, Andy, and their little boy, Ethan. As luck would have it, or lack of, Brian was not a fan of Andy.

Brian was perfectly pleasant and nice but as soon as they left Brian said, "I'm so glad that's over. Maggie was great.

Their son was adorable. Her husband on the other hand, a know-it-all asshole. I don't like him. He talked down to me the entire time about things no one cares about."

"I know he doesn't really make the best first impression, but I really like Maggie and hoped we'd all hit it off and have another couple to do things with."

I was disheartened. I was hoping we could all be great friends and do things like double date nights and share a sitter or weekend BBQ's in the time we had left there. It didn't look like it was going to happen though.

That's something no one ever tells you. Making friends as an adult is one of the most difficult things to do because there are so many players involved. The husbands need to like each other, the wives need to like each other, and the kids need to get along and play nicely. If just one of those is not a team player, you're screwed. It's dating on steroids.

"Why do we need to do 'couple' things? Let's just do our own thing."

"Because I think it'd be fun. You're just going to have to suck it for my sake. Ok?" Maggie and I clicked so quickly and easily. She was my best and only friend there so if Maggie invited us over for dinner, we were going.

I still had April and Mia to talk to but it wasn't the same. They didn't understand married life, dealing with a child, being alone in a new place or any of the other struggles that went along with military life. Sure, they could listen to me vent, but they'd never fully be able to empathize. Never mind the fact that we were all so busy, our conversations didn't last long. We were all slowly disconnecting from one another.

Brian let out a loud groan, "Ugh, fine, but it'll be limited interaction. I am not dealing with that guy in large doses."

"That works for me."

Of course, just as I had started to find my place in Alabama, the moment of truth had come.

"Hey, babe. I have some big news," Brian said beaming with excitement.

"Ok, what is it?" I asked reluctantly.

"I've been selected for flight school. I need to report to Florida in about a month."

"A month! That gives us little to no time to pack, find a place to live, say goodbye to the few friends I have here. Why so soon?"

I was crushed. I'd barely begun finding my way in Alabama and was going to have to start back at square one soon. Flight school was even more intense than the schooling he'd just finished so it was a given I'd be alone ninety percent of the time. The hours were extremely long, training vigorous, and sleep was elusive.

"Look, I know it's not ideal but those are my orders. It'll be another big adjustment, but we can do it. I'll figure out how to balance studying, training, and my family. It'll all work out," he said optimistically.

Great, I thought. Live out your dreams while I have yet to even get my degree.

I spent the last few weeks in Alabama slowly packing, house hunting online, and hanging out with Maggie and our kids. I knew military life would be difficult, but Maggie and I had grown so close in the few short weeks we knew each other. I could feel myself slipping into a minor depression.

"What's wrong? You've been sulking since I told you about flight school. I thought you'd be happy?" he asked one day while I was packing our life into a box.

"I'm happy for you, but… I feel like I'm finally fitting in here. Just the thought of having to do it again makes me anxious. It's been hard for me."

"Yeah, but I thought you said you had a great time at that mommy and me class. Then you met Maggie. You've been fitting in just fine here."

"That's what I said but those women were really mean and clique-y. I was too embarrassed to tell you that. But most of the women I've met here have not been nice to me or they just ignore me. Maggie is my only friend, besides Mia and April of course, but they're not here and they don't understand this military thing. Shit, I barely understand it most of the time. Honestly, things haven't even been great between me and Mia since she blindsided me with her engagement to YOUR friend."

Things had been very rocky between us. I felt like her entire relationship with Scott was kept as a secret. She had been so hurt about Brian and me getting so close so quickly but I at least talked to her about things. She had kept silent on everything when it came to Scott. It left me with an uneasy feeling.

"I'm sorry, babe. I know it's been a rough few weeks and I'm sorry we have to move but that's what you, what we both signed up for. I told you it wasn't going to be easy," he said indignantly.

"I know that. It's just…. this isn't what I expected." At the ripe age of twenty-one, I felt like I was already an old woman. A husband, a baby, actual bills to pay, and trying to maneuver socially through Air Force culture was a lot to handle.

"You're just going to have to find a way to get used to it. With this pilot slot, I'm automatically committed to six years of service. What do you want me to do, turn it down?"

Ugh, *way to make me the bad guy in all this*, I thought.

"No. I don't want you to turn it down. It's the whole reason you joined. I'll manage. It'll be fine. I'll be fine," I said with a fake smile and forced cheery optimism. My lack of sincerity didn't bother Brian. He gave me his million-dollar smile, a quick peck on the cheek, and went back to packing.

Before I knew it, it was time to say our goodbyes to the few friends I had and prepare myself for life in a new city and new home with new people. Thankfully, when we got to Eglin Air Force Base just outside of Valparaiso, Florida, we had a great little apartment within walking distance from the beach, and it was beautiful. There was a great boardwalk with tons of eateries, cute clothing boutiques, and little shops that had a wide array of little tchotchkes. There was a big park and pool in our complex along with a gym that had a small play area for the kids. I had a great feeling about Eglin from the start.

During the next few months while Brian was in flight school I found little things to do here and there with Nina. We did story time, lots of time at the beach and pool, and I even joined a kid friendly running group.

Unlike in Alabama, most of the women there were nice and fairly normal. There were still a few bitches here and there, and of course there's always at least one clique, but I was able to reinvent myself depending on the group or day. I wasn't from there, I wouldn't be for more than a few months, what did they care what I was actually like.

There, if I wanted to be the chic and put- together young mom, I could. If I wanted to be the bohemian, all-natural hippie mom, I could. If I just wanted to be my regular self, I could. I wasn't hurting anyone so why not appeal to all different sorts of women and expand my social circle at the same time. Brian was rarely home and when he was, it was the same as in Alabama; he was studying or sleeping. It was rare we actually spent quality time together or heaven forbid, go on an actual date. I needed companionship.

As much as I missed spending quality time with Brian, I felt worse for Nina. With his crazy hours, by the time he got home, she was already asleep for the evening. I was starting to think she'd forget who he was. Nina was my little buddy. She was always with me and always so happy and eager to 'listen'.

There were times I felt guilty because on the rare occasion Brian was home early, we'd totally forget he was there and go on with our routine. He'd be excluded him from our little girl time while lying on the floor playing with blocks or chasing her around since she'd become an official crawler.

Despite Brian and I being a little off, things were looking up. I felt great. I was finally back in shape and looked great, minus the stretch marks. I was getting adequate sleep and I decided the timing was perfect to finish up my final semester of class work.

"I think I'm finally ready and in a good place to go back to school. I'd just do part-time, not that I have a ton of classes left anyways and put Nina in daycare part-time. What do you think?"

"I think that's a great idea. It'd be good for you to do something positive and get your diploma. I know you've been wanting to finish up since we had Nina. Were you thinking of finishing up here and getting a job at the next duty station or just want to finish it?"

"To be honest, I haven't really thought about that yet. I don't know if I want to leave Nina in daycare full-time just yet to go off and work. She's still so young. I just know I want to get my degree and everything seems to be lined up to do it here. We can talk about it later down the line though."

"Ok. I am on board with whatever you decide."

The University of West Florida had a satellite campus not far from our apartment so I registered to take two of the classes that I couldn't take online at my old school and would still be transferrable towards my degree program. I enrolled Nina in part-time daycare so I could attend classes and have some extra study time.

The night before classes started I was like a little girl anxious for her first day back to school. I picked out my outfit two days in advance (a cute pair of coral cropped skinny jeans with a loose white t-shirt and nude sandals), had all new notebooks and pens. I even woke up early the morning of class to do my hair and get ready so I'd be presentable.

I was so nervous I woke up even earlier than when my alarm was set to go off. It had been almost a year since I'd been in a classroom. I was about the same age as most of the people who were in my class, but I wasn't a normal college student anymore.

Brian had already left early for training so I had a little bit of time alone to have a cup of coffee and piece of toast before I had to wake Nina up and get her ready for her first official day as a part-time daycare baby.

I felt a tinge of guilt at leaving her for the first time. She'd been to daycare at the gym, but I was always within viewing distance of her. I actually had to leave her there with strangers.

The woman in charge of her room was a plump old lady that reminded me of the mother from *Everybody Loves Raymond*. She had her blondish white hair short and curled, some light makeup and red lips, but rather than being a little overly pushy, she was quiet with the grown-ups and silly with the babies.

When Nina saw her, she had no problem crawling away from me to Ms. Sheri. I was relieved but sad and felt a little betrayed that the little person my life revolved so much around could be easily swayed towards anyone that held a shiny object. I gave her a temporary reprieve. Anyone as beautiful as my Nina could get away with anything.

I walked into my class and was surprised at how young the professor looked and how large the class was for a small satellite school. It was in an old building that was desperately in need of a few new coats of paint, some air freshener, and slightly more comfortable seating. I picked my seat to the right of the podium that was center stage and a few rows back. Enough to be able to pay attention and not so front and center I'd draw attention to myself. Other students trickled in and seats filled up. I alternated between nervously looking around to feel out the other students and checking my phone to make sure the daycare hadn't called about Nina.

A few minutes in to the lecture, and I was already bored. It was just an elective and one I wasn't particularly interested in, "Exploration of World Classical Music". I simply registered because it was a check in the box for something I needed to get my degree at my home university. It was a 'beggars can't be choosers' type of mentality when picking my electives.

I half listened and jotted down a few notes when there was a slight whooshing of the door flying open and a girl about my age hurrying in. She scanned the room for a suitable empty seat. Even though the entire first row was vacant. There was one right next to mine in the inconspicuous enough spot I had staked out so she walked straight towards it.

I gave a small smile and turned back to paying half attention. It was a struggle to keep my eyes open. The material itself was boring, but the young professor I thought would be interesting and vibrant about the subject was even more boring and so monotone that I'd have preferred to listen to nails on a chalkboard for an hour.

While gathering my things, the late girl struck up a conversation.

"Hey! Are you new here? It's a pretty small campus, if you want to call it that. I haven't seen you around before. I'm Sadie." She stuck out her hand, and I noticed how pretty she was and definitely friendly. Sadie was slightly taller than me, thin, and nicely tanned. If she had been about an inch taller, I'm sure she could have been a model. She had blond hair that had been cut into a cute little bob and big brown doe-like eyes.

I shook her hand back. "Yeah. It's my first semester here and probably the only semester I'll need to take. I'm finishing up everything else online through my old school.... I'm Nelly by the way."

Oh my God! Why did I just say that, I thought? I'd given her a fake name and she seemed nice—she could be a new friend here. I didn't even think twice about giving this friendly stranger a fake name. Well, it was already out in the universe, and I figured I'd only be spending a little bit of time in class and by the end of the semester, we'd be moving again. I tried not to sweat it. It would just be a fun little game for me. I'd begun slightly portraying different versions of myself when it seemed appropriate so this would be exactly that. I could go on to have fun with it and figure out what little role I wanted to play during my few hours out of the house. Why not? I'd always wanted to be an actress. This was my shot, minus the audience, salary, and fanfare.

"Nice to meet you! Oh, you're married? You look really young to be married." She noticed my wedding band.

"Oh, yeah, he's in the Air Force. He's training to be a pilot. We got married young. I'm twenty-one. I'll be twenty-two soon though." I looked at my ring and twisted it around my finger. As I said my age, I realized how really young that was. *My daughter better never get married that young,* I thought.

"Wow. Must be something special then. I was engaged, but it didn't work out. I wanted some freedom for a little bit longer. I'm only twenty-seven and in no big rush," she said genuinely. I slightly envied her. Sadie was gorgeous and could have gotten any man she wanted but she decided to just roam different pastures—only be accountable to herself. It seemed like a liberating way to live.

I made a 'humph' sound. "Must be nice. Well, I better get going. I want to get a start on some of the assignments and get ahead while I can now that we have the syllabus. It was nice meeting you, Sadie. See you later." I waved bye and left.

I thought about the kind of person Sadie seemed like on my way to the public library. I used to be that person. Carefree, no responsibilities, great friends. Instead, I'd become the epitome of responsibility, a little uptight, some friends, definitely not a Mia or an April, and I was definitely not carefree anymore. I assumed having a husband and baby would do that to you. I didn't want to dwell on what I used to be or what I could be doing in that moment. What was the point?

I loved my daughter and would never regret having her. I loved Brian too, but things were definitely not what they used to be. Sure, we still talked and held hands occasionally but when we talked, it wasn't about our hopes and dreams or silly things like. It was about bills or whose turn it was to load the dishwasher.

Even our sex life had changed. I've always been a pretty physical person. I have the type of personality that craves physical touch. Since Brian had been in training, if he even came home, he'd go straight for the pillow with barely a peck on the cheek. Some nights, he just opted to sleep on a cot in the barracks he was so tired. When we did have sex, it was noticeably less passionate than it was before having Nina. It was definitely less frequent. I was lucky if Brian wanted to touch me once every two weeks. I didn't like to think about it. It was depressing. I pushed all that out of my mind for the time being and vowed to study and talk to Brian about how I was feeling at some point when he wasn't so exhausted.

Two days later at my next class, Sadie was already seated in the spot she'd sat in on the first day and waved for me to sit with her. She was the only person I knew and the class was so boring that I was happy to sit next to someone who could help keep me awake during the lecture. I'd take notes and Sadie would scribble ridiculous phrases or draw obscene pictures of our professor and pass them to my desk. We'd always stay and chat a little after class and that became the routine.

I liked her a lot. She was cool to hang around and was funny. She showed interest in *me*, or I should say in Nelly. Nelly was the young, laid back wife trying to find her way in the world and had no issues with spending most of her time alone in a new place. She was an independent young woman that liked her space and didn't feel the need to spend every waking moment with her husband. Nelly was cool too.

Everything Sadie and I talked about wasn't always a lie. I just chose to omit certain portions of my life or embellish a little. *Did we have kids?* Us? No, not yet. We liked our freedom. (I felt horrible leaving the fact that I had a daughter who I loved more than anything out and I really have no idea why I did that, but I did. Whenever I talked to Sadie, I wanted to be cool and have no baggage other than my husband who was never around.) *What did we do for fun*? Oh you know, try to surf (never surfed a day in my life). Reading, I like to read a lot (that was true). Just relax. Go bar hopping (in my good old days). *How much is your husband gone?* All the time! (Honest answer).

I have never been a pathological liar. It was just fun to create this other woman who was the person I had imagined I would be. Nelly would disappear in a few months when we got new orders, and I'd go back to just being me. Our next duty station would be long-term (at least two years), and I had no desire to pretend to be someone else for that long. I was just pretending. What I was doing, that was just two days a week for a few months. The true issue was that I didn't really know who I was. How could I at 21?

After a few weeks of class, Sadie asked if I wanted to go out with her and some of her girlfriends to a few of the bars downtown. I said of course, as long as my husband was ok with it.

"Hey, Brian, a girlfriend of mine from class wants to go out this weekend. Would it be ok if I tag along and you stay and watch Nina?" Due to his schedule, I couldn't remember the last time he'd been alone with her. They needed that one-on-one time anyways.

"No, not at all. I think you deserve a night out. What do y'all plan on doing?" He sounded excited for me to actually have a friend to hang out with.

"Nothing big. Just dinner and a few drinks." A slight omission on my part. I worked hard so I deserved to have fun. I didn't want to feel guilted into staying home, despite Brian never having given me a reason to feel guilty.

Saturday arrived, and I felt like a college sophomore all over again. Excited to get dressed up, a rarity, and go out dancing, even more rare. It made me really miss Mia and April. I thought about all the times we'd gotten ready together in the dorms and how much things had changed. I felt a twinge of guilt and sadness for not keeping in touch like I should have.

I missed them. I immediately picked up my phone and sent a quick text to them both, "Thinking about y'all. Miss you girls tons. We need to skype soon! I love y'all! XOXO".

April responded immediately, "That's so sweet. I miss you and little Nina tons too. Love you! Give beauty a kiss for me!" I never heard back from Mia, unsurprisingly. She had told me Scott didn't like her being on the phone all the time. I tried to forget about it. I was going to have a great night with Sadie and her friends. I hadn't met them yet but if they were like Sadie, it'd be an awesome evening out.

Before I left the house, I did a double take in the mirror. I looked really good. Almost like my old self. I made sure all the bottles were ready for Brian, Nina's pjs were laid out, and all the other little things he would have forgotten to do were done. I wanted to make it easy on him but I also wanted Nina to be kept on schedule, which I promptly wrote down for him. Brian looked at me and whistled.

"Wow! You look gorgeous! You sure you don't have a hot date?" He walked over to kiss me and fondle me a little. It was a glimpse of the old Brian and it made me want to stay and see what else of the old Brian would come out if I did. He gave me a long kiss and then my phone went off. I pulled back.

"Sorry, sweetie. Sadie is waiting for me downstairs. I better get going." I gave him another long kiss and then walked over to Nina and gave her a kiss. "Not sure when I'll be back but call if you need anything or there's an emergency. I'll come straight home. I'll text you when I'm on my way back. Love you." I walked out the door, took a breath, and became fun Nelly.

Sadie gave me a hug as I got to her car. "You clean up well, young lady."

"Thank you, ma'am." I winked at her and hopped in the front seat.

We sped off to our first spot to meet up with two of her friends for cocktails. It was an upscale place. The kind where you need to know someone to get in and get a good spot. There was music on but not blaring. We could easily hear each other without having to yell across our small table from the corner booth. We all sat back drinking our dirty martinis talking about the guys in the bar. It was so laid back. I was correct in my assumption. Sadie's friends were awesome and laid back.

We were in no rush to move on to the next bar where, I was warned, we would definitely dance. It was the best time I'd had since my wedding. Pure fun and no worries. I felt like a normal twenty-one-year-old. I checked my phone to see the time and saw a text from Brian. It was a picture of Nina looking peaceful, beautiful, and sound asleep in her crib.

It read, "Not too bad for my first time! Everything's good. Have fun."

I snapped back to my normal self for a minute and felt guilty. Here I was out drinking like I hadn't a care in the world. What was wrong with me?

A waiter walked over with a tray of shots, something fruity, compliments of a group of young guys at a table across the room from us. *So cliché,* I thought, but it was a free drink. We all downed our shot left before they could come over and kept us hostage there with cheesy pick-up lines.

The rest of the night was fantastic and a blur. I drank way too much. My alcohol tolerance was that of a twelve-year-old. After leaving the first bar, I was already tipsy. I remember dancing and laughing a lot. Sadie dropped me off and I somehow managed to get to my apartment in one piece. Although, I did initially try to use my key on the wrong apartment door. I got in the house and passed out on the sofa. When I woke up the next morning, my head was pounding, my throat and mouth were as dry as a desert. I had been moved to bed and carefully undressed and re-dressed in my pajamas. I felt a big surge of love for my sweet husband who took care of me and our daughter while I was passed out drunk. My makeup had smeared all over the pillow. *Great, now I have to do more laundry*, I thought. I looked at the clock and saw it was already noon.

I jumped out of bed and felt my head pound again and the room spin. Coffee, coke, and ibuprofen was what I needed, and fast. I washed my face and headed out to the living room.

"Hey! You're up. Have fun last night?" Brian was abnormally cheery. The house was surprisingly clean and Nina was already taking her nap.

"Hey… (pound, pound, pound in my head)… I'm up. It was a lot of fun. Thank you so much for everything. Was Nina good last night? This morning?" I headed straight for the coffee.

"Nina was great. She slept like the dead, kind of like you did. She was good this morning too. I think she misses you though." He was so upbeat considering I had pretty much checked out for almost eighteen hours.

I felt bad that I had missed Nina waking up. She was always so excited when I crept into her room. I'd hear her talking to herself in her crib, and I'd quietly open the door, tiptoe towards her, and clear my throat so she'd know I was there. She'd always turn around and squeal as though she hadn't seen me in days. It was always the best part of my day.

"I missed y'all last night. Maybe we can have a date night soon. I need to find a good sitter first though." I desperately needed the ibuprofen to kick in.

"Sure. Date night sounds fun. Who with?"

I gave him a puzzled look. "With you, who else?"

"Oh ok. Just checking. I thought you might want to go with your new friend Sadie." He was starting to take on a tone of anger in his voice, and I felt a pit in the bottom of my stomach.

Please let this ibuprofen kick in. I felt so sick. "Brian, what are you talking about?" I was lost.

"Oh nothing… but do you mind explaining what the fuck this is and why she thinks your name is Nelly?"

He handed me my phone and there was a text from Sadie that read, "Had a great time with you last night. You're full of surprises. Hope to see you soon!" Seemed innocent enough and then I really felt sick. There was a picture. It was me sitting on top of her, face to face, at a bar and we were definitely kissing, and it looked intense. I ran to the kitchen sink and vomited.

9

The Bottom Fell Out

I was sick to my stomach for two reasons: one, the obvious hangover; and two, my obvious ignorance to what I had done. I was in shock. I rinsed my mouth out and splashed some water on my face and tried not to get sick again while cleaning out the kitchen sink. I looked up at Brian.

"I… I… I have no idea what happened. I mean, I had a lot to drink. Whatever it looks like, it obviously meant nothing. I swear. I'm so so sorry. I just don't know what happened." I felt horrible. What was I thinking last night?

"Really? You have no idea what happened? This picture looks like it says a lot. That was what you were doing on your laid back 'girls' night'?!" He said using air quotes. I had never seen him so angry. I wanted to crawl into a hole and die.

"I'm sorry. Whatever that looks like, it was all just for fun. A big joke. Nothing serious. I don't even remember doing that! I swear! Please tell me you believe me." I was pleading with him and trying not to be so loud that I'd wake Nina up.

He could barely look at me. "Even if I did believe you that it meant nothing, why the hell is she calling you Nelly?"

"It was just a stupid joke. I said I hated my real name but always loved the name Nelly so she thinks it's funny to call me that." I was a horrible liar, and it was an absurd lie at that. I knew it as I said it. I didn't want to tell Brian the truth. He'd think I wasn't just a cheater, which I wasn't, or at least I didn't think I was, but he'd think I was crazy too.

Brian finally looked at me. It was a look that bordered somewhere between disgust like he knew I was lying and pure hurt.

"You know, I had no problem with you going to school. I want you to meet new friends. I want you to be able to go out and let loose every once in a while. But, what you did or what you can't remember you did, this is a complete betrayal of our marriage and MY trust. What... did you just want to go back to school here so you could re-live your college days? Because if you did, I'll tell you, that ship has sailed. We have a kid for God's sake. What the fuck is wrong with you? Did you think it was ok to come home like that? Although, I guess I should be thankful you made it home at all. I'm sure Sadie would have been glad to take you home with her," he said with venom in his voice.

"Brian, please. You know that's not why I went back to school. And I know that I'm not a regular twenty-one-year-old college kid anymore. I know all that. You don't think I'm reminded of that every day when I'm picking Nina back up from daycare so I can come home to clean, cook, and change diapers! I know that! Trust me, I really do. I just wanted one night out where I could feel like myself or just be carefree and not worry about anything. Don't you understand that?"

"I understand wanting to have fun but not the kind of fun that makes you forget you have a family."

"I'm sorry. You're right, I should never have gotten that drunk and totally irresponsible. I'm sorry. You know that's not me. Maybe it was three years ago, but not anymore. I love you and I love Nina with all my heart. It was just a terrible mistake. I'm sorry." My ibuprofen still hadn't kicked in, and I wondered if I'd thrown it back up with everything else.

"I really don't want to hear your 'I'm sorrys'. It shouldn't have happened in the first place! And don't even try to manipulate me into feeling guilty for not finishing school or having responsibilities. I have responsibilities too! I'm busting my ass and working eighteen-hour days training. It's my job! It pays well and keeps you and Nina taken care of. And you decided you wanted to follow me. You didn't want us to be apart. You could have stayed with my parents and finished school. You made the choice to have our daughter, to drop out a semester early, to stay. I never forced you to give up school or any part of yourself. If you're unhappy with how things are, find a way to fix it! But don't lie to me and go off to have some stupid lesbian rendezvous! I'd love a night out to go wild but can't. I know where my responsibilities lie. Do you?"

"I really don't want to get into this now. I feel horrible and frankly, you seem to have no clue about my happiness. You're so wrapped up in flight school that you're barely here! And when you are, you certainly don't ask me how I'M doing. Just asking about my day doesn't count. If you were here more, you'd probably know more about your own wife!"

I knew he had made several valid points, and I definitely am not making excuses for my behavior. It was horrid, but I was alone. Having someone show interest in me made me feel important again, worthy of something more than just being able to change a diaper standing up or making a good dinner. I was an individual. Even though I still had no clue as to exactly what all happened with Sadie, I didn't want to be painted as the only bad guy or player in the situation.

"You feel horrible? How do you think I feel? Knowing my wife is a liar and running around town doing whatever she wants while I'm here taking care of our daughter! You want to talk about this later, fine. Just find someone else to talk to. We talk now or I'm done."

"Done? What do you mean done?" Was he really giving me an ultimatum?

"I mean done. I'm leaving. So you better start talking. Make me understand why you'd want to hook up or make out or whatever with someone else and why you're so unhappy. To be clear, I could care less if you'd hooked up with a man or a woman. It's all cheating to me! Talk."

I took some more ibuprofen and swallowed it with my coke and saltines, took a deep breath and started talking. I told him everything! Just about everything anyways. I skipped the part about lying to Sadie about a few things like my name, how opposite I truly was of who I pretended to be with her, and the part about having no kids. I know I should have told him but let's be real, wouldn't you have someone like that committed? I wasn't crazy! Not by a long shot, I just wanted to be… I don't know, liked maybe, live vicariously temporarily, and have an escape of some sort. So, anyways, I left that part out but was totally honest about everything else.

"Brian, please believe me and know how incredibly sorry I am for my actions last night. I really don't know what happened. You have to believe me."

I still have no clue to this day, just what Sadie told me which wasn't much. She claimed what was in the picture was all that happened. She had never lied to me up until that point about anything that I knew about yet, so I had no reason to doubt her.

Brian stayed quiet so I just kept talking.

"I've been really lonely here. It's been hard being away from everyone I love, every place I love. I still don't even have a favorite place to eat yet. I know you think it's silly but that helps make a place feel a little more like home. I've given up everything. Yes, I've done it willingly, but I didn't think it would be this hard. Remember that mommy and me class in Alabama?"

"Yeah but what does that have to do with anything? Did you make out with one of those moms too?" He had a bite in his words.

"No. I lied about how the class went. They were so mean. They completely ignored me and I was too embarrassed to tell you that. It just made me feel even more like an outsider. That's how I've felt since we started moving. And I hate to admit this, but I'm a little envious of you. You get to live out your dream and I'm not. I'm just a housewife without a degree. Having a degree is kind of essential for me to live out part of my dream. I've felt alone. You're so wrapped up in training that it's like you've checked out. When you are home, your mind is elsewhere," I said with shame. Shame for my behavior, and shame for finally voicing my lack of confidence.

"So now this is my fault?"

I started to get angry. "You're missing the whole point. I'm not blaming you for anything. I'm telling you this is how I feel! The whole thing with Sadie… it's about my insecurities, my stupid desire to… I don't know. Just be different, fit in… I don't know what. I just know I'm sorry."

Brian sat in silence and took the rest of what I'd said in. I didn't know if he was understanding me or trying not to throw something at me. I finished talking just as Nina started to stir in her room. Naptime was over and that meant, I was back on duty. My head felt better, but I was drained emotionally and physically. All my body wanted to do was sleep. I got up to get a bottle and small snack ready for Nina.

Brian stood up from the couch and said, "I'm going to go for a walk. I'll be back soon."

He left me standing there with a bottle in one hand and veggie puffs in the other. I had just poured my heart out, and he left. I couldn't believe it. I knew it was a lot to process but a small nod of understanding or a big fuck you would have been better. I'd at least know where he stood. Instead, he just left.

I went about the rest of my day with Nina. I tried calling and texting Brian but he ignored me. I had started to feel like a nagging wife with the "Where are you?", "Answer me, please", "When are you coming home?". No response. No response. No response. Bedtime for Nina came and went, and still no Brian.

While he was gone, I sent Sadie a text. "Sorry about last night. Had too much to drink. Big mistake. Probably won't be going out for a while."

She responded, but I deleted it and her contact information without even checking the message. I needed to start over as myself. I planned on just slowly distancing myself from Sadie until the semester was out.

It was almost ten o'clock and I still hadn't seen or heard from Brian. I was extremely worried but also utterly exhausted and trying to recover from my girls' night out. If he didn't want to talk to me, there was literally nothing I could do. I certainly wasn't going to drag Nina out at that hour to conduct a search and rescue mission. I did my best not to worry settled in for the night.

Brian woke me around two a.m.

"I'm home," he whispered. He sounded like he was being sweet to me, and then I smelled the whisky on his breath and the beer coming out of his pores.

I wiped my eyes and rolled over to see him propped up in the bed staring at me. "Hey. I was really worried about you. I'm glad you're home. I…"

"Sshhh. Just don't talk right now." He put his pointer finger to my mouth and was smiling. Definitely drunk. Guess he had his guy's night out.

"Brian. I'm really sorry. I never ever wanted to hurt you. I love you. Only you."

He gave me his gorgeous smile. I felt butterflies again. "I know. I should have come home but I just needed to think." His speech was slow and words heavy. I wasn't even angry. I had no room to get upset after my previous evening's actions. I just wanted him to love me again (if he'd stopped) and not be angry.

"I understand. I just wish you'd told me you were ok. I know I laid a lot in your lap with zero notice. I should have kept my promise to be more open and honest with you about my feelings but I know how much stress and pressure you're under." I put my hand on his chest. He smelled like a bar. My stomach did a small lurch at the thought of alcohol.

"We both have done a shitty job at talking to each other. What you did was shitty. It was wrong, period. Just wrong. But I love you too and this needs to work, not just for Nina but for us. You and me need to work." He made a crazy hand gesture pointing back and forth between us.

He continued, "I've thought about it and I know you really want to take these classes but… I just don't feel comfortable with you taking the one class that Sadie is in. I don't. You've lost some of my trust and staying there, with… her… it just doesn't sit well with me. I'm sorry," he said with his eyes half closed.

I looked at Brian's glazed over eyes. He was still so handsome. I just wanted to look into his perfect face forever. I looked down and then back up into his half-open drunk eyes.

"Ok. I'll drop the class. I'll do whatever you want me to if it means I can gain your trust again." I truly meant it. I wanted nothing more than to be a perfect, happily married couple. I loved Brian as much as I did when we first met. Nina cemented my love for him and our bond. I wanted to be a great wife, a perfect wife.

He leaned in and kissed me. There was more passion in that one kiss than we'd had in months. He was back. It felt like it was just Brian and me again. It was bliss. We slowly undressed each other and made love like he was going off to war tomorrow. I felt whole and happy.

Later that morning Brian woke up and was the one paying the price. He had a headache, felt nauseous, and was exhausted.

I doted on him like a mother would a sick child. I still felt incredibly guilty and wanted nothing more than to solidify my place as his loving and loyal wife. He should have been at work but I called the duty officer for him and said he had a stomach bug and wouldn't make it in that day. I thought things were well on the way to being back too normal.

Fresh coffee was brewing and I gathered a plate of fresh bacon, toast, and fried eggs with some ibuprofen. I even decided to skip my class. It wasn't that difficult of a decision considering I was about to drop the class anyways. I needed to avoid Sadie to start rebuilding Brian's trust in me.

I took Brian his breakfast in bed. He gave me a cold, "Thanks," and got up to get ready for work.

"What are you doing? I called in sick for you so you could rest."

"I have to go in. It looks bad if I miss," he said with a shortness in his words.

"What's wrong? I thought things were at least a little ok with us. I know I've royally screwed up but after last night, I thought," he cut me off before I could finish.

"I was drunk last night. Ok? I meant most of what I said but I'm still really angry about everything and need some more time. I don't trust you." He pulled up his pants and tied his boots.

"I gotta go. We'll talk more later if you want but I really need to leave. I'm already late." He took a piece of toast and bacon to go and left.

I sat down on the bed and cried. I didn't know he could be so dismissive. I knew it was delusional of me to think things would just snap back instantly but I really thought after his drunken confessions and the way he kissed me, we were on our way back to each other.

I spent the rest of the week walking on eggshells. Anytime I tried to talk to Brian about anything, even how his day went, he responded with one-word answers or grunts. Then he would get up to play with Nina or go to the bedroom. I'd had enough.

"Brian, you need to get over it! You can't keep punishing me and treating me like a live-in maid and nanny. It's rude and I feel disrespected. Just talk to me already! I've apologized a thousand times, I dropped my class, and deleted Sadie's number. I haven't even left the house in a week. What else do I need to do?" I begged.

"It's been one week. You think trust can be rebuilt in one week? I don't think so. Show me you want to be here. Show me I can trust you again."

"I have been! And yes, it will take longer than a week for you to trust me but you have to meet me halfway. I can't be in this alone. You need to make an effort to talk to me and be present so we can work on our marriage. Stop ignoring me all the time."

He finally stopped playing with Nina to look at me. "I don't mean to ignore you. I'm just trying not to be so pissed at you."

"Let's do counseling then. I've already looked into it and we can go to a marriage counselor and it won't cost us anything. We have to do something. This isn't healthy and I don't want to live like this. I can call right now if you want."

"I don't want to talk to some stranger about our problems."

"That's the problem. You don't want to talk at all! We can go back and forth like this all day but I'm willing to talk and work on us. You need to be willing to do the same."

After a long pause, "Ok. Call the counselor."

We did several sessions with our marriage counselor, Linda. She was a perfectly pleasant woman, but it seemed like we did all the talking and she'd just nod her head and ask stupid questions like, "Why do you think you feel that way?" or "What do you think the reason behind it is?"

I almost smacked her during one session and wanted to scream, "If we knew the answers to all your ridiculous questions, why the hell would we need you?!" We wanted her to give us some more insight and tools on how to fix our relationship, not whatever she was doing.

Going to Linda didn't do much except give Brian and I a place where we could talk openly about everything and not have things turn into an explosive fight. With an outsider looking at us, we had to find ways to communicate like adults since a real adult was watching us. We were able to really hear the other clearly and that brought us closer, not Linda herself.

Everything seemed like it was well on its way to being back on track. It was just in time since Brian's parents were flying in for Christmas, New Years, and Nina's first birthday. Considering I'd distanced myself from Sadie, my closest friend there, and any other acquaintances I had, there wasn't going to be a big party for Nina with other little people. It was just going to be us and the grandparents.

The visit was great. Nancy and Henry were wonderful as always. They were more than happy to watch Nina while Brian and I had a night alone. Dinner and a hotel suite on them! They completely spoiled her in the short amount of time they stayed and blamed it on the fact that we lived so far away. We were one big happy family.

Two days after Christmas, Brian and I left Nina with Nancy and Henry to attend a holiday party for Brian's unit at flight school. I was excited to finally have an opportunity to meet the people he worked with. I wanted to impress and make Brian look good by being a gracious pilot's wife. Even Brian seemed happy to take me out and introduce me to the guys (and a very few of the girls) he worked with and his superior officers.

When we got to the ballroom at the Officer's club where the party was being held, things were already in full swing. The unit had gone all out. There was a DJ, open bar, dance floor, and a big tree with the Secret Santa gifts we were requested to bring. I wasn't too surprised at how many guys there were. The women were so outnumbered they stood out like sore thumbs. Then my heart dropped.

I was chatting nicely with Brian and the wife of one of his buddies, Jessie, about how gorgeous the weather was, even in December, and other niceties when I spotted her. She was in line for the bar and turned to the side to speak to a gentleman. It was Sadie. What in the world was she doing at the bar at a unit function? She had never mentioned anything about being affiliated in any way to the flight school. I kept smiling without hearing what Jessie was actually saying.

"You ok? You look a little flustered?" Brian whispered in my ear.

"Um, yeah. I just need to use the restroom. I'll be right back." I gave Brian a quick kiss and made my way outside the ballroom. I needed a minute to gather my thoughts and pour over every conversation Sadie and I had ever had. Did I miss something?

When I returned a few minutes later, I scanned the room to look for Brian. I wanted to go home. I planned on telling him I felt sick and wanted to call it an early night. He was standing at one of the cocktail tables laughing with none other than Sadie and the gentleman she'd talked to earlier in the bar line. *Fuck my life*, I thought. What were the chances? Brian had no clue who Sadie was, especially since that awful picture showed mostly me and her face had been covered by mine. I took a deep breath, walked over, and figured I'd act like we'd never met and find the quickest escape route.

I put on a big smile and Sadie acted like it was the first time she'd ever met me. Even though I had planned on doing that first, I was extremely offended and also pissed that she got the jump on me with the act.

Brian introduced me to Captain Nichols and her husband, John. He pointed to Sadie. Now I was really confused. If she was an instructor, why was she taking college classes, and how did she even have time for that? She said she called her engagement off, but then she was married? Brian seemed to never have time for much of anything because of the demanding schedule so how did Sadie. I pushed the thoughts out of my head. I needed to focus on acting normal and I would sort through everything else later.

"Nice to meet y'all." I gave an awkward smile and shook both their hands. If she'd lied about what she did for a living and the fact that she was married, what else had she lied about? I took a big drink from my glass of vodka tonic.

"You know, it's kind of stuffy in here. I'm going to step out for a minute and get some air," I said as politely as possible.

"Ok. Want me to come with you?" Brian asked with concern.

"No, not at all. I'll be right in." I smiled and once again, made another quick exit.

I stood on the deck overlooking a small inlet wondering if I should tell Brian about Sadie. I was so engrossed in my thoughts that I never even heard footsteps behind. I jumped when I heard a voice.

"If you're thinking about telling your husband about who I am, don't. It won't be good for him or his career. Trust me," said Sadie. I couldn't tell if she was trying to warn me out of kindness or as a threat.

"What about your career? I'm sure it won't be good for that either. Female superior officer having a fling with a subordinate's wife! Great headline, don't you think?" I felt so betrayed by her, even though I was just as bad as she was.

"No. It wouldn't be good, but I'm telling you it'll be worse for him. He's just starting out and has more to lose than I do. Right, Nelly?" she said with a sly smile.

We were both liars and knew it. "I won't say anything, just answer a few questions for me first."

"Shoot." She looked so at ease as though this was entirely normal for her.

"Ok. First, why were you taking that class?"

"I'm a lifelong student of learning and like to take random classes if I have the time." She smiled and just shrugged her shoulders as if that was a satisfactory answer.

"Why did you tell me you weren't married and didn't like attachments?"

"I don't like being attached. My husband and I are not happily married at the moment. And it would appear that your behavior and the little stories you told me about yourself, show your marriage isn't too great either."

"Our marriage is fine. We've worked on it. Don't worry about us," I snapped back. "Just tell me that we didn't do anything other than make out that night you sent me the picture."

"Do you want me to tell you that or do you want the truth?"

"Give me truth. Stop playing games, Sadie." I almost wanted her to lie but needed to know.

"Well, you were very touchy feely with me after the second bar and I've always thought you were attractive but honestly, things were pretty innocent. We made out, a lot. You wanted to go home with me but I wouldn't have been able to explain that to John, so I made up an excuse about needing to be responsible, and I took you home. On the way home though, you were very… overly friendly to put it kindly…. very grabby. I thought it was cute." She smiled as though this was a normal conversation and she'd just given me great news.

I turned away from her and said, "It was all a mistake. I love my husband. I should never have done that. It was just a mistake."

"If you say so. I'm not judging. But, remember what I said, don't say anything." She said the last three words slowly and with a lot of emphasis. Now that I had the whole story, I was going to keep quiet. Brian and I were finally making headway, and I wasn't going to ruin it. I rationalized thinking he'd already assumed the worst so why pile anything else on, despite the more innocent version she'd just given me. What he didn't know wouldn't hurt him. I also didn't want to ruin his career. I still couldn't tell if Sadie was trying to threaten me into silence by using Brian or not so that was extra incentive to stay quiet.

I walked away without saying anything to Sadie. I just wanted to go home and forget the whole night had happened.

On the drive home though, I felt guilty. I didn't want to start the New Year with more lies. We were both communicating so well with each other. Surely Brian could handle whatever I told him. We were at a stoplight about ten minutes away from our apartment when I looked to Brian and started talking.

"You know I love you, right?" He nodded. "Ok, we've been so open and honest lately and I don't want to ruin anything so I want to be honest with you, right now. Captain Nichols is Sadie. She's the one from that picture. I'm so sorry. I didn't know she..."

He was silent for a moment.

"That bitch." I was shocked. I'd never heard Brian talk about a woman that way. "What a manipulative bitch." He was more talking to himself than me.

"Brian, I'm sorry. I didn't know who she was and she never told me she worked for the Air Force." I was starting to tear up already.

Brian looked at me and shook his head. "You don't understand."

"What are you talking about? I just told you Sadie, your superior, is the one I kissed. What don't you understand?"

He pulled over, put his head down, and took a few deep breaths. "Since we're being honest, I have something we need to talk about. I don't want to lie anymore either."

I swallowed hard but nothing could have braced me for what he was about to say. "Ok. What is it?"

He was nervous and starting to sweat. He could barely look at me.

"After I saw that picture and those texts, I was so angry. I couldn't believe you'd cheated. The night I left, well, I went to one of the bars on the boardwalk and 'Sadie', whose first name is Jennifer was there. I don't know where the other name came from, but we started talking and drinking and one thing led to another and..."

"Please tell me you did not sleep with her. Please tell me that at least Brian. I don't care what you may have thought I did, just tell me you didn't." I was already crying.

"It meant nothing. I just was so angry and hurt. Afterwards, I told her she could transfer me to another class, and I apologized for being unprofessional. She said it was fine. I acted out of anger and was too ashamed to tell you before. I'm sorry."

"You fucked her! And then came home and made love to me! Did you use protection? Do I need to get checked? God! Why would you do that?! I didn't sleep with her! It was a fucking kiss. How could you do that? Want to get even with me? That's not even, that's just pure revenge. Did you hate me that much that you thought it was ok to sleep with someone else?"

I stopped crying and just felt my whole being turn into a ball of rage. My knuckles were white from holding them in fists so tightly so as not to start throwing them Brian's way.

"I know! I just… I thought more happened and… nothing I say will excuse it, I should have told you weeks ago. I should have done a lot differently. And I did use a condom. I'm sorry. Things got out of control…," he said meekishly.

"Shut up! Don't say another word to me or I swear I will kill you. You played the innocent, hurt husband so well. Made me feel like a piece of shit for a kiss! A damn kiss. I dropped my class, one that I need to get my degree by the way, to prove to you that you could trust me. Meanwhile, you fuck your instructor, came home to sleep with me, and have been sitting in her class this entire time! Talk about trust. You're a pathetic and disgusting hypocrite! How dare you? Are you still sleeping with her?"

"No! Absolutely not! I swear to you, it only happened that once. Everything is strictly professional now." I knew he was telling the truth but it meant nothing to me.

I wanted to scream and hit him but instead, I got strangely calm and quiet. "Get out of the car, please."

"Are you serious?" he asked.

"Get out of the car, please."

"We're still seven miles from home. Please, just let me take you home, and I'll stay at the hotel with my parents. Please," he pleaded almost so silently I had to strain to hear him over the pulsing of my heart in my ears.

"Brian, get out of the fucking car! I can't even look at you!" I was using every part of my being and self-will not to hurt Brian. I seriously considered running him over with the car. He looked at me one last time and slowly got out of the driver's seat with glassy eyes. I got out of my seat and walked around to the front to get in.

"I love you and I'm sorry. It was a mistake. Please. Don't leave like this. Just talk to me." Brian looked pathetic.

I got in and before I closed the door, I said, "I'll have your shit packed up and send it to the hotel with your parents. Find another place to live. I'm sure Sadie or Jennifer or whatever the fuck her name is will take you in." I drove off without even looking in my rearview mirror.

10

Picking up the Pieces

I drove the rest of the way home with my mind reeling. I couldn't understand how Brian could have betrayed me in such a way. He had every chance to tell me what he had done. Instead, he continued to make me feel guilty. Pour my heart out in counseling while he opted for the easy way out, only talking about his feelings towards my actions. I wanted to cry but I didn't want to give him the satisfaction of possibly seeing me puffy faced if for some reason he made it home before I did.

I flew into the apartment like a bat out of hell and then remembered Nina was already down for the night. His parents looked at me and could obviously tell something was wrong.

"Hey, sweetie. Everything ok? Where's Brian?" Nancy asked.

To tell them what a lying piece of shit their son was, or take the classy route and kindly tell them they should talk to Brian? No. I opted for brutal honesty. I let my anger get the best of my judgement.

"Your son, my husband, screwed one of his instructors. So, he can stay with you two at the hotel until you go home and then, he can move into the barracks, the street, I really don't care," I scoffed storming past them.

I grabbed a trash bag from the kitchen and headed straight for the bedroom closet. I wasn't going to let Brian have the good luggage, so his clothes could smell like plastic and vanilla lavender until he figured out what to do with them.

"What? That can't be. That doesn't sound like Brian at all. Are you sure about that?" Nancy asked with pure shock.

I really did feel bad for his mother. No parent wants to hear about all the bad stuff their child has done. We like to think the best of them. Nancy was so sweet and didn't deserve for me to break the news in quite that way. I didn't think about it until days later and did apologize for my behavior. Henry, his stoic self, just took it all in.

"Well, it is Brian alright. He told me himself on the way here. He cheated. He's a cheater. Brian is a cheater. I don't want him here. I can't even stand to look at him right now." I was frantically throwing his clothes into the trash bag. I ripped the side of the bag in my frenzy and got really angry.

"Shit. This damn bag." I opened up the doors that led to a small balcony outside of our master bedroom and decided it was easier to throw everything overboard. He made this mess of our marriage, the least he could do was pick his own stuff up. I'd save him the trip up the stairs. Nancy looked at me with wide eyes, like a deer caught in the headlights.

"Please don't do that. Just stop." I was still grabbing his items and throwing them over the balcony. "I know you're angry and you have every right to be, but be an adult or at least let me pack his things. We'll sort all of this out when Brian gets here. Where is he?"

"No, Nancy. WE won't sort it out. Brian and I can try to sort it out but right now, it's not even an option to discuss it.

You don't know the whole story, and I'll spare all the details but what he did was completely inexcusable regardless of the issues we had. You don't get to come in here and fold his stuff nicely for him and make it easy for him to feel better about what he did. He's a grown man, and he's had women taking care of everything for him his entire life. It stops now."

I was starting to get tired and out of breath from walking back and forth from the closet to the balcony so I sat on the bed to think and catch my breath.

"You're right. This is up to you and Brian to sort out. But he is still my son and I won't let you disrespect his things or his home."

"Fine. I'm done anyways. I'd say he has enough clothes down there to last him a while." I finally let the tears come.

What was happening to us? Things used to be so perfect, and now, it was the complete opposite of perfect--it was pure shit.

"Nancy, I'm sorry for all this. Do you and Henry just mind heading back to the hotel? I'm home now and can take care of Nina. Thank you for staying with her."

"Are you sure? You don't want us to wait until Brian comes home so you two can talk?"

"No. I told Brian not to come home. I really cannot be around him right now. He's probably walking or took a cab to your hotel so you should probably meet him there. I really need to be alone with my daughter and think."

Nancy and Henry didn't say anything else. After a few minutes, I heard them outside picking up Brian's things. I laid back on the bed and cried. I ran through every conversation we'd had since moving to Eglin and doubted it all.

Did he really need to stay and work such long hours? Was he really spending nights in the barracks after long days? Had he only slept with Sadie once? Was he still sleeping with her? Why didn't he just tell me when we were in counseling? My phone rang, and I ignored it. It was Brian. It rang again. Hit ignore. Rang again. Shut phone off. I had some serious thinking to do. I didn't know if I could get over his infidelity. His utter betrayal.

It had been four days since I'd seen or spoken to Brian, and the only reason I finally relented was because it was Nina's first birthday. Just because I wanted nothing to do with Brian, it didn't mean I wanted that for Nina. He was still her father, and a good one at that so I sent his parents a text and we all agreed to meet at the park by our apartment. I didn't want Brian stepping foot in MY house.

Nina and I got there a few minutes late. I partially wanted Brian to sweat it out and think I was going to keep Nina home, but I also got caught up feeding her lunch before we left.

Nancy and Henry looked timid. I didn't blame them. After the last time they saw me, I'm sure they were scared I was going to go flip out again and do who knows what in the middle of the park. I wasn't that crazy yet.

Nina toddled over to Brian. She was so excited. To her, it seemed like an eternity since she'd seen her dad. Brian looked great which made me even angrier. It would be like him to not lose any sleep over his wife kicking him out. Me, I hadn't slept well in almost five days and had big bags under puffy eyes from bouts of crying.

"Hey. Thanks for meeting us. I missed you two," Brian said sheepishly. He seemed awkward, but to be honest, the entire thing was awkward. The only normal person there was Nina, sweet and innocent Nina.

"I didn't come here for you. I came so Nina could see you. She misses you. As far as you and I are concerned, I'm considering getting a lawyer." I squinted to keep the sun from totally blinding me.

"Lawyer? For what? You can't seriously be considering a divorce? You won't even see me or give me a chance to talk to you," he said with fear in his voice.

"Actually, I am serious. You slept with someone and then came home right after and slept with me! I kissed someone, the person you actually screwed, and you kept silent. Made me feel guilty for it and still kept your mouth shut. I left school for it. You're still seeing this woman every day at work! Why wouldn't I be serious? What you did…. it's disgusting! It's totally unforgivable!"

"Don't you think I know how fucked up what I did was? I know that. I hate myself for it…," he said desperately.

"Good. You should hate yourself. You're a hypocrite and a liar." We were arguing in whispers to keep Nina and his parents from hearing. They had wandered to the swings, but I kept seeing Nancy glance over at us.

"Let's do counseling again. We can talk about everything and get it all out in the open." He looked at me with pleading eyes.

"You had your chance. We did counseling, remember? That was the perfect opportunity for you to speak up and you didn't. And what else is there to get out in the open unless you're keeping even more from me!" I could feel my voice getting louder.

"No, I'm not keeping anything else from you. I just thought in counseling we could just talk and find a way to move past this. I'm sorry. I'm really, really sorry."

"Just keep your sorrys. You should have thought about that before. I don't know how I can get past it. I can't even stand to look at you. I know I screwed up big before, but what you did is much, much worse. Two wrongs don't make a right, and even if they did, your part of the equation isn't equal to mine. I don't want to do counseling again. And being here, just seeing you makes my soul burn. I'll be calling a lawyer later today. I want a divorce. I'll let you have the afternoon with Nina but bring her home by five."

I couldn't believe I'd said the words. I'd thought I may want a divorce but hadn't been sure until I saw Brian that afternoon. I truly didn't think I could forgive him.

The next few weeks were miserable. I was up half the night crying and then slept part of the day, or when Nina allowed it. My appetite was nonexistent, and I walked around with a pit in the bottom of my stomach, always feeling sick.

Brian and I communicated solely through text messages. I couldn't bring myself to hold a conversation about anything other than Nina the few times I did see him to drop her off at his temporary home— a cheap motel room that had nothing more than a TV and tiny 'kitchenette', which consisted of a small fridge and a tiny microwave. It was truly depressing. It looked like the kind of place a hooker would go to meet a John. I still didn't feel bad for him.

I hadn't contacted a lawyer like I'd promised. I couldn't bring myself to actually make the call. Deep down, I really wanted to forgive Brian, but I didn't know how. I would start to forget about it and miss him, and then I'd see him and be filled with hatred towards the man I loved. I'd given up so much already to be a family with him, ending it seemed so anticlimactic. I was torn.

His graduation date quickly approached, and he'd already gotten orders for the base in San Antonio. No matter what happened between us, we could both move back and be close to family. He invited me to his graduation ceremony, but I didn't think I could handle seeing him walk the stage and shake all the instructors' hands as he got his award. I'd probably cause a scene. Now I understood a little why my mother was so crazy half the time. Men! They all seemed pretty awful no matter how much love was supposedly involved.

I was becoming more and more sick over the entire mess. My body couldn't handle all the stress of being a single mom and contemplating a divorce, not just a mere separation. After much pushing from my mother, of all people, I relented and made an appointment with my doctor to see about the magic pill, Xanax. The appointment was pretty routine but apparently something I said raised flags with Dr. Conway so he recommended doing a full panel of bloodwork to make sure nothing else was going on. If I was stressed before, I was even more so after seeing Dr. Conway.

I thought about all the worst things that could show up: cancer, a never-ending flu, or an STD! Brian did sleep with two women on the same night so I couldn't rule it out.

Dr. Conway called a few days later and said everything looked normal but he wanted me to come back in for a follow up. *No big deal,* I thought.

I went in and sat on the table with the horrible white paper that crinkles every time you move a centimeter. Dr. Conway entered with a nurse and a portable machine with a monitor attached. I thought it odd since it was supposed to be a regular follow up.

"Well, Mrs. Roberts, like I said on the phone everything seemed to check out but your HCG levels were a little high. Based on your history of ovarian cysts and some of your other medical history, I think it could be an ectopic pregnancy. I just want to do a quick check and make sure everything looks good," he said with a big cheery smile.

"Um, ok. Should I be concerned?"

"Let's just see. Hmmm, ok. Warm jelly..." He started moving the sonogram machine over my stomach like he was looking for clues.

"Everything look ok Dr. Conway?"

"Well, that solves that!" He stopped talking as though he'd explained something to me when all he'd done was confuse me even more.

"Solves what?"

He pointed to the screen and printed something. "Just wait one moment," he said while he turned the sound on.

"Congratulations! You see those two little blimps, if you want to call them that, to the bottom right of the screen? Looks like you're about nine or ten weeks along with twins!"

I was dumbfounded. Brian and I had only had sex twice in the past few months, and I managed to get knocked up, again, during one of those little trysts.

"Are you sure? I haven't had symptoms really. I thought my feeling sick, and moodiness, and exhaustion were just from the stress of everything. Are you sure?" I asked hoping the answer would change.

I couldn't be pregnant. The timing was horrible. Brian and I were not in a place to have any more children, let alone two at once!

"I'm sure! We're going to have to refer you to an OB in the area and get you started with your prenatal care. I'll put everything in for you and you should get a call in a week or two.

"Congratulations." He kept saying "congratulations" like it was a good thing and I just wanted to tell him to shut up. I wanted to get out of there quickly so I could think.

Three weeks later I was sitting in the waiting room alone for my first appointment at the OB clinic. I hadn't told Brian yet. I wanted to wait and have it confirmed by an actual OB/GYN. I couldn't even imagine how that conversation would go with Brian, "So, I'm still leaning towards a divorce but am most likely pregnant with twins." My life was turning into a soap opera with every minute that passed.

My name was called and I pushed my sleeping beauty back into the dark room the ultrasound tech worked. She started scanning my belly and immediately said, "Oh! There they are! Let me measure how big they are and get you a more exact due date and see how far along you are."

"They". Definitely twins. Looking up at the screen, I was in love already, just like when I saw Nina on the screen for the first time. No matter how bad things were with

Brian, those two little lives would not be punished. They would be loved and cherished.

"Ok. It looks like you're thirteen weeks and four days along and due around September fourteenth. They're fraternal twins. If you want, I can look to see if I can determine the sex. It can be a little more difficult this early on but still pretty accurate. Want to see?"

"Sure! If you think you can see, I'd like to know. Thank you." I watched as the two little people moved their little arms up and down like they were already fighting for more space.

After a few minutes of her looking, she said, "It looks like they're both boys."

I was going to have sons.

The pregnancy with the boys was much different than my pregnancy with Nina. I wasn't nearly as sick, my ass wasn't nearly as fat, but I started showing at fifteen weeks. I'd worn extra-large clothing anytime I saw Brian. I wasn't ready to tell him or anyone else for that matter. I was still trying to figure out what having two little boys meant for us. I still loved Brian but didn't want to get back together in the hopes that having more children would fix everything. I'd seen my mom get pregnant to keep a man or save her relationship and it failed with flying colors every time.

I did the unthinkable and called my mom for advice.

"Hey, girl! What's up with you? Haven't heard from you in a quick minute. How's my grandbaby?"

"Hi, Mom. She's good. Big, beautiful, and smart," I got quiet.

"What's wrong?" my mom asked with worry.

"Brian and I separated. I don't want to get into all the details but it doesn't look good and I'm pregnant. It's twins."

She was silent for a full minute before talking. "Well, shit! I have to say, I did not see any of that coming. Did he do something or you? If he did something, I'll kill him," she yelled.

"Mom! It doesn't matter who did what to who. The bottom line is we're not together. The pregnancy was not planned. I do love Brian but don't want to get back together just for the kids. I need actual advice here. So, if you could just try and be empathetic for one minute, that'd be really helpful," I said already regretting calling her.

"Ok, sorry. You want my advice. Kids won't fix anything. But I know how much you guys love each other. If there's anything worth saving, even a small chance, you should try and make it work. It's that simple. But if either of y'all cheated, good luck. That's a hard thing to move past."

I was surprised at how much sense she made. "Ok, thank you. That helps a little. I gotta go. Nina is going to be up soon, and I need to take a quick nap before she gets up. I'm exhausted."

"I bet you are cooking two babies in there! Listen, no matter how things turn out, I love you and those babies. God will take care of y'all. Love y'all lots. Send pictures!"

It was a few days before Brian's graduation ceremony and what my mom said made sense so I called him for the first time since we'd separated.

"Look, we need to talk before we move. Do you want to come here? You can spend some time with Nina before she goes to bed and I'll make dinner. Nothing extravagant. We just need to get some things out in the open and cleared up."

"Of course! I'd love to come by." He sounded happy, as though I'd welcome him home with open arms. He'd gone out of his way to be overly kind since he'd come clean about his infidelity. I felt sorry for him at times. He understood how badly he'd screwed everything up but I couldn't help it. I still wanted to punish him so I kept him away and stayed cold.

"Good. Come by later tonight around five."

He came and even brought flowers, like it was an actual date. I wore a large tunic so he couldn't really tell that I had a bump and thanked him for the flowers. Nina was excited as always to see her daddy. It was always in those moments that I wanted us to be a complete family again. Just for her. To give her everything I never had.

After Nina went to bed, I got down to business. It was time to lay it all out on the table.

"Ok. Time to talk. Do you have anything to say first before I start talking?"

"I just want to say again how sorry I am, for everything. If you still really want a divorce, I can't blame you. I fucked everything up. But I love you, and I love Nina. These past weeks have been hell. I can't imagine going any more time without seeing you or her every single day. I just can't. I need you both. I'm sorry. Just tell me what I can do to make that happen again. Please. Just tell me we can be together again and make this work," he said tearing up. I'd only ever seen him cry when Nina was born.

"Brian, I wish it was that simple. I really do. I still love you which is why I haven't actually filed anything yet. It's just…. what you did… I'm having a really hard time forgiving you. I have been trying, whether you realize it or not. The truth is, I don't know what I want. I want to stay married but I feel like if we do, I'll find ways to always punish you for hurting me and that would make everyone miserable."

"Then let's do counseling again. We have to make this work. We have a daughter. We both still love each other. We can work it all out. I know we can." He reached out to grab my hand but I pulled away. I knew if he touched me, I'd crumble and give in. We needed to do more talking first.

"Look, we can talk about that in a few minutes. I really need to talk to you about something else first. We need to talk for a number of reasons but I can't really keep hiding it because it'll be obvious soon and you also have the right to know."

I pulled out the sonogram picture of our two little boys and slid them across the table.

"I'm pregnant. We're having twins. And they're both boys. I'm almost sixteen weeks along. And yes, do the math, they're yours in case you were wondering or had doubts. You are the ONLY person I've slept with." I stopped talking so I could let the news marinate. He just kept looking at the pictures and smiling.

"Why didn't you tell me sooner?" He wasn't mad, just perplexed.

"I was confused, still angry, and nervous. I didn't even know I was pregnant until I was almost ten weeks along. It was a lot for me to take in and I didn't… I still don't know what I want to happen with us. I was hoping I would have sorted it out by now but I haven't so I figured I should tell you sooner rather than later."

"How far are you now again? When are you due? How are you feeling? Are they moving?"

In that moment I realized how much Brian had missed. I had done everything all alone and deprived him of watching two more of his children grow. He didn't even know when they were tentatively supposed to make their appearances.

"I'm sixteen weeks, due September fourteenth. I've been feeling good. Taking care of myself. Not sick like I was with Nina and not nearly as fat. And they are very active. All boy, that's for sure. They may be little soccer players. Who knows?" I said wondering what the future would hold.

Brian looked sad. "I'm just sorry I haven't been here. I wish I could have been with you through all this."

I looked down. I could feel myself starting to get emotional and caving in to Brian. Anytime I looked at him, I saw the cheater and hated him, but I also saw the man I fell in love with. My heart was torn in two. But deep down, I knew. He was it. We had to make it work.

"Come home."

"What?" Brian sounded genuinely shocked. I'd been so steadfast about wanting a divorce.

"Come home. Things will probably take a long time to get back to where they used to be, but I want you home with me. With Nina. With our little boys. I love you so much still that it hurts. I want to find a way to not be angry with you and to make us work, so come home. You're graduating in a few days, the movers will be here next week, let's just make San Antonio our fresh start."

"Ok. If you're sure. I'll have my things here tomorrow."

The next week we were so busy preparing for our move that I didn't have time to be angry with Brian. We got everything sorted and ready to go. I decided last minute to attend Brian's graduation ceremony. I was proud of him for finishing and getting slotted as a C-130 pilot, but I also wanted to rub it in Sadie's face that she didn't destroy my marriage. I wore the tightest dress I had to show off my baby bump and walked around like the Queen of England, sucking up all the attention. Not long after the graduation ceremony, we found out 'Sadie' was being dishonorably discharged. Apparently, Brian wasn't the only trainee she'd had relations with during her time at Eglin.

The next day, we were off to San Antonio. I was starting to feel like a nomad. We were going to be homeless when we got to San Antonio since we hadn't bothered finding a place to live while still in Florida. We had, however, already placed our names on the waitlist for a house on the base to make things easier. In the meantime, we waited it out in a hotel until a house opened up for us.

Very, very slowly, things felt a little more normal. I think the excitement of the pregnancy helped move things along further but we still had a lot of work ahead of us. We found a new counselor in the area that was fantastic! Much better than Linda. She called us out on our shit and gave us homework assignments that helped us rebuild our trust and teach us how to communicate better.

We were finally starting to get in a good place so we decided to break the news to our family that we were working things out and already twenty-one weeks along in our pregnancy. Everyone was shocked on both fronts. My mom pulled all the dirty details out of me. She had a few choice words about everything but it wasn't her life. She'd made her own shitty choices in life, now she needed to let me make my own choices and be supportive.

Just as Brian and I were moving into our new house on base, and things were looking up, his command gave him orders. He was set to leave in exactly one month for a short-term deployment to Kuwait for four months. I'd be on my own, again.

11

Bundles of Joy

I was twenty-five weeks along when Brian left. I turned into a blubbering, distraught pregnant woman. I had to keep it together enough to take care of Nina. All I wanted to do was lay in bed all day crying. I threw a pity party about my husband being gone for the next four months. My doctor had already prepared me for the fact that I most likely would not make it to a full forty weeks since the boys already measured big.

I put on my big girl panties and prepared myself for the likelihood of delivery without Brian. I started making arrangements for family to come in and help whenever I went into labor. It was all overwhelming, and it didn't help I felt depressed.

I was thrilled to be back in my home state of Texas but it was still a new city that I was trying to get accustomed to without my husband. I wanted to be a hermit and stay inside with Nina all day but forced myself to snap out of it.

I started volunteering with Brian's unit, planning functions for the families of those service members that were deployed and loved it. I was making new friends, keeping busy, and Nina was making new friends too. Before I knew it, our once dismal social calendar was buzzing with playdates, mommy's night out, and random community events happening on base or downtown. San Antonio quickly became our home.

I was so busy the time seemed to fly by. In the blink of an eye, I was thirty-one weeks. I went in for a standard OB appointment with Nina in tow. She was ecstatic to be a big sister and loved hearing the boys' heartbeats. Nina was already a little mommy. I had been extra tired from incubating two children, my feet were swollen from the Texas summer heat, and I felt a little under the weather. Despite all that, I still felt good—happy and optimistic about everything in my life and what the future held.

Brian would miss the birth but after talking to several other wives, it wasn't uncommon. Other women had done it before, and under much worse circumstances so I was trying to find the silver lining—it could always be worse; someone would always have it worse. It was all part of the new positive attitude I was trying out. The doctor came in and looked a little concerned.

"Well, we need to do a few lab tests, and we need a urine sample from you. Your blood pressure is starting to get high and with you carrying twins and not having family close by, we want to take every precaution to make sure it's not preeclampsia. If it is, we'll admit this evening and deliver in about a week."

"I'd have to stay in the hospital for a week before you deliver me? No. I'd rather just stay home with Nina for a week." I had never left Nina for more than a few hours and certainly not overnight.

"We're not saying it's definitely preeclampsia, but you have all the symptoms and it could be life threatening to you, the babies, or both. If it's not preeclampsia, nothing major to worry about. It could just be an off day for you, maybe too much salt this morning. But if it is, we need to monitor you. I want to let those babies grow a little longer before we deliver. That's the reason for the time delay. Do you understand?"

I badly wanted Brian to be with me. Life threatening? Those are words you never want to hear.

"I understand. I just was expecting to go home after this and go about my day. If I have no choice, let's run the tests and I'll start to make arrangements if I absolutely HAVE to be admitted."

As soon as I left the doctor's office, I called Nancy to fill her in.

"Hi, sweetheart! How are you feeling? Did the appointment go ok? How excited was Nina to hear her brothers?"

"Hey, Nancy. She loved hearing them. It was really sweet. I'm ok, I guess. I wanted to let you know the doctor was running some tests. He thinks I may have preeclampsia..."

As soon as she heard "may have" preeclampsia, she cut me off and took over.

"Ok. I'm packing my bags right now and will be on the road in exactly one hour. Don't worry about Nina or anything else. Just relax, and I'll be there soon!"

It was such a blessing and relief to have a mother-in-law like Nancy. I was thrilled I wouldn't be totally alone, but having Nancy come wasn't the same as having my husband there.

I also called my mother to fill her in and let her know Nancy was already on the way so not to worry.

"What? You think because you married a rich white dude, you can let her be your mother now? Why can't I come and help?" she asked, feigning contempt.

Oh God I thought. More dramatics. I didn't even know if I actually had preeclampsia yet and here my mother was giving me grief over not inviting her first, sending my blood pressure even higher I'm sure.

"Mom! First off, they're not rich. Compared to you, yes, it looks that way but they're not. Secondly, you are six hours away and Nancy and Henry are only two. If I have to be admitted tonight, you wouldn't make it in time anyways. And do you even have the money to come down here?"

She was silent for a minute. "Well, you should have called me first at least. When do you want me to come?"

How to answer politely? I really do love my mother but having her around was always exhausting, and it was like having a full-time job. She was crazy, loud, easily offended, and very drama filled, if you haven't noticed already.

"Um, I don't know mom. I just need to figure out what's going on first. I haven't thought past getting Nina taken care of for tonight. I still need to send Brian an email and let him know what's going on. I'll get back to you when I can figure out when it's a good time for you to come and help."

Thankfully, that answer seemed to satisfy her, and she dropped the subject. Once I was done pacifying her, I sat in my car and emailed Brian filling him in. With the time difference, I was sure he'd be asleep and wouldn't get it until he woke up in a few hours. Until I heard back from him, all I did was worry. I was worried about all the possibilities of what could go wrong. I wasn't fully prepared to welcome two little boys into the world just yet. Their room was ready, car seats installed, clothes washed and folded, but *I* wasn't ready yet.

I drove home listening to Nina humming offbeat to the song on the radio and forgot about all my worries until it slowly crept back in. Nina would have to share her momma. All these little sweet moments would be harder and harder to have with two newborns vying for my attention. Would she be ok sharing me for the first time in her short life? How would I have enough time, arms, and love to go around threefold? Would I even be good at parenting all these children alone until Brian came back? There were times I felt like I was failing miserably with just one!

As soon as we got home, I started to pack my bag just in case and write out Nina's routine and favorite things for Nancy so she would be prepared. If I was going to be gone for a week or more, I wanted Nina as comfortable as possible and kept on schedule. My hand was starting to cramp from my lengthy list when my phone rang. It was an odd number.

"Hello."

"It's me. I just got your email. Are you ok? The boys ok?" Thank God it was Brian.

"Yes, and yes. I'm still waiting to hear back with my lab results but the doctor thinks it's preeclampsia so I'm just preparing to get admitted if he's right. He wants to make sure I can be monitored safely, but it looks like I may have these babies in the next week or sooner. Can you come home?"

"I don't know. I'm sorry. I can talk to my Commanding Officer but you'll have to go through the Red Cross to make it an official emergency. Then the C/O will have to sign off on it. He's still asleep, but I'll talk to him as soon as he's up. I promise. Is my mom on her way?"

"Yeah. She should be here in two or three hours…. My mom was pissed I didn't invite her to come help." I was so disappointed that Brian wasn't sure if he'd make it home and was trying hard not to let him hear it.

"You sure you're ok? I really am going to try and come home. I don't want you by yourself. I want to be there with you. It's just not that easy to up and leave from where I am."

"No, I know that. I do. It's just… I'm really scared about something happening and not having you here to help deal with it. I wasn't prepared to have to leave Nina already. We don't even have names picked out yet. I'm just scared and overwhelmed. It's still too early to have them."

"I know. I'm sorry. I'll try. Send a Red Cross message as soon as we hang up so my C/O will have it. It'll help with official documentation. Ok? I love you."

"Ok. I love you too. Look, I need to finish things up around here before your mom gets in. I'll send the message and email you as soon as I hear from the doctor. Love you." I hung up and fought back tears.

Sure enough, by the time Nancy got to the house, the doctor had called. Definitely preeclampsia. I needed to be admitted that night. I was beyond disappointed and fear crept in. I had held out hope that he was wrong and it was just the food I'd eaten that morning. I kissed Nina goodnight and had a neighbor take me to the hospital.

My temporary home was a depressing, jailhouse looking hospital room with a view of a hideous parking lot where I tried not to go crazy. I had been hooked up to monitors for three days and would have either loved to just have the boys so I could start recovering and head home or I could have just started an underground market for best 'contraband' items in the maternity ward. The food was awful and I missed Nina. Nancy brought her every day to visit for several hours but it wasn't the same. We were confined to a small twelve by fifteen-foot room with nothing but a small TV, uncomfortable beds, and an awkward gliding rocker. There were no toys so trying to keep Nina entertained was a huge undertaking.

Brian wasn't on his way home but I'd been reassured that "should things get serious" he'd be on the next flight out. I guess a woman pregnant with twins and dangerously high blood pressure that demanded constant monitoring, and a toddler at home didn't constitute a serious situation. Thank you, United States Military.

I hoped his commander would change his mind if they had to do an emergency C-section. I knew he still wouldn't be there for the birth, but he'd be there soon after, exhausted and jet lagged no doubt, but it would definitely calm my nerves down. I'd been so anxious during my stay that I was too nauseous to eat.

"Ok, your blood pressure is still dangerously high and there are no signs of it getting better unless we deliver the babies."

There wasn't much I could do but go with it. I may not have been ready but every hour that went by was another hour I was putting myself and the boys in jeopardy. "Ok. When do we do it?"

"We can have the OR ready in about an hour and all the paperwork done now. Are you ok with that?"

"That's what I've been waiting for doc. I just need to make sure I get in touch with my husband and mother-in-law. I'll do that now."

The doctor left, and I sat in the rocker. It was the last time I'd be so tranquil and at ease about such a stressful situation. I slowly got up to grab my phone. I sent the Red Cross message through our Family Readiness Officer, and then an email to Brian so he was ready for it. I called Nancy and then sat back down just enjoying the quiet and the hum of the air conditioning unit. It was the calm before the storm.

A mere three hours later, they had arrived. Two perfect little boys. The nurses briefly brought the boys up to my head so I could get a quick look before they were whisked off. One looked just like Brian's baby pictures and the other looked like a good mix of both of us. They were beautiful but so tiny compared to what Nina had been born at. They were nearly a full eight weeks early. Baby A (the one who looked like Brian) was the bigger of the two. He came in weighing three pounds fifteen ounces. Baby B weighed just three pounds eleven ounces. I didn't want to name them without Brian so we kept referring to them as 'A' and 'B'.

Brian had called his mom while I was having the C-section. He was going to be leaving the following day to come home. When I was in the recovery room and heard the news, I was elated. We would all be together.

After the doctors were done putting me back together, they wheeled me to my room. The boys were having trouble breathing on their own and needed IV's to be fed so they would be staying in the NICU for a few weeks to give them more time to develop. They warned me that Baby B was having much more difficulty breathing on his own than Baby A so they had intubated to help. I was terrified. All I wanted was for them both to be healthy and thrive so we could all go home in a few weeks. I had a nurse help me into a wheelchair as soon as I was able to move my legs. I had to see them.

I looked at my little angels. Nothing could have fully prepared me to see them in their incubators. Monitors hooked to their little feet and cords everywhere to allow oxygen to pump into their tiny bodies. I put my hands through the holes in the side of their temporary home and touched their little hands. My finger looked gigantic in their palms. It hurt to not be able to actually pick them up, hold them, and comfort them.

I sat there for what felt like hours before a nurse touched my shoulder.

"Mrs. Roberts, you really need to get some rest and eat." The nurse sounded more like she worked in a yoga studio than a hospital.

"I will. I'm just going to stay a little while longer," I said still looking at my boys.

"The boys will be checked again soon and if you plan on nursing, you need to start pumping. Get the juices flowing kind of thing. You have two little mouths to feed. You need to get a good jump start," she said sounding like a cheerleader.

I reluctantly gave in and left the boys. I was back to being a human dairy farm.

To my surprise, Nancy and Nina were there waiting for me in my room. I gave Nina a big smile, and she walked over cautiously to give me a hug. I looked disheveled, bruised, and battered in my wheelchair. I couldn't blame her for being hesitant.

It was a short visit, but I told Nina all about her little brothers while Nancy walked down to the NICU to meet her newest grandchildren. I tried not to let Nina see me cry when she was getting ready to leave, but I couldn't help it. I had just had two babies that I couldn't hold and were having trouble making it on their own, my husband wasn't there yet, and I was having to spend more nights away from Nina.

She said, "It's ok mama. No cry. I wuv you." It made me cry a little more listening to her sweet voice comfort me.

I smoothed her hair and gave her a kiss. "Thank you so much, Nina. You're such a good big sister already and the best little girl I could have ever asked for."

She gave me a big wet kiss back and headed off with Nancy.

I spent that fourth night in the hospital waking up to pump every two hours. When I wasn't pumping, I'd take a short cat nap and then wheel myself down to the NICU to check on the boys. By the time morning rolled around, I felt like a zombie. I kept forgetting to eat, and frankly, didn't have any appetite at all. I force fed myself at the nurse's request.

Brian arrived two days later. I had never been so relieved. We got on a schedule, taking turns with each of the boys and Nina. If I'd gone another day without Brian, I was sure to collapse. The exhaustion and stress of it all was taking a toll. Another thing we had to do was give the boys names. We couldn't keep calling them Baby A and Baby B.

Brian and I were in the NICU together looking at them when he broke the silence. He had been just as unprepared as I was at first to see them.

"Well, they're just perfect. We have the three most perfect kids in the world."

"We really do. But we need to give them names. What do you think about Jacob and James?"

"I like Jacob for that one," he pointed to Baby A, "but James doesn't fit the other one. What about Joseph? Jacob and Joseph."

I thought about it for a minute. Joseph wasn't my first choice but it was a good name and if I was naming one, he could name the other. "Jacob and Joseph it is then."

Jacob and Joseph were five days old when I was officially discharged from the hospital. They both were doing well and Joseph no longer needed to have the intubation tube but they still weren't strong enough to leave yet, especially Joseph. He still had slight trouble breathing compared to Jacob. I fought the hospital hard to keep me admitted so I wouldn't have to go home just yet but they needed my room for someone else.

I missed Nina and wanted to be home with her but with Brian was home I felt a little les guilty devoting more time to the twins. I wasn't comfortable leaving the boys at all. They were still so fragile. What if something went wrong while I was at home? How could I forgive myself?

That afternoon I cautiously left to head home for the first time in a week. My anxiety once again crept to an all-time high. I knew the boys were constantly being monitored in the hospital and Brian was there, but I still had that need to be with them constantly. I felt extreme guilt. Guilt for leaving them, and guilt for having spent so much of my energy on them and neglecting Nina.

I was home just long enough to take my first decent shower in over a week, eat some real food, and spend some quiet time with Nina while Nancy got a much-needed break. It had only been about three hours when I got a frantic call from Brian.

"I need you to stay calm. You need to come back to the hospital now. Jacob is fine but Joseph just had a seizure and has had to be intubated again to breathe. The doctors are running tests right now to see what's going on."

My heart stopped for a minute. "I knew I should never have left the hospital."

"Just relax and head back here. Ok?"

"Ok. I'll see you soon." I turned to Nina. "Sweetie, mommy has to go back to see your brothers."

"NO! Stay and play! Please!" She started screaming and crying, getting louder and louder by the second. I tried calming her down but she was relentless.

"No. Momma stays. Sit. Don't leave. Sit."

I lost it and screamed, "Just stop it! You have to be a big girl! I have to go now!"

I immediately felt like a horrible parent. She was barely two. What did she understand about life and death or healthy and sick? All she knew was she was happy to finally play with her mommy and I was cutting it short. Nancy looked at me still trying to figure out what was going on.

I gave Nina a hug and said, "I'm sorry sweetie. I shouldn't have yelled at you. I'm sorry. It's just your brother, Joseph, is really sick right now, and I need to make sure he's ok. I'll be back later. I promise. Ok?"

She wiped her nose on my arm and nodded. I gave her a kiss and painfully stood up to get my things and leave. I quietly told Nancy what happened and left as quickly as possible.

The entire drive to the hospital, my heart raced. I just wanted Joseph to be ok. I would have done anything to make sure that would happen. I parked and ran to the NICU unit. Brian looked awful.

"What happened? Is he ok?" I was out of breath.

"I don't know. I was in there with my hands on their chests when he started seizing. They've been running tests and won't let me back in to see him yet." He was shaken up.

I started crying. "I knew I should have stayed with them. How's Jacob? What kind of tests are they running on Joseph? I don't understand why no one has come to talk to you."

"Just be calm. Please. They'll talk to us when they have more information. Just be calm. Jacob is fine. He's perfect."

I stopped asking questions and sat down in a hard, plastic chair that faced the large window looking into the NICU. My heart hurt. Seeing all those doctors and nurses surrounding this tiny little creature.

He was sick, probably scared, and didn't have either of his parents in there to lay a gentle hand on him. Brian walked over and sat down next to me. He grabbed my hand and we just sat there in silence until the doctor came out.

"We have your son stabilized, but we have to keep him intubated. It could be a number of things so we've done some lab work and should have some answers in twenty-four to forty-eight hours." The doctor stopped talking and left us with more questions than answers.

"Well can you explain what any number of things could be? Does he have an infection, was it a fluke, does it have something to do with his heart? And can't you put a rush on the lab work? Twenty-four to forty-eight hours seems like a long time to wait." Brian clasped my hand tighter as a silent request to calm down a little.

"We can't narrow anything down right now. His symptoms seem to point to several possibilities and I don't want to give you any wrong information. Unfortunately, that's as quick as we can get the results back. I did request there be a rush on them. Once they're back, we can give you a definitive answer. Until then, just bear with us and continue to be here with your boys. The physical touch will help." He didn't wait for a response from either of us. He simply gave us a half, pathetic looking smile before turning on his heels and disappearing around a corner.

Brian and I scrubbed down before entering the NICU to see the boys. Joseph looked so frail and doll like. Jacob was sleeping soundly next to him and looked strong. The contrast between the two was jarring. We stood on opposite sides of their incubator so we could put our hands through the holes and touch the boys. I hoped they knew it was us. I held onto the hope that our hands would magically heal Joseph a little, or at least give him some comfort that we were there.

After a few hours of sitting there and talking to the boys, I remembered I never called Nancy to fill her in or talk to Nina. Brian hadn't eaten yet so he volunteered to run home and check on Nina. He planned on only being gone an hour or two tops. He was just as reluctant to leave as I was but we both knew we had to be reasonable about keeping ourselves healthy and we couldn't keep neglecting Nina. We'd been so wrapped up in making sure the boys were growing stronger that we'd only spent minimal time with her. I felt like we were failing as parents all around.

Irrational thoughts started floating around in my mind. If I could have just kept my blood pressure in check, the boys would still be growing in my belly instead of fighting to grow stronger. If I hadn't eaten that last McDonald's number 2 and super-sized it, things would have been fine. The boys would be ok and Nina would have had some extra time as the complete center of our universe. I know how unreasonable that may sound. I couldn't have predicted anything or kept my blood pressure low any more than I could have demanded they arrive on their actual due date. It all just happened. Thank you, Life.

About an hour after Brian left, I dozed off in the chair in front of the boys when I heard alarms and monitors beeping. It took me a moment to realize where all the commotion was coming from. Joseph. I looked at him and there he was shaking. Another seizure.

I started screaming for help even though three nurses and a doctor were already running towards us. I wanted to thrust my hand into the incubator and help him but the staff was already swarming around him and had gently guided me out of the room. I was shaking and crying. I picked up the phone and called Brian.

I sat alone in the hallway waiting for Brian. I shook my right leg. I felt my heart beating in my throat. My mouth was dry as though I hadn't had water for days and I had a hard time swallowing. I looked down at my hands and realized my left hand was bright red from squeezing it so tightly.

Ten minutes later, the doctor came out. "I'm so sorry, Mrs. Roberts. Joseph went into sudden cardiac arrest. We weren't able to restart his heart. I'm sorry...."

I felt like I had gone deaf--there was buzzing in my ears. I couldn't have heard him correctly. I sat down and just stared at him. "What do you mean you couldn't restart his heart? Get your machines back out and keep trying! Tell them to try again! Do your job!" I was sobbing.

"I'm sorry. We tried everything we could. Is your husband on his way?"

I was crying so hard that I never even heard Brian run over. The doctor explained everything again and left us alone. He said he'd send a grief counselor to speak with us.

We both sat outside of the NICU and cried. We were both so confused as to how we could have had him one minute and then lost him so suddenly the next. We had spent thirty-two weeks preparing to meet and care for these boys and now one of them was gone. The pain I felt was so intense it was as though I could actually feel my entire heart shatter. There was a physical ache and hurt running through every inch of my body. If I hadn't been in the hospital, I would have curled into a ball and died myself.

A nurse eventually came out. "I'm so sorry for your loss. If you'd like, you can go in and see him now before we take him to the hospital mortuary. Someone will come and give you more details as to what needs to happen next. Again, I'm so sorry." The yoga-sounding nurse touched my arm and slowly stepped to the side so we could walk into the NICU.

Brian and I leaned on each other to walk in. If he wasn't there to hold me, I would have collapsed from the agony and aching in my heart.

Brian helped me walk over to the bassinet Joseph laid in as my legs shook. They had moved Jacob into another incubator already. I gasped, trying to suck in as much air as possible and brace myself. He looked like an angel. He was peaceful. All the tubes and IVs had been removed and he looked like a normal baby--just resting his eyes for a nap. I smiled at him with glassy eyes and reached down to pick him up. It was the first time I'd actually held him in my arms.

I sat down in the rocking chair and hummed to him. Tears continually streaming down my face. I stared at his face and tried to imprint every part of it into my mind. I didn't want to forget a single thing about him. I bent down to smell him as my tears wet the top of his head. He was still so warm and sweet. I couldn't accept that he was just gone.

I'd felt him kick and he was so strong. I couldn't wrap my head around how he could have taken a turn so quickly. It's something I still don't understand even now. Brian just watched silently from the other side of the bassinet. He made no move to come closer. When I finally looked up, Brian just stared in shock. His eyes were red and blood shot.

"Do you want to hold him?" I got up to walk towards him but he took a step back.

"Just give me another minute. I… want to but, I just need another minute." His voice was shaky.

"Ok. Whenever you're ready." I sat back down in the rocking chair and continued humming and staring. He was our beautiful angel.

I stopped rocking and whispered to Joseph, "I love you my sweet, sweet baby boy." Then I thought, *How am I going to go on*?

12

Shattered Glass

The next few days and weeks were a blur. I went through the motions of everyday life. I accepted all the casserole dishes from the spouses in Brian's unit, continued pumping breast milk, and sitting with Jacob in the NICU while he grew stronger and bigger. I spent time with Nina and tried to act normal with her, but it all took every ounce of effort to do so. It felt like I was using all my energy to simply breathe.

I couldn't even bring myself to plan a small service for Joseph so I let Nancy and Brian make all the decisions. The day of the funeral arrived and I couldn't move.

"Babe, you have to come. I know how difficult this is. Please, wear your sweats if you want to. I don't want to do this alone," Brian pleaded.

I was so tired. I hadn't showered in a few days and my eyes were swollen from the constant bouts of crying.

"I just can't. I'm sure everything you and your mom picked out is beautiful, but I just can't go." I rolled over in bed and cried myself to sleep. Not going to Joseph's service is something I've always regretted and still haven't forgiven myself for, I doubt I ever will.

Nancy temporarily moved in with us to help take care of Nina until she knew we were all ok and Jacob was able to come home. My mother kept harassing me to come stay but I certainly didn't have the energy or patience to have her stay with us. Even Mia and April called and offered to come and help. I just didn't want any company.

Three weeks later, the doctors said Jacob could come home. He was thriving on his own and eating like a champ. Everyone was ecstatic, but I felt nothing but fear and anxiety. I'd already failed one of my children, I didn't want to fail another. I requested they keep him for another couple of days just to be safe. They eventually agreed but I know it was more out of pity for the grieving mother than out of necessity.

Brian seemed to be coping much better than me. He turned into super dad. He'd take me to the hospital in the morning, spend some time there with us, and then he'd leave so he could help his mom with Nina and grocery shop or run other errands. He even took Nina to a few play dates.

Every night when I'd come home from the hospital, the house would be clean and Nancy or Brian would have a dinner that I would barely eat on the table. I started to retreat into myself. I rarely spoke unless it was to Nina or Jacob. When I tried to talk, my throat would tighten and I'd have to fight back tears. I was barely a functioning human.

The day we brought Jacob home, Brian was elated, but all I could do was cry.

"I don't understand why you're not glad we can finally bring him home. He's been in the hospital for six weeks now. This is a good thing. He's strong. He's healthy," Brian said with so much optimism in his voice.

"I am glad, but bringing him home just reminds me even more that we should be bringing two babies home. And what if something happens to him? We're not at the hospital anymore where they can just swoop in immediately to fix it."

"They wouldn't have discharged him if he wasn't healthy. I wish we were bringing both our boys home too, but we need to be grateful we still have Jacob."

"Grateful? Yes. I'm grateful Jacob is healthy and coming home, but I still don't understand why Joseph isn't."

I knew I was depressed and didn't care. I'd have these hideous bouts of anger and rage inside me where I thought I may hurt someone or myself just to feel the pain. Then there were days where all I did was lay under my covers and cry.

"There's nothing anyone could have done. It's horrible what happened but we have two other children to take care of. We have to start picking up the pieces. We can grieve, but we also need to pull it together for Nina and Jacob. I need you, and the kids need you."

"If you hadn't had left, maybe things would have been different. Maybe I wouldn't have gotten preeclampsia. Maybe I could have gone further to term," I said bitterly.

He looked at me with hurt. "Don't you dare blame me for what happened. I had no say in when I deployed. I know you're angry but don't blame me. There is nothing anyone could have done. I understand you're hurting, but so am I. He was my son too. You don't get to be the only one who grieves and falls apart. Don't you think I wouldn't love to just lay in bed all day while everyone else did everything for me and for Nina? One of us has had to pull it together. I've given you four weeks of a pass but it has to stop. Now. I'm not saying you can't grieve. I am too, but you have to try and make this your new reality. You have to."

I couldn't look at him. I knew what he was saying was right, but I still felt the need to blame someone, other than myself. I didn't want to just make this our new reality. I'd been prepared to have three children and had mapped out in my mind how our lives would be. I had all these great dreams for the boys growing up— being best friends. We were going to be a big happy family of five. I hadn't prepared for Joseph to die. I couldn't imagine what our lives would turn out to be.

"Brian, you just don't understand. I know you were his father, but I carried him for thirty-two weeks. I felt him grow and move. I just…. it's not as easy for me as it is for you. I was his mother."

"Don't play the 'I'm his mother' card. I loved him just as much as you so I do understand. I really do, but life goes on. We have to take care of the children we have. Here and now. I've been trying to be patient, and loving, and sympathetic with you, but you don't respond to anything. You're practically wasting away in front of us and none of it's healthy. Either snap out of it or see a doctor or the counselor the hospital recommended. You need to figure it out. You have to come back to us."

"I'm trying Brian. I just feel lost… I'll try harder," I said defeated.

And try I did. We got Jacob settled in at home. I forced myself to eat more than a bite or two of food at every meal. I made plans to take Nina back to our regular playdates while Brian made plans to head back to work since he would not be going back to Kuwait. I even saw the grief counselor a few times. She recommended medication but I refused.

After about two weeks home, Nancy decided it was time for her to return to her life and husband. She said it looked like we had things under control.

Outwardly, I looked like I was returning to normal, if you want to call my life normal. But inside, I felt like I was dying. By the end of every day, I was completely drained from having put on my best face and acting my way through life. Whenever I took Nina and Jacob to play dates or a doctor's visit, people would look at me with a sad smile and make comments like, "You look wonderful!", "You're so brave!", "I don't know how you do it after all you've been through!", "Let me know if you need absolutely anything! We're all here to help."

I always wanted to smack them and answer, "I'm not brave. I'm putting on a show for everyone else's benefit. I'm doing it all because I have to."

If I didn't, I was sure Brian would have me medicated. The false offers of help infuriated me. Did they really want to help me clean my house, feed my children, or watch them for a few hours while I slept? It was doubtful.

I know most people have the best intentions, and let's face it, talking to a mother who lost a child is probably one of those conversations no one ever preps you for so you don't know exactly what to say. Guess what? The best thing is to say nothing! At least for me that was the best thing. I would have been fine talking about the weather or how shitty our husband's work schedules were.

I didn't want to constantly be reminded of the son we'd lost. All that did was make it more difficult to move forward. Honestly though, I didn't really want to pull myself together, but like Brian had pointed out, we had two other kids so I had to do something, even if it was faking outward happiness. I was becoming a pro at it though. Every once in a while, I believed that I was actually happy.

Jacob had just turned four months old and by the looks of him, no one would have ever guessed he'd been born a preemie. He was the perfect baby. He was always happy and smiled at everyone, especially Nina. He ate well, slept well and shit well! He rarely ever cried unless he was hungry or needed a diaper change. Like I said, perfect. Nina was just as happy as he was and had been the model big sister since bringing him home. She rarely ever threw a tantrum. It was as if she knew that I was still on the brink of madness and she didn't want to push me over the edge. Sweet, smart girl.

Brian was back on his schedule of working long hours so he could catch up on all the flight time he'd missed while we'd been in the hospital. This meant spending more time alone again. I had just gotten done putting both kids to bed when my phone rang.

"Hey! Did I catch you at a bad time? Are you spending time with Brian right now?" It was Mia. I was extremely surprised. It was rare that we talked anymore which was probably due to the fact that she was still engaged to Scott, my number one fan.

"Oh no. He's still at work and I just got done putting the kids to bed. Everything ok?"

"Yeah. Everything's great. Why wouldn't it be? How are you?" She sounded extra chipper.

"I just don't hear from you that often anymore is all." I was irritated that Mia didn't seem to think that was a problem.

"It's life. Things are busy on my end, and well, I know you've been dealing with a lot so I wanted to give you some more time. How are you? How are the kids?"

"Things are good. We're all adjusting. It's good. Have y'all set a date yet?" Not that I really cared.

"Not yet. I was actually calling because it looks like we're moving to San Antonio. Scott just got a job there, and I was able to find something so we're going to move. We'll set a date once we're officially settled in!"

Deep down, I was happy for her, but I was also envious of how fantastic things seemed to be going for Mia and Scott.

I took a second to process the news. I was thrilled Mia would be in the same city, but we'd been so distant from each other that I didn't know if it would actually matter if we lived in the same city or not. On the other hand, we could take it as an opportunity to work on our friendship. We'd been so close once and I desperately needed that again. I wasn't jumping for joy that Scott would be as close for Brian. I didn't know what kind of an influence he'd be.

I gave her my best excited voice, "That's great! It'll be so nice to have you close. You can see the kids more. We can hang out. It'll be so much fun. When are y'all set to move? Any ideas on where you want to live?"

"I'm really excited to be a short drive away from you and the fam. We're actually heading down this weekend to go house hunting, and we have to be moved in within a month. Scott starts work in about three weeks so it's all going to happen quickly."

"That is fast. Well, if you two need a place to stay while you house hunt, our door is always open." Foot in mouth disease at its finest!

"Are you sure? I know you have your hands full right now with two kids under the age of two."

"Well, Nina is technically two and a half. Sure I'm sure. I wouldn't have offered otherwise. Brian should be home this weekend, and I'm sure he'd love to catch up with Scott," I said in dismay she'd actually accepted the invitation.

"If you're sure. I'll talk to Scott and let you know. I'll text you tomorrow."

"That sounds good. I'll let Brian know y'all may be staying with us this weekend. I'll talk to you tomorrow."

I hung up and hoped something would come up on either end and their stay would fall through. I really wasn't up for playing host yet. I mean, Scott had enough money that they could stay in a gorgeous hotel along the river walk.

As my luck would have it, Scott was surprisingly cheap or he just wanted to make my life a little more miserable during their stay because they gladly accepted my invitation to be our guests.

Mia sent me a text the next day, as promised. "Hey! If you're still ok with it, we'd love to stay with you guys! Just let me know. XOXO"

My reply, "No problem at all. Can't wait to see y'all!"

The next two days were spent cleaning and stocking the fridge with groceries and beer along with a secret stash of vodka that I figured I'd need. I made sure they had access to get onto base since neither of them were military and emailed detailed instructions on what to do and where to go when they got into town.

"Are you sure you're ok with Scott and Mia staying here?" Brian asked the night before they were set to arrive. Ever since we'd lost Joseph, Brian usually talked to me like a child, always concerned and never trusting me at my word.

"Yeah. It'll be fine. I'm sure Scott has grown up a bit since I last saw him. Besides if things go bad, we can politely kick them out. I sent Mia a text earlier today and told her to warn Scott to be on his best behavior so we should be good. I think it'll be nice to have our friends here. Scott's your best friend and Mia's mine, so it'll all work out," I said with a small shrug and smile.

"Ok, but if you feel like it's too much to have extra guests in the house, just let me know. Ok?"

"Yes, Brian. I'm perfectly fine. I've been managing just fine the past couple of months. I think I can handle a weekend of entertaining friends." Even though I'd put on my 'brave face' and done all of my wifely duties with "umph" and a smile, excluding sex, Brian still felt the need to treat me like a child sometimes. Sex was out of the question for me for the time being. I wasn't ready yet and wasn't going to fake that.

When Scott and Mia got in the next day, I was surprised by a few things. One, Mia had packed on about twenty pounds since I'd last seen her. She'd always been thin, fit, and gorgeous. She was still pretty but her face was fuller along with everything else.

Two, Scott looked surprisingly handsome. I didn't remember him looking any degree of attractive when I'd first met him.

And three, Scott was being overly nice to me. I know I was having him as a guest in my house, but he was never the kind of person to be nice if he didn't want to be. It was refreshing to not see him as an asshole. The weekend was looking up. If this was how it would be all the time I thought, it'd be great having them live nearby.

Brian ended up having to stay at work after all on Friday. There was some training exercise that he somehow had forgotten to put on his calendar. He was expected to run a few flights from eleven p.m. until six a.m. Saturday morning. After that, he'd be able to have the weekend off.

Since things were surprisingly pleasant, I wasn't too upset that Brian wouldn't be home. When Scott and Mia arrived, he not only greeted me with a big hug but complimented me.

"You look great! I'm so glad you're doing well," he said with all sincerity.

I gave him a puzzled look and then looked to Mia who gave me a big smile. "Ok. What's the catch here Scott?"

He laughed. "No catch. You look good. I know you've been through a lot. I'm really glad to see you're ok."

That definitely wasn't the same Scott I remembered but I was going to run with it. "Well, thank you. I really appreciate that. Come in and make yourself at home."

I gave them a quick tour and started cooking a nice dinner. The kids were excited to have company. There was plenty of wine and beer to keep all the adults happy and pleasant, even though we missed Brian.

Scott looked like a natural when it came to the kids. He was patient and silly and Nina couldn't stop laughing. It had been a long time since I'd been able to make her laugh like that. I got lost in my thoughts when Mia interrupted.

"What are you thinking about? You look sad."

"No, not sad. I'm just so glad Nina is laughing. She's having a lot of fun. I'm surprised at how good he is with them. He doesn't come off as that type of guy. I would have thought he'd be the kind of guy to use a fly swatter to keep them at arm's length." I nudged her a little and smiled.

She laughed and said, "He actually loves kids, and I've always told you he was nice. He wants to have kids soon but I'm not there yet. Eventually, just not yet."

"It's a lot of work. You're ready when you're ready. I don't know if I would have had kids yet if Nina wasn't such a surprise but I'm glad I did. Without Nina or Jacob, who knows where I'd be now."

"Well, you're doing a great job with them. They're happy kids and Jacob is so adorable. I love all his little rolls!"

I started laughing. "Who doesn't love a baby with rolls?" I got all the plates out to set the table and served dinner.

We had a great time. It was like we were all old friends. I excused myself to put the kids to bed since it was past their bedtime at the late hour of eight thirty. When I got back, Scott and Mia had cleaned everything up and had glasses of wine poured and waiting.

I grabbed my glass and sat on the couch to finally relax after a long day. Scott and Mia grabbed the bottle and wandered to the living room to join me.

"You know, Scott, I may have misjudged you. You're not as big of a douche as I thought," I said laughing afterwards.

Thankfully he joined in my laughter. "No, I'm not. I just liked giving you a hard time. I also was a pretty big prick back then."

"You say back then like it was ten years ago. We're not that old. Either way, I'm glad you two were able to come and stay with us. It's nice being able to catch up." If only he'd been that nice when we'd first met.

We talked and drank for nearly two hours straight before Mia got up. "Sorry guys, but I'm beat and don't want to be totally hungover while we look at houses all day tomorrow. I've got to get to bed."

"Mia! Don't be such a party pooper! Stay up a little bit longer. I haven't seen you in so long." I was definitely one drink shy of being on my way to drunk.

"Tomorrow. I promise. Babe, you coming to bed?"

"I'll be there in a little bit. Love you." She bent down and gave him a quick peck. We could hear her snoring within ten minutes. That was new. I just hoped she didn't wake the kids or keep me up when I went to bed.

"I'm serious, Scott. You're so much nicer now. If I would have met this Scott four years ago, I would have liked him."

"I know. Truthfully, I was surprised you were into Brian. You seem like you're a little above his class."

"What are you talking about? If anything, I'm surprised Brian put up with me. My family is freaking crazy! You saw my mom at the wedding." I laughed just thinking about her in that skin tight white dress.

He laughed too. "No. That's not what I mean. Not that Brian's not a good-looking dude, but you know, you're kind of better looking than him."

"Please. I think most women do look better than men. You guys aren't meant to be beautiful creatures. You're supposed to be rugged and lumberjack-y and handsome in a Clint Eastwood type of way."

"I guess. Still. You were more my type than Brian's type," he said with a dangerous tone to his voice.

He looked at me and there was something there. A small spark and a flutter in my stomach. It was something I hadn't felt since I'd gotten pregnant with the twins. It was eerily quiet except for the snoring coming from the guest bedroom.

I looked away and set my glass down so I could excuse myself. I absolutely could not let anything go beyond innocent flirtation. He set his glass down and grabbed my arm as I went to stand up. I didn't move. I let him slide over next to me so closely I could smell his cologne and see every crease and feature of face. Scott set one hand on my thigh and the other on the back of my neck gently. I could just barely feel his warm fingertips on the nape of my neck.

"Scott. We can't," I was whispering.

"Just one kiss." He was already leaning in. I could have moved but didn't. It had been so long since I'd felt anything other than anger or pain. It felt good. He kissed me with such force I felt my head spin.

His lips were so soft. His smell intoxicating. He moved his hand off my neck and up into my hair pulling my head back so he could kiss my neck. He moved down, lifting my shirt so he could kiss the rest of my skin. He slid his hand between my thighs, and I could feel a smile form while my stomach slightly shook. I didn't want him to stop.

Before I knew it, I was sitting on top of him and undoing his belt. I slid his pants down and slowly made my way back up so I could slide him inside me. I pulled his hair and put my face in his neck. I cried the entire time we had sex. Not from guilt, but pleasure.

Down the hall, my kids and Mia slept peacefully. Their worlds remained temporarily unchanged. But I felt something change inside me as we both came. I felt like I'd been reborn.

13

Reckless

I woke up the next morning with a dry mouth, pounding head, and a fully awake house. Brian was home and it smelled like he was making breakfast for everyone. I was starving and in dire need of something greasy and a Coke. I slowly got out of bed so I could wash my face. I looked at myself in the mirror and didn't feel disgust towards myself for sleeping with Scott, rather I felt calm. It was peculiar.

For the first time in nearly four months, I was calm instead of secretly seething at anyone who crossed my path. I wasn't exactly happy, but I didn't want to cry. I almost felt normal. I'd definitely had too much wine, but knew what I had done. I was one hundred percent OK with my actions. The mystery was whether or not Scott was OK with it.

I made my way down the hall and heard everyone laughing at something, presumably something Nina had done since she loved to be the center of attention.

"Hey! You're up!" Brian handed me a plate of food.

"Yeah. Thanks for letting me sleep. I didn't realize how late I went to bed. You must be exhausted after working all night. Why don't you let me finish up out here and you can get some rest?" I sounded cheery, not a care in the world.

"I'll take a nap when the kids go down for their naps. I wanted to catch up with Scott and Mia before they started their big day of house hunting," Brian said, blissfully unaware of what had occurred in his living room hours before.

"Yeah, Brian was telling us about the training exercise he was doing last night. It sounds like pretty amazing stuff," Mia said.

"I'm sure it is." By the sound of her voice and the way Scott was acting, I could tell he hadn't said anything and wasn't planning on it. Fine by me. It was a one-time thing anyway.

Scott looked at his watch. "Shit. It's nine forty-five. We're supposed to meet the realtor in fifteen across town. We gotta go. Thanks for breakfast. We'll see y'all this afternoon!" Scott and Mia grabbed their things and left for the day.

"Well, things seem to be going well. Scott's not so bad, right? He told me that y'all were able to clear the air last night and things are good. Cordial at least."

"Yup. I guess I misjudged him. We actually had a good time last night. All of us did. It was nice to catch up." I turned around to grab a mug out of the cabinet and smiled. I heard Jacob crying and put my coffee plans on hold to get him a bottle. I spent the rest of the day back on schedule like nothing had happened.

"You are in a great mood this morning. It's nice having them here," Brian said.

"It is. I've really missed Mia. I feel good today. Thanks for noticing," I replied.

Scott and Mia got back in the middle of naptime and were excited that they'd found a house and put an offer in. It wasn't too far from the base so if they got it, we'd practically be neighbors. Brian was passed out cold and Mia wanted to stop by the store and get a few things so she could make dinner for us as a thank you for our hospitality. That gave me the perfect chance to talk to Scott.

"Glad y'all found a place. Hopefully it works out.... Look, we have to talk. About last night, it was great. Really. It's hard to explain but I needed that, but just for last night. Can we both promise to keep it to ourselves?"

"Oh, absolutely, not a problem," Scott said adamantly.

That was easy. "Really?"

"Yeah. It'd be better if no one knew." He said with a smile and gave me a look. There it was again, that spark.

I walked over, grabbed his hand, and took him out into the garage, opened the passenger door of my car, and let myself go. We got back inside just as we heard Mia pulling back up to the house. I tiptoed to my bathroom to get myself situated without waking anyone as Scott went to help Mia with the groceries.

Our second indiscretion in less than eighteen hours. I know it sounds awful and like I'm a horrible human being, but I felt even better than after the first time. I sat down on the toilet to pee and tried to really think about what the hell I was doing and why. I didn't have a good answer other than I simply wanted to. I noticed a change within me and I liked it. I heard Brian getting out of bed so I hurried up and finished in the bathroom.

"Hey! Have a good nap?"

"Uh. I feel like I could sleep all day. Kids still sleeping?" He was rubbing his eyes and getting his stuff together to shave and shower.

"Yup. Mia just got back from the store. She wants to cook dinner for us tonight. I'm going to go help her put everything away." I went to head out and Brian grabbed my hand and smiled. He leaned in and kissed me.

"I said it earlier, but I'm really glad to see you so happy. It looks good on you." He smacked my butt and hopped in the shower.

"Thanks. See you out there in a little," I said with a small twinge of guilt.

I loved Brian but not the way I used to. I know, once again, I sound awful. Things had always been a bit fractured and broken after my kiss with Sadie. Brian screwing her further exacerbated and increased the cracks in our marriage. And well, everything kind of went shitty after that. I never truly had enough time to properly process our life, my life. I STILL had yet to finish my degree.

There were so many things I hadn't planned on and little monkey wrenches had been thrown all along my path. I felt like it was finally my time to do something for me, even if that meant sleeping with Brian's best friend and my best friend's fiancé.

In retrospect, if I really want to analyze my behavior, I'd say I wanted to completely break everything. It's just like when you go too long with a broken bone and the doctors have to re-break to set it properly. I guess that's what I was trying to do in the most selfish way possible.

The rest of Scott and Mia's visit went by quickly. Scott and I didn't have any more meetups. It's not that I didn't want to, we just didn't have the opportunity. Instead, we went back to acting like cordial acquaintances. When they left, I went back to feeling empty and I replaced my genuine smile with a fake one.

A few days later, I sent Scott a text. "You free in a few hours?"

"Yeah. Why? (Insert smiley face with a wink)."

"Just dropped the kids off at daycare. Meet me halfway?"

"Just tell me where…"

I googled the best halfway point and found there was a large wooded national park situated exactly between our houses. Perfect. I gave him the name of the park and told him to meet me there in an hour and a half. I grabbed a large blanket, my purse, and was flying down the highway.

We met and had another few great rounds of sex. I was like an animal. When I finally got up from our secluded spot in the woods, that looked more like a place you'd take someone to murder, to check my phone, I saw I had seven missed calls. Two from the daycare and the rest were from Brian. *Shit*! I listened to the messages.

Mrs. Roberts, Nina had an upset stomach and got sick. Please come pick her up within the hour.

Mrs. Roberts, we still haven't received confirmation that you'll be picking Nina up soon. Please contact us immediately.

Where are you? The daycare just called. I have to leave work early to get the kids.

Why aren't you answering your phone? Call me back….

Damn it! I grabbed everything and put my panties and pants back on. "I gotta go! Nina got sick, Brian had to leave work early. Shit. What am I going to tell him?"

Scott was up and getting re-dressed too. "Damn. Sorry. Tell him you were at the gym or lost your phone."

"I'll figure it out. Gotta go. Talk soon?"

"Yeah. We'll talk soon." He grabbed me for one last kiss before I pulled away and ran to my car.

I made it home in record time and called Brian on my way. "I'm SO sorry. I had my phone on silent and had gone to the gym and then went for a long walk and just forgot my phone in the car. I'll be there in twenty!" It was more like forty, but I blamed it on traffic.

As soon as I got in the house, I checked on Nina. She was back to running around and acting completely normal. "Must have been something she ate. She seems fine." I looked over at Brian and mouthed "I'm sorry" while I felt Nina's head.

"What the hell happened? Since when do you leave your phone in the car or not check it? The daycare said they tried calling you three hours a go!" He was rightfully upset.

"I know. I know. I'm sorry. It's just been one of those days. I'm kind of in a funk. I'm sorry. It will never happen again. Trust me." I wasn't sure if I was talking about Scott or not.

"Look, I gotta get back to work. Turn your phone ON please. What if there's an emergency?"

"Ok. Turning it on loud now. Have a good day at work." I showed my phone to him as proof I'd hear it next time.

I sat down on the sofa and watched Nina playing on the floor and Jacob in his swing. What was I doing? Brian was right. What if there had been a serious emergency? I needed to snap out of it or be more careful.

The next two weeks Scott and I continued to meet at random places whenever we both had time. He and Mia were getting ready to close on the house they'd put an offer on so he was coming to town and finalizing all the paperwork. Scott texted me before he got in.

"The bank gave me the keys early. Meet me at the house tomorrow. 2201 Mulberry Drive."

I replied immediately. "Don't know if I can… have the kids all day tomorrow."

"Please. I want to see you and show off the new pad… I'll make it worth your while…"

After a few minutes of debating if it was a good idea, I responded. "Ok. I'll come around naptime so the kids can sleep in the car. See you tomorrow!"

It was just a short fifteen-minute drive to Scott and Mia's new home. I pulled into the driveway and the house was gorgeous! It was a mini-mansion. The facade was made with red brick, white window shutters, three-car garage, and surely a ton of bedrooms. He spared no expense. It was what I'd always imagined my dream home would be.

Scott opened the garage door so I could pull in. The kids had fallen asleep as predicted so I quietly got out and left the door open so I wouldn't wake them.

The garage door led to a massive kitchen slightly which we left slightly cracked so I could hear the kids if they woke up. We christened the kitchen, living room, and master bedroom before I got the full tour of the house. It was beautiful. Four bedrooms, two family rooms, a man-cave, pool in the yard plus plenty of grass, my dream home.

"This is really the perfect house. Mia's one lucky lady."

"What if I didn't want Mia to be the one to enjoy it?" he asked raising an eyebrow.

I laughed. "Please, Scott. Stop joking. I need to go check on the kids."

"They're fine. I'm serious. Do you want to be the one to move in? All this sneaking around is exciting and all, but don't you want to have freedom… not have to hide? I think we have something here." He was dead serious.

"We can't do that. Be realistic here, Scott."

"Why not?" He asked sounding wounded.

"A number of reasons. One, you and Mia are engaged. Two, I'm married. And three, I have two kids for starters. How do you think all of this would really work? As wonderful of a time as I'm having, we don't know each other. This is just sex. It's fun. Don't ruin it."

I walked towards the kitchen so I could make sure the kids were still asleep and we could head home. I didn't want to have that conversation with Scott. I thought he was in it for the same reasons as I was. We barely ever spoke unless it was about mundane or unimportant things. We didn't have deep conversations about our dreams and what we wanted out of the grand scheme of life. We didn't really know each other at all, and now he was talking about me leaving my husband. For what, a fling? If that's what it was.

"This is fun, but I think it could be more. Don't you? Just think about it," he said somberly.

"I'll think about it but I really have to go. A neighbor is going to watch the kids tomorrow so I can run a few errands, are you staying in town for the night or heading back?"

"I'm staying. Want to come here around ten?"

"That works. I'll see you then. I really have to go." As I got in the car Nina woke up.

"That Mr. Scott? Mama?" She asked while rubbing her eyes.

"Oh, no sweetie. Go back to sleep. We're going home now."

I drove home thinking about what Scott was actually proposing. I'd never entertained the idea of leaving Brian or my kids no matter how I felt. I loved my kids and I loved Brian—he was the father of my children. I loved my kids enough to keep them in a two-parent home until they were both eighteen at least. By then, I'm sure Brian and I would be on stable ground so they would never have to worry about it.

What did I even know about Scott other than what I'd heard from Brian or Mia? We had some sort of connection, sexually at least, but I didn't know if I could see myself being in a real relationship with him. And, truth be told, I'd never sought out more information than what was necessary in getting to know about him. We'd never been anything more than acquaintances by association.

I didn't even know what I wanted. All I knew was that when we spent time together, I felt good. I was happy. I didn't have to think about anything in my real life. I didn't have to deal with any of the pain I still felt from losing Joseph. I didn't want to change any of that.

When I got home I put the kids in their beds to finish their naps. I laid down on the couch and thought about what I really wanted. It was something I thought about the rest of the day. Even when Brian came home, I kept trying to remember what things had been like and how I'd felt when we first met.

Brian used to be able to barely graze my arm or give me his million-dollar smile, and I'd feel giddy and my heart would melt. I really wanted all of that back but the thought of putting so much effort into something that may never happen again was not only discouraging but overwhelming. If we loved each other, it shouldn't have to be so much work. Right?

Then there was Scott. It was all easy and fun. Could I live my life without ever having to think about things too much? Just be provided for and carefree. Would that be worth ruining my kids' lives? Brian's life? Mia's too?

I told Brian I had a headache and needed to lay down early. While he put the kids to sleep, I pretended to be asleep. I laid there awake most of the night just thinking. I slipped out of bed and sent Scott a text around three a.m., "How about a date first? Then maybe I can consider your proposal."

To my surprise, he responded right away, "Absolutely. Already have the perfect place. Just tell me when you can get away."

"Tonight? If you're staying in town again..."

"It's a date."

I had my first date set since my last first date with Brian nearly three years ago.

Later that morning, I called Brian at work. "Hey, do you mind if I go run some errands after you get back? I want to get some shopping done and hit the gym."

"That should be ok. It's going to be an early day here anyways. Just don't spend too much money on junk. I love you."

"I won't. I love you too."

Perfect- I'd have at least three hours for my first official date. Plenty of time to talk and see if Scott and I actually had anything in common other than a mutual physical attraction.

I put a nice outfit in my tote bag so I could leave in my workout clothes and not arouse any suspicion. When Brian got home, I gave Nina and Jacob goodbye kisses and thanked Brian for staying with the kids while I did my errands.

I drove straight to Scott's gorgeous house and parked in the open garage, making sure to close the door behind me. He didn't know I was already there so I quickly changed into my nice clothes and put a little bit of makeup on in the powder room.

"Scott? Where are you?"

"I'm in my cave. Come in here. I have a surprise for you."

I made my way to his adult-sized playroom. He had laid out a picnic in the middle of the floor, candles and all. I immediately thought about Brian's picnic after our awkward first date. It was the first real sense of guilt I'd felt since I'd started our full-blown affair. I pushed it away. I wanted to see what could potentially happen with Scott. Brian and I had a ton of issues to work on and I thought it was a lost cause.

Since Joseph had died, we'd gone through the motions of marriage but that was it. We didn't speak about our grief. It was this big elephant in the room that we tiptoed around all the time. I don't think Brian, I certainly didn't, wanted to wake the emotional beast that was slumbering inside me.

"This looks amazing! What are we eating?"

"Well, I got some fresh sushi, spring rolls, and even decided to splurge on some caviar and crackers for you. Fancy, huh?" He said, very impressed with himself.

"Very. Thank you. We could have just gone somewhere that had actual tables and chairs though. You didn't have to do all this."

"I know. I thought it would be nice. We can still go out if you want," he said disappointed.

I felt sorry for him. I didn't want him to feel bad after the work he'd done setting up. "No. Probably better this way. No offense, but I don't want anyone I know to see us. I'm supposed to be shopping and working out. Remember?"

"Right. Good call.... Well, come sit. Join me. Let's get this 'date' started."

"Ok. Let me lay some ground rules though. This is a real date, even if we're in your house. That means no sex and very minimal touching. I need to get to know you." I looked at him and tried to give him a serious look but ended up laughing. "I'm serious though! No touchy-feely stuff."

"If you say so, but you do know me," he said smiling and swirling his finger on my forearm.

"You know what I mean, Scott. We don't really know anything about each other. I don't even know your parents' names! Your middle name. Favorite food, music, color. Stuff like that. Yesterday you asked me to seriously consider leaving my husband. I can't just do that on a whim. I need to know if we're compatible on more levels than one. Make sense?"

"Yes, ma'am. I'll be a gentleman then. Best behavior for tonight."

"Great. Now we can get started."

We had a great time. He was much funnier than I thought, and so goofy. I laughed a lot. He told me his middle name, Walker (made me think of Chuck Norris), and all the other things I wanted to know. He was an only child. His parents were very well off and had given him a sizeable trust to do what he wanted when he graduated college. He'd chosen to invest some, spend some and save some. Reasonable. He was very reasonable and surprisingly smart. Despite his spoiled upbringing, he was surprisingly normal. My first impressions could be chalked up to being an immature college kid. I finally put the brakes on the great time we were having and got serious.

"Scott, do you love Mia? Do you love Brian? What are we doing? What do you really want from this? What you're asking of me… it's a lot. I've thought about it and, honestly, I don't know what I want to do right now but I need to know where your head is here."

He took a minute before answering. "No, I don't love Mia anymore. We get along, but we've turned into friends. We've been together for a while now and I think we're both scared to just end it after investing all that time. And I do love Brian. He was like a brother to me growing up. I know this is all fucked up, but I liked you from the first… well maybe second, moment we met. I really like you and I think we have a lot in common and we could have something great. You're obviously not happy with Brian or else we wouldn't be here right now. Am I right?"

"Are you really willing to give up your relationship with Brian for a woman you just really like? And what about my kids, the ones I share with Brian? Have you thought about the fact that you'd have an instant family overnight? It's kind of a package deal. There's a lot between me and Brian that you don't know about and that's probably a good thing. And no, I'm not particularly happy with Brian right now, but that's not all his fault. I do still love him. Life has just kind of thrown up all over us, and things are...," I let my voice trail.

"What do you want then? Tonight has been great. Sex is amazing. I don't want to keep hiding and sneaking around. We need to figure this out before Mia moves here in two weeks. Once she's here, it'll be much harder for me to end things."

I sat there and let the silence drown us. Finally, I blurted out, "Ok. Let's just go away. Just you and me. I'll figure everything else out later."

"Ok. Where to?"

14

PARADISE

Several hours had passed since I'd left Brian with the kids to run my errands. He called around nine, but I was too nervous and scared to pick up or call back so I hit the 'decline' button on my phone every time. Finally, he sent me a text.

"Where are you? Are you ok? I'm starting to get worried"

I finally sent him a text back. "I'm sorry. I need time away to think. I will call and come home when I've sorted some things out."

I quickly shut my phone off so I wouldn't have to read a response or reject another phone call. Cowards way out, I know, but at least I didn't just disappear which I had seriously considered. I thought by leaving, even if it was with Scott, I could gain some more perspective on my life. I missed Nina and Jacob already, but I'd just felt so weighted down by everything. I needed distance, even from them.

The next few days were spent hiding out in Scott's house until our flight left for Hawaii. His parents owned a timeshare on the island of Oahu so we stayed there. I'm not sure what he told his parents about his reason for the trip. I would've loved to go someplace exotic, but I didn't want to risk running into Brian or the kids at the house. If I did,

I ran the risk of changing my mind about leaving so I was content making do without my passport.

Scott had a week to kill before starting his new job but had a few odds and ends to do before we left, hence the reason for the delay. One of the main things was breaking off his engagement with Mia.

In just the short amount of time I'd been at Scott's, I gained a little more clarity about myself and what I wanted. Top of the list was finishing college. I was only short three classes from completing my degree and had yet to finish. I wanted to be able to fulfill my dreams of being able to help others. I still wanted to make a difference in people's lives. I didn't just want to be a housewife who only took care of her husband and children all day. I loved them, but I needed my life to amount to more than that.

I know raising children is important, someone has to do it, but I still didn't know if that was the only thing I was meant to do. I got married extremely young, I'm still young, and all of my adult life, which started at nineteen, had been spent taking care of Brian, then kids. I felt like I'd lost my identity somewhere along the way. I assumed when Scott and I got to Hawaii, I'd be able to think more clearly with all the distance from my life. I was sure of it.

When Scott got home from his new office he had news.

"Mia and I are officially over. I called her while getting settled in and told her things just didn't seem to be working out. I told her I loved her like a friend but couldn't see myself in a marriage with her."

"Just like that? Wow. And... how'd she react? I can't imagine well."

Knowing the firecracker Mia was (or used to be) she'd probably be fuming and want to cut his balls off.

"She didn't say much of anything actually. She was surprisingly quiet. So, I guess it went well."

"Hmmm. Mia didn't text me about your conversation. Not that I don't believe you, but she knows I know she's planning on moving here. She hasn't bothered to call or text about a change of plans. Seems odd."

"I think she was relieved to be honest. Anyways, it doesn't really matter now. It's done. I just want to get out of here and go on our little trip. How are you? Still excited or having second thoughts?" He sauntered over and pulled my hips in close to his.

"No, not at all. I'm excited. The sooner we leave the better. I'm having a great time with you. I think once I'm out in the fresh air smelling the ocean, I'll be able to sort a lot of stuff out," I said while running my fingers through his hair.

He pulled me in closer and kissed me. I had those exciting butterflies.

We were finally on our flight to paradise! Just taking off and seeing San Antonio disappear below me was cathartic. I felt my stress blowing away behind me with the wind of the airplane engines.

Since I had never bothered to go back home, Scott generously offered to buy me a small wardrobe, which I graciously accepted. What girl doesn't love shopping? I did some serious online shopping in those two day before leaving and had everything overnighted to the house. Whatever didn't work, I just sent back. Everything else, I packed. I was ecstatic to go on my first adult vacation.

The air smelled fresh and clean when we stepped out of the airport and walked through the parking lot to our rental car. It was gorgeous. Palm trees everywhere, clear and sunny skies--perfect weather. It was a tropical paradise.

As we drove to the condo, I forgot about everything. I didn't have kids or a husband back home. I wasn't a college dropout or a philandering wife. I was just a young twenty-three-year-old with no commitments or responsibilities. It was liberating. In that moment I decided. *This is what I want.*

I wanted the ability to just jet off to some beautiful island if I wanted to, sleep in past six am, go to school, and not worry about having to plan classes around daycare schedules. I wanted my freedom. I wanted to be happy again. Having a little wiggle room thanks to Scott's trust fund money was certainly to my advantage, but I didn't care if he was in my little fantasy life or not. He was an added bonus.

I loved my kids and I loved Brian, but at that minute, in that place, I loved myself more. I accepted that I was being more than selfish but I was OK with that. I didn't want to be what others thought I should be. I didn't feel as though I was meant to be a wife or a mother. I decided on a fantasy life with Scott.

"I think I know what I want," I said abruptly to Scott as we pulled into the complex.

"Oh, yeah. What's that?" He parked the car in front of our building and looked at me.

Matter of factly, I said, "I'm going to leave Brian."

"Ok.... any other big announcements with that little piece of news?"

"Yes, actually. I'm done with my marriage from this point forward but here's the catch. I cannot go back to San Antonio. I just can't. I want an entirely fresh start."

I was smiling like a crazy person, enamored with the thought of starting over in a new place like I was the star of some Hollywood movie.

"What about your kids? What about my job? I'm set to start when we get back. Do your big plans including me in your 'fresh start'?"

I shrugged and looked out the window. "I'd like them to. I understand you may not want to pick up and leave what little you do have back in San Antonio. I mean, you just closed on the house and have a new job, and that's great! It really is. It's just, I haven't been happy there. And I think that if I really want to be happy, I have to leave everything. I have to figure myself out and find my own path. I can't do that with a husband and two kids. I love them but I need space, more than just living in a different house ten minutes away from them. I need to figure out my life with full freedom, with you."

He looked out the front window. "Well, I get it, I guess. I really would like to join you wherever you plan on going, I just don't know if it'll be feasible. I could easily rent out my house but my job, that's another story."

I could see the wheels turning. Scott was trying to figure out how he could insert himself into my new life and play leading man.

"I know. And I'm sorry. I wish I could have had this 'a-ha' moment sooner but I didn't. Why don't we just head to the beach, unwind, and we can talk about it tomorrow?"

"Fine."

His mood shifted from being excited to stand-offish. I didn't blame him. I was sure that wasn't what he had planned on hearing, especially since he'd whisked me off to Hawaii on the whim that I would leave Brian, move in, and be one big happy family with him and my kids.

We spent the rest of the evening in relative quiet. We both silently stewed over my proposed plan. I didn't want it putting a damper on the trip too much though. I was going to enjoy my mini vacation and relax as much as possible.

I went to bed that night peacefully. I was invigorated with the idea of starting over again, somewhere new.

That night, however, I had nightmares of Nina and Jacob drowning in a pit of tar while I stood back and laughed. I woke up early the next morning and pushed it out of my mind. I put my swimsuit on, grabbed a towel, and headed to the beach. I left Scott a note telling him to join me when he woke up.

As I laid there in the sand, I tried to iron out the details of my new life. Instead, the breeze washed over me and I dozed off listening to the birds and the waves crashing onto the shore. I woke up twenty minutes later to my phone going off.

"Hey. You're awake. Are you going to come join me down here? It's beautiful out," I said shaking the sleep from my voice.

"Yeah, I just woke up and saw your note. I'll be down in a little. We should talk," Scott said solemnly.

"Ok. Good talk or bad talk? I want to be prepared for whatever you throw at me." I tried to sound light hearted but my heart was already racing.

"Depends on what else you've thought about. Just… I'll be down in a minute." He hung up and I sat there anxious about what he'd have to say.

Ten minutes later, Scott strolled onto the beach casually as though he didn't have a care in the world. He laid his towel down next to mine and cleared his throat.

"Alright. Well, I definitely wasn't expecting you to want to leave absolutely everything behind. I don't fully understand but it I know things have been rough for you the past few months. At the same time, I can't just leave San Antonio. I committed to the job, just bought that house, so I have to stay and see how things go."

"So…. what are you trying to say? We'll just be friends, go back to acting like we hate each other, what?"

"It all depends on if you've thought anything else out. You didn't give me much last night. Have you thought about where you want to live? Are you going to get a job? Go back to school? Work out custody with Brian?"

"I have done a little more thinking this morning. I want to stay here. Things here are so calm and people aren't in such a rush. I love the beach. I could get used to this. I know you can't just quit your job, but maybe they'd let you work from a home office and you could stay here with me. It would be like being on vacation all the time. We wouldn't have to worry about anything."

"You haven't even been here twenty-four hours, and you think you'd love living here? I really don't get what's going on in your head. I could probably get away with fifty-fifty work from home and office but that's it. And I've been here enough to know that living here is definitely not the same as vacationing here. You'll get sick of it. Then what are you going to do? Say you stay here, and I live here fifty percent of the time, what are you going to do when I'm back in San Antonio?"

"I'll get a job. I'm sure there's something I could do. Waitressing, a receptionist, administrative work, something. I can make do. I'll see the kids when I'm better. When I'm all sorted out, so-to-speak."

"There's a lot of what-ifs and unknowns in your plan here. Here's what I'm proposing. We finish our vacation and go back to San Antonio. You can start divorce proceedings and live with me while you finish school, I'll even pay. You get your degree, then you can work, or not work, if you don't want, and maybe sometime down the road, we get married."

I wasn't even divorced! I hadn't even told Brian I wanted a divorce yet and Scott was already talking about possibly getting married. He wanted me to go from my married house to his house all in the same breath. It sounded tempting, but I had a funny feeling about it. I knew he could afford to pay for me to finish school but I didn't want to feel like I owed him anything for it. I wondered if the payment would be a marriage.

"I don't know Scott. I need to settle things with Brian and the kids first before I can consider divorce. And I don't need you to pay for anything. I already have student loan debt. I can take on a little more for three classes."

"Ok, well why don't you just move in then? If you don't like the house since it's so close to the base and your family, I'll rent it out and we can get something somewhere else."

Always the problem solver, I thought.

Red flags went up everywhere. I could hear those little ding-ding-ding noises going off in my head but dismissed them. Scott was overly willing to bend over backwards and accommodate my needs when we'd still just barely started getting to know each other. We'd been sleeping together for over a month, but we'd only just had our first date a week ago. Now we were on vacation together like a seriously committed couple, talking about moving in together, and getting married. I ignored my gut because it sounded like life would be easier with Scott.

"Hmmm….. IF you rent the house out, and I can pick the new house, I think I could live with that."

He smiled at me and leaned over to kiss me. "You got yourself a deal."

The rest of the trip was smooth sailing. Everything was perfect. We ate at all the nicest restaurants and bars. We had a fabulous time. When it was time to leave, I could feel myself tightening back up like a clam. I decided I needed to call Brian before I got back and let him know everything. I owed him that much.

I'd called from the condo's land line so he answered hesitantly, "Hello?"

"It's me. Are you free to talk right now?"

He cleared his throat and I could hear him sitting up in bed. It was late in Texas, and I'd forgotten about the time change. "Where are you? What the hell is going on? Why aren't you home yet? The kids miss you. I'm worried about you."

"Look, I'm sorry. I shouldn't have gone about any of this like I have. I'm sorry. I just… I can't take it back now, but I am sorry. I'm not coming home."

"What do you mean you're not coming home? The kids miss you. I miss you. Whatever's going on with you, we can work it out."

"I can't. It's a lot to explain but in a nutshell, I haven't been happy for a while. Probably started with our first move to Alabama, but especially in San Antonio, I haven't been happy. Joseph's death…," I couldn't even say his name without feeling a lump in my throat, "I'm just not happy and it has nothing to do with anyone but me. I want a divorce. Don't worry about me fighting for custody or alimony because I'm not planning on doing that."

"What? I don't understand. So, you're not happy and haven't been. You want a divorce. And you don't want custody? Are you telling me your cutting ties off with all of us? Even your children?" I could hear the anger rising up in his voice.

"It sounds so harsh when you say it like that. Right now, I need to be alone, completely alone. I can't work on myself if I'm still taking care of two kids that don't even know how to wipe their own asses. I need to find what makes me happy."

"Unbelievable. Un-fucking-believable. How could you do that to your kids? Forget me, I'm an adult. I can find a way to cope with you up and leaving me, but what about Nina and Jacob. They've been devastated the past week without you here. You haven't even bothered to ask how they are. Fuck! What is wrong with you? How could you be such a selfish bitch?" He was practically hissing through the phone. If I'd been next to him, he may have lunged at me.

"Brian, please. This is something I have to do… for me… I just… I'm sorry." I thought he'd be slightly understanding. I assumed he'd had some inclination about my unhappiness, especially after Joseph.

"I don't get it. I've given you everything. I've been supportive. I've been patient. I've loved you with all my heart. We've had issues but you've never given me pause to think we weren't on solid ground. How do you even plan on supporting yourself? No job, no work experience, no money. You're obviously somewhere and you haven't even used our account once!"

"I'm sorry. You have every right to be angry. I didn't set out to intentionally hurt you or the kids. I'm just in a shitty place right now and I'm trying to work through it." Time to drop the bomb about Scott. "I haven't been alone. Scott has been helping me. He's…" Brian cut me off mid-sentence.

"Scott? My best friend, Scott? You've got to be fucking kidding me. This just keeps getting better. I really hope this is some kind of twisted joke you're playing. If it's not, you're more fucked up than I thought. Wait until I see him."

"Brian, please. It's not his fault. He didn't plan on hurting you either. Everything just sort of happened and really quickly. He understands that I need to figure out a lot of things. He's not pushing me to be anything I don't want to be or to be something I'm not."

"No. Don't. Just shut up. Don't go on and on about needing to find yourself when you're hopping from my bed to his. You're running. You're a damn coward. You'd rather leave your family than face yourself. You think you can just run off and play house with him! Of all people. You have no idea what you're getting yourself into. You're a damn cheater. That's all you are. Don't sugar coat what you're really trying to do."

"It's not like that Brian," I said emphatically, also wondering what he meant about Scott.

"It absolutely is. If you really wanted to find yourself and work through your issues, you'd do it alone! Or turn to your husband, for fuck's sake. Not with another man. Jesus Christ. You're throwing everything away for something that's probably going to end badly. Are you fucking him just because he has money?"

"Brian, I'm done. I've told you what I needed to so I'm hanging up. Give the kids kisses for me and tell them I love them and I'm sorry."

"I'm not telling them anything. You want to run off with Scott, fine. As far as the kids are concerned, they don't have a mother." The line went silent.

I sat there with my heart racing. I waited for tears that never came. There was nothing but the ringing in my ears and the sound of the waves crashing outside.

Later that day, Scott and I hopped on our plane back to Texas. Goodbye Paradise, back to Reality.

15

Clean Up on Aisle 12

I sat somberly the entire flight back to San Antonio. Scott seemed to have left his mind back in Hawaii with not a care in the world. I had just destroyed my marriage and torn my family apart in one big swoop. I was going down in flames the way I was, but it was too late. I'd gained too much momentum and couldn't stop like a wrecking ball into a building. It was done. All that was left for me to do was look forward and figure out my life. Figure out who I was, apart from being a wife and mother.

Scott arranged for us to meet with a realtor the same afternoon we got back with the goal of fining a placed where I'd be more comfortable. I wanted as much distance from my old life as possible.

The very first place Shayna, our young and gorgeous realtor, took us was incredible. It was a new high-rise condo building. There was a doorman, fitness center, clubhouse, and pool. It even came fully furnished. I was sold as soon as we walked in the front door. It was in a great area with lots of bars and shops within walking distance and it was farther away from Brian and the kids.

As we walked out of the building, I whispered to Scott, "This is it! I love it!"

"You sure? We still have a few more places to check out?"

I nodded. "I'm positive. Let's sign the papers today!"

We signed the papers later for a spacious two-bedroom condo with a balcony overlooking the pool area. It had a fantastic closet the size of a kitchen. Although I didn't have anything to fill it, I figured Scott would solve that problem. All my old clothes were at home and I'd decided, I didn't want them. I wanted everything to be new and fresh.

We moved in two days later and Scott's house was officially on the market as a rental property.

Being in our new condo was like being on vacation all over again. The furniture was ultra-sleek and modern. It was nothing at all like I would have chosen, mostly because I had children and they tend to destroy nice things. It looked like something out of a catalog.

I went shopping and bought all new clothes, even panties and bras. The clothes were just as beautiful as the furniture—they were a far cry from the sweats and t-shirts I normally wore to run errands in. It was all expensive and name brand. I'd never even owned a Coach bag, now my big closet had three of them.

I spent my days leisurely. If I wanted to work out, I worked out. If I wanted to go lounge by the pool and read a magazine, I did. If I wanted to sleep until noon, I could. I didn't have diapers to change, kids to feed, daycare or a babysitter to call to run an errand alone. I even started looking at schools.

Things were better than great! I was living the high life. I didn't worry about anything. Scott had started his new job and was more than generous with his money so I did as I wanted. About two weeks after we'd gotten settled in, my mother called.

"What the hell do you think you're doing?" She was pissed, really pissed.

"Hi Mom. I'm doing really well. Thanks for asking by the way. How are you?"

"I don't give a shit how you're doing! Brian finally decided to call me. Told me about your little stunt. I thought I raised you better than that! Get your shit together and go home to your kids. Grow up," she scolded.

"I do have my shit together. And you know what, you didn't raise me. I raised me along with everyone else. I have shit to work out so I'm working it out. Don't judge me. You've made your fair share of fucked up decisions. You have no right to tell me what to do. Just let me be," I said, my voice full of annoyance.

Silence impregnated the air for a minute. "I may not have been around as much as I wanted to be, but I wasn't there for good reason! If you recall, I was working jobs to provide for you all! I never, ever abandoned you. Y'all knew how much I loved you and still do. I don't know exactly what's going on with you, but please, don't run from your kids. They need you. If you want to throw your marriage away, that's on you. Don't make them suffer." She hung up without waiting for me to respond.

Her input fell on deaf ears. I had already made up my mind. Why put my kids through having a dysfunctional mother? In my mind, it was better to just cut ties then. Whenever I was ready to deal with everything, and whenever I was able to find my own identity, I'd go back and be their mother, however much or little they wanted.

I went back to la-la land in my pretty, new condo. Playing house with Scott was great at first. I never worried about anything. We'd been together for a little over two months and we were still in that 'honeymoon' phase. He was always overly giving. He'd often come home with a new outfit or purse for me just because he thought I'd like it. Later, I figured out it was just one of his many ways of trying to control me. For every item he'd bring in, two of my new pieces that I'd chosen would disappear. I didn't pay too much attention to that right away though. I thought it was all so sweet, just a part of the new romance thing.

He was never physically abusive, just liked to control little things. It all clicked as to why I rarely heard from Mia when she was with him. Friends was another aspect he liked to have a say in.

I'd met a nice girl named Sandy, slightly older than me, at the pool and we hit it off. She loved the same kind of music, clothes, and bars. Sandy had an older, well-to-do husband. We'd gone shopping together a few times while Scott was at work and had the best time. She was the first friend I made since leaving Brian.

When Scott met her, he was polite enough but shortly after their first meeting, he'd said, "I think that girl's a bad influence. I think you should stay away from her."

I had no idea what gave him that impression but he was adamant. "Scott, I don't know what you're talking about. She's really sweet. We have fun. No harm, no foul."

"Don't question my judgment. She's not good for you. Stay focused. You have me. That should be enough."

I should have run immediately, rather I let it slide and just adjusted when I went to the pool so I wouldn't run into Sandy. When she'd text, I'd tell her I was busy. Eventually, she got the point and didn't bother to text again.

I'd gotten accepted to University of Texas at San Antonio to finish school. That part of my life was back on track. I was finally going to get my degree in just one short semester. I was beyond thrilled. Scott absolutely refused to let me take out a loan and paid in full for the entire semester before I even had a chance to fill out my financial aid paperwork. I had more little red flags fly up when he insisted on coming with me to register for my classes. I thought it was really odd.

"I'm taking half the day off tomorrow so I can come with you to register for your classes," he said nonchalantly.

I felt like a child all of a sudden. "You really don't have to. It's only three classes I need, and they're pretty standard."

"I know. I just want to make sure you're getting the best possible classes you can. That's all." He kissed my head and went back to work at his computer as if that settled everything.

I sat on the sofa perplexed at first. I didn't put up a fight though since he was the one footing the bill. I reasoned away at Scott's investment in my education and our future. I just chalked it up to him looking out for me in a sweet and creepy kind of way.

After one of my classes let out, I decided to run to the grocery store to pick up a few things. Rather than going to the one close to the condo, I decided to take a detour and wound up at the base commissary. I told myself I wanted to save some money, as though it were an issue all of a sudden.

I still had my military id and base access so I went. I had yet to actually contact a lawyer to start divorce proceedings, a big point of contention between Scott and I. I couldn't bring myself to do it and make everything so final.

I was walking slowly through the aisles grabbing an item here or there— soy milk, fruit, coffee, normal stuff. Then I spotted a familiar face. Nancy. And she was pushing my kids. I could feel myself internally panicking. I tried to turn away quickly but she spotted me. I heard a tiny little, excited voice.

"Momma! You're home! Grandma, look! Momma's home!" She was so loving, so innocent, so forgiving about my months' long absence. Jacob just stared at me blankly. Nancy's face, once welcoming and warm instantly turned rigid and hateful. I could hear her whisper.

"Sshhh, Nina. Let's just say hi, and then we need to finish our shopping."

I felt my face turning red and perspiration forming on my forehead and armpits. I reluctantly turned my cart and slowly walked towards them. I hadn't seen my kids in three months. They had changed so much and looked so much older! They looked like little people, especially Jacob who would be one soon.

He had four teeth already, long hair, just adorable. He was shy too.

Nina looked like a little girl, not the baby-faced child I left a few months ago. She was beautiful! Big bright eyes, her hair had grown longer and she was so verbal.

I was looking at two completely different children. It was so amazing to see how much they'd grown and I missed it. All of it.

"Hey, sweetie. Look how big you are. And your brother!" I said rubbing their heads.

"Yeah! I'm a big girl now. I get to help grandma a lot, and I get to help daddy when grandma goes home to visit grandpa."

My heart broke. What did I do? She was already growing up too fast.

"I'm so proud of you, Nina," I had to fight back tears and could feel my eyes getting glassy. I hadn't been prepared to have a little reunion in the middle of the grocery store. "Hey bud.... you're so handsome and so big." He just looked and smiled shyly. He didn't even recognize me.

"Momma, are you going to come home today? I really miss you," she said, her voice bursting with hope.

I smoothed her hair back, "Um, no sweetie. Not today."

"But why?" She asked, full of disappointment.

"Well, it's hard to explain, but I'll see you soon. I love you both." I gave them both kisses and mouthed a "thank you" to Nancy who up until that point, had barely looked at me or spoken. I turned to leave, and she grabbed my arm. I could feel her nails digging into the inside of my arm. This from a woman who had probably never even killed a fly. She leaned in and smiled so the kids wouldn't see anything other than a 'happy' picture.

"What you've done.... it's.... disgusting. Stay away from my son and my grandkids. They deserve better," she hissed.

I pulled my arm away and left. My cart was left standing in aisle twelve while I power walked to Scott's car. I got in and realized I was shaking. What had I done? I had abandoned my children. I was no better than the dad I barely knew. Actually, I was worse. He was at least partially excused. He had a disease. He physically couldn't help being addicted, at least that's what I'd always been told about drug addicts.

Me, I was just running. A coward, like Brian had said. I was running from that constant feeling of loneliness, pain from losing Joseph, fear of not being the perfect wife, fear of failing at being a good mother. Rather than confiding in my husband, my best friend, I shut him out. It was easier for me to run and live in a fantasy than it was to try and be happy with MY family. I needed to grow up. Be an adult, be a mother, but the allure of just escaping was still so strong.

On the drive back to the condo, I thought about my kids. I tried to imprint their faces in my mind and figure out what I was going to do and what I truly wanted. I realized my heart was still with Brian and the kids. I sat in the car crying, trying to rationalize my behavior. Trying to justify the hurt and pain I'd inflicted on those I should have given my life to protect. It was useless. There would never be a good reason. My phone rang. I wiped my eyes, cleared my throat, and answered.

"Hey!" I sounded cheery and happy. "I just pulled in. Be up in a minute."

"Oh ok. I was wondering where you were. I know class let out a while ago." Scott sounded skeptical.

"Yeah. I stopped by the grocery store but then couldn't remember everything we needed so I ended up having to come home to check and make an actual list. I'm just now getting out of the car. See you in a few."

I hung up and started making my way to the lobby. Scott was waiting for me.

"What are you doing down here? I told you I was headed up." I looked at him strangely and then gave him a hello kiss.

"Yeah, but I thought I'd be sweet and walk you up."

"Ok.... Thanks."

We rode the elevator up in silence before Scott finally spoke. He didn't say anything until the doors opened and we began our short walk to our front door, "How was class?"

"Good. The usual. How about you? Work ok?"

"Yeah. It was a pretty good day. Look, I've been thinking. We've been together for a while. You've been living here, I paid for your school, your car. I think it's time you talk to a lawyer. Move on." And there it was—expectation, payment, commitment.

I looked at him and anger rose inside of me. "Scott, first of all, don't hang your money over my head. I never asked you to do anything for me! Don't make it seem like I owe you anything. Secondly, we've talked about this. I'm just not ready. It makes everything so.... so..."

"Final? Yeah, I know. If you're really ready to move on, that shouldn't matter. And to set the record straight, I don't think you owe me anything but I've done a lot for you and feel like you're stringing me along."

"Don't rush me! I'm done, I am. It just makes everything so absolute. It's a big deal. A marriage is not the same thing as just breaking up with a boyfriend or a fiancé."

"I get it. But it's been a few months now. Shit or get off the pot." He walked into the bedroom and slammed the door.

I threw my purse and books on the couch and sat down. He was right. I needed to make the jump and start divorce proceedings or break it off with Scott and figure out my life all over again. Everything was in a state of limbo.

If I left right then it would look like I was a money grubber, but if I stayed, I'd probably end up unhappy, always feeling like I'd have to work my debt off and 'repay' Scott for all his so-called generosity.

I got up and walked to the kitchen to pour myself a drink. I heard a weird noise coming from our bedroom. I grabbed my drink and walked over. I slowly opened the door and there was Scott. Sitting on the bed crying.

"Scott? You ok?"

"I love you and don't want to lose you. I just want you to pick me," he sobbed with his shoulders bouncing up and down.

I was so taken aback, and frankly, very uncomfortable. His behavior was completely out of character for him. I almost thought he was joking, but he kept on.

"What are you talking about? I did pick you. I'm here aren't I?" I took a sip from my drink and passed it to him.

"You're here, but you're not. I just need to know what you want. Why haven't you called a lawyer yet?" He was whining worse than a child.

"I told you why already. I just need more time. Everything will work out. Don't worry." I sat down next to him and grabbed his hand and noticed there weren't any real tears coming out of his eyes. I looked forward. My decision became easy instantly. I had to break it off with Scott.

He'd been a great escape and lots of fun in the beginning, but seeing his true manipulative and controlling colors was not what I'd signed on for. It was great when it was easy, but it wasn't anymore. I was beginning to understand why Mia seemed all too happy for their engagement to end.

Seeing my kids in the store was the slap in the face I needed to get back to reality. I needed to find my way back to them, and Brian if he'd have me. Time to clean up my life for real this time. No more running.

16

CAN WE WORK?

I spent the next few days internally plotting how I could break things off with Scott while simultaneously fixing things with Brian. He hadn't bothered to contact me at all since our last conversation, not that I blamed him, but it didn't bode well for me. I told him I was done and leaving. What more was there to discuss?

I acted normal with Scott but after our argument and his crocodile tears, I needed to end things as quickly and painlessly as possible. I worked up the nerve to call Mia for advice. She'd been with Scott for much longer than I had so it was a safe bet she knew him infinitely better than I did.

I dialed her number and waited. No answer. She was either busy or knew that I had been the reason for her break-up and hated me just as much as Brian probably did.

I sent her a text. *I really need to talk to you. It's important. I'm sure you're angry, and I'm so sorry. I'm trying to make things right. Please call me back.*

No response immediately. An hour later she called.

"What do you want?" she said shortly.

"Look, I just want to say first, I am SO, SO sorry. I've been a horrible friend, wife, just a bad person in general. I never should have gotten with Scott, and I certainly never should have left Brian and the kids. I just really need to get my life back on track. I just…. Scott has gotten unusually… um…. not really controlling I guess, but manipulative."

"Oh, that. That's him alright. Guess you're finally seeing his true colors," she said bluntly.

"Yes. And he's not mean or anything but the past few days… it's been weird. Anyways, I've realized how fucked up I've been. I ran into Nancy and the kids, and I have to go back to them. To Brian too. I just don't know how to nicely break up with Scott. He's done a lot for me and he's already kind of thrown the money thing in my face."

"My advice to you is to dangle a younger and more attractive version of yourself in front of him. He likes shiny and new things. Our relationship was great at first but truthfully, I was miserable after the first year. If you think he's manipulative now, just wait. It gets worse," she chuckled.

"That's the thing, I don't want to wait, and I don't have time to find someone new for him. I need to start making things right, now. I've destroyed everything, Mia. You have no clue how horrible I feel. I've been so selfish." My voice wavered and cracked slightly.

She actually sounded like she felt sorry for me. There I was confiding in her about her ex-fiancé, and she wasn't cursing me out.

"I can imagine. You really did screw shit up. I'm glad you figured it out, but Scott won't just let you drop him that easily. I tried to break things off with him a few times but he's got a few loose screws. Anytime I tried to break up, he'd threaten to kill himself or he'd get scary drunk to the point I thought he had alcohol poisoning."

"Jesus. He didn't hurt you, did he?" I asked. I was terrified I'd be guilted into staying or be responsible for a terrible outcome if I couldn't be guilted.

"No. I was never scared of him hurting me, but I really did believe he'd hurt himself. He seems like he's got it all together but something really isn't right with him. I really don't know what to tell you. When he broke up with me, I wasn't sad. I didn't even care that he left me for you. I felt sorry for you because I knew you didn't know what you had just gotten yourself into. I was happy to be done with him. I can't help you. You gave me my way out, now you have to find yours."

"That's not what I really wanted to hear. Why didn't you warn me at least?"

"I'm sorry. By the time I'd actually heard y'all two were together, it was too late. Plus, I was pissed and still think it's fucked up what you did to your family. By the time I could have warned you, I didn't want to." At least she was honest.

"Thanks." I felt trapped. At least Mia didn't completely hate me, but she didn't help me either.

"Hey, I'm not telling you anything you probably don't know about yourself already. If you're really serious about making amends with Brian and being in your kids' life again, just leave. Don't give Scott any warning. Just leave. Hopefully Brian will be forgiving but with what you did.... I don't know. I wish you all the luck but it looks like we're two completely different people and have changed a lot. I hope you get what you want and don't fuck it up again."

She hung up. Not only did she not give me any helpful information, but it sounded like our friendship was amicably over. She left no wiggle room for us to ever be friends again.

I deflated in an instant. I had dug myself into this giant hole and couldn't see a light to even claw my way out of it.

I left the condo and drove around for hours. Just thinking. I thought about my kids, how Brian and I met, how happy we were after having Nina, and how things fell to shit pretty quickly after he went active duty.

I thought about how I never opened up enough to Brian after we moved. I didn't talk to him about my fears and insecurities. I suffered silently. Everything was my fault. I saw the exit that led to the base and took it without thinking. I drove straight to Brian's office, got out of the car, and walked in.

No one looked at me or said hello. I'm sure they thought I had a lot of nerve just showing up unannounced after turning Brian's life upside down. I didn't care. I needed to talk to him and see where he stood. I stood in front of his office door. My heart was pounding and my hands started sweating. I turned the doorknob and walked in.

He looked at me in shock. "What the hell are you doing here? Shouldn't you be playing house with Scott?"

I took a deep breath. "Brian, I'm sorry. I'm sorry for everything."

"You should be more than sorry. You have some balls just walking into my office in the middle of a workday. Whatever you have to say, you could have emailed, called, sent a text, not just show up."

"I know. I just couldn't wait to talk to you. I know I have no right just showing up like this. None. How I've treated you and the kids, what I did… I've been making myself sick. When we talked last, you were right. I'm a coward. I am. I ran away and did the unthinkable, and

I'm sorry. I can't take any of that back. I can't get that time back. I missed so much with Nina and Jacob. With you. I'm sorry." I could feel my throat tightening up. It was the first time I'd seen him and he acted like I was just some stranger on the street. He didn't even want to look at me.

He was looking at his computer screen, clicking away and then stopped. He looked at me with those piercing blue eyes. I thought I saw them soften for a minute but the second they did, he looked away again.

"What you did made me sick. It still does. You have no clue what the kids and I have gone through, especially Nina. She's been devastated. And my mom said she saw you. Nina was so happy. And now…. all I hear about is how mommy's coming home soon. What am I supposed to say to that?"

"I don't know. I'm sorry. It's taken me a long time to figure it out, but I'm ready to work on everything! I'm ready to go see a therapist by myself or together. I want to be their mother again. I want to be your wife. I just want to come home and make things right…. I…"

"Stop it! No!" He had stood up, and then realized he was yelling. He looked at me harshly.

"I loved you so much. I still love you, but what you did. Just up and leaving. You didn't even give me the chance to talk to you so we could work through things. I may have been able to forgive you for sleeping with Scott, but just leaving to start a new life like we didn't exist! No. I can't forgive that. If you came here thinking I'd welcome you with open arms and be happy and say 'Sure, come on home', you're fucking delusional. It's not going to happen. I'm not going to let you break Nina's heart again or give you the chance to break Jacob's," he said sitting back down.

I looked down like a child being scolded. "I didn't come here thinking you'd be happy, but I thought there was at least a chance we could work things out. I love you. I love the kids. I'm sorry. You have no idea how much. I want to make things right for everyone. Please, Brian. At least think about it."

"There's nothing for me to think about. If you could leave us so easily the first time, why would I think you'd be willing to come home and stay? What's going to keep you from leaving again?" he asked with a waiver in his voice.

"Because, I just won't. I will do whatever it takes for you to trust me and believe me. Like I said, I'll go to counseling. You can take away the car or the phone or whatever makes you comfortable. I don't care. I just want to work things out."

He laughed at me. "Great idea. Then you'll really feel trapped and do God knows what. You need to leave." He looked at his computer screen again blankly.

"Brian. Please. Just think about it," I pleaded.

"We're done. You made it clear months ago that you were done with our marriage, our kids. It was hard on all of us. We are finally getting back to normal, our new normal without you. I can't have you just come back like things aren't different. I will never believe you. I will never trust you. I don't want to live like that. And I don't want to get Nina or Jacob's hopes up to only have them crushed. I have to think about them. You made your decision when you left without even having the respect for me or our marriage to talk to me! I've already talked to a lawyer about how to proceed from here."

He opened one of his drawers and handed me a large envelope. Inside were divorce papers and papers that terminated my parental rights.

"Brian...." I continued to plead while holding back tears.

"We're done. You can send those papers to the address in the envelope. I would have sent them, but I didn't know your new address. Close the door on your way out."

I got up and walked away, crushed. I expected him to be angry, but I thought he might be a little happy or at least relieved I wanted to come home, be a part in Nina and Jacob's lives. Not only did he want a divorce, he wanted me completely out of the kids' lives too. I had to figure something out to make my family whole again.

17

Home Again

After my disastrous and disheartening meeting with Brian, I did the unthinkable. I drove the three hours to my mom's house. I couldn't be with Scott anymore and Brian didn't want me. I had no place else to go. Scott called several times and I ignored his calls every time. I didn't want to talk to anyone.

I parked and walked into my mom's house using my old spare key. I didn't say anything to anyone. I just went straight to my old room. A second later, I heard the heavy thumping of my mom's footsteps coming up the stairs.

"What in God's name are you doing here?" she asked out of breath.

"Mom, I've ruined my life. I ruined Brian's life. I ruined the kids' lives. I have nothing. I just want to go to sleep. I've had a long day. I feel like shit. I need to be alone. I'll talk to you when I'm ready." I sounded like a pre-pubescent child.

She closed the door softly and left. It was one of the few times she actually did what I asked and did it quietly.

I turned my phone off and slept the rest of the day. I got up only to pee and get a drink of water. When I finally had enough sleep, it was three am. I walked into my mom's room and sat at the edge of her bed.

"Mom?" I shook her foot. "Mom?"

She groaned and rolled over to look at the clock. "Girl, you had better be ready to talk if you're waking me up at this time."

I laid everything out on the table. I was surprised she understood me at all considering I went back and forth between sobs and gasps for air in between sobs. I was mortified and felt so much shame telling her how screwed up her oldest child was.

When I was done, she sat completely up and turned her table lamp on. "We all make mistakes. Your mistakes were pretty damn fucked up, but you're admitting to them. That's a start. But honey, let me tell you, and you may not like what I'm about to say. You will probably never be able to make things right with Brian. The kids, maybe, but that's up to Brian now. You left. That's all there is to it. I'm glad you're home, and you're welcome to stay but if you stay, you pull your weight around here."

"Yes, Mom." I just wanted to be babied for one minute. Have her lie to me and tell me things were all going to work out.

"I have to get back to sleep. I have an early shift. We'll talk when I get home." She turned the light back off and was snoring thirty seconds later.

I was wide awake. I got back in the car and drove to the nearest park to watch the sunrise. I sat on a bench and turned my phone on. I had twenty-five missed calls from Scott and forty text messages from him.

They started off casual: *Where are you?* Then worried: *Are you ok?* And finally worked their way up to frantic: *Call me back ASAP. I need to talk to you.* Then they ended with crazy talk like: *Come home or I'll slit my wrists.*

Slit away, I thought. I was done. I'd destroyed three lives already, what was one more.

It had been a long time since I'd spoken to April, but I needed a friend. Someone to comfort me somehow. Based off of our last brief conversation a year ago, I remembered she didn't live far from my mom, about an hour. I got back in the car and drove to her last known address. I drove fast, hoping to catch her before she left for work.

I pulled up to a small house with cute little daisies planted in front of the porch and a big Texas star hanging on the front of the small carport. I knocked. Thankfully, April answered.

"Oh my God! What are you doing here?" She gave me a big hug and stepped to the side so I could come in.

I looked awful. I had bags under my eyes, no make-up, disheveled hair, and two-day old clothes.

"Hi. I'm sorry to just drop in like this. I know you're probably getting ready for work. I just really didn't have anywhere else to go and I remembered you lived close to my mom so here I am."

"Oh, don't worry about it. I don't leave for work until about eight thirty. Sit down. Are you ok? Want some coffee?"

"Coffee would be great." I went into the whole saga and got her pretty caught up on my disaster of a life thus far. "That's it. Now, I'm here."

She let out a deep breath, raised her eyebrows, and said, "Wow. I don't really know what to say. That's a lot to take in."

"I know. Again, I'm sorry for just showing up. I didn't come here to impose or have you solve my problems. I just needed a friend to listen. Maybe advice if you've got any.

I'm at a loss. I can't see my way out of this hole. I know it's been a long time since we've actually been in the same room together or had a conversation longer than five minutes, but I'm free falling here. I just need help. You've always been so level-headed and a great friend," I said as I looked at my wrung hands.

"Jeez. I don't know. I knew after... Joseph... you were depressed, but I didn't know how badly. Why didn't you talk to Brian or come to me or Mia or someone sooner?"

"I just couldn't. I didn't want to talk about it. I blamed myself for everything. And it wasn't just Joseph. It was everything. I got pregnant so early, didn't finish school, my marriage was teetering between great and then awful. I thought I needed to suck it up and be the perfect mom and wife, so I didn't say anything. Then I felt all this resentment. I just didn't want to deal with anything. I wanted to start over instead of talking about all my issues. I'm trying to put things back together but I don't know if it'll happen. I've hurt so many people," I said, suddenly realizing how exhausted I was.

"Ok, you want my advice?"

"Yes. Anything."

"Well, here it is. Move on, alone. Based off of what you said Brian's reaction was, he's not going to budge. Can you blame him? I'm sorry, but I wouldn't take you back either. I would at least try and convince him to let you see the kids. And then get on with your life. Start over alone and re-build. Get to know yourself better. Maybe one day, Brian will be ready to let you back in, maybe not, but at least you'll be on stable ground yourself. And you can be there for your kids.

Be strong enough to be present in their life. That's all you can do." I heard sorrow in her voice.

It all sounded reasonable and logical but wasn't what I wanted. It was all or nothing. "You're right. Thanks for letting me just drop in. I have to get going." I set my coffee down and stood up.

"Don't leave. I didn't want to upset you. I'm just being honest. Please, at least finish your coffee. I haven't seen you in so long. Where are you even going to go?"

I smiled at her. "April, you're so sweet and kind and loving. Thank you. Thank you for being there for me, especially now when I've done nothing to deserve it. I wish I'd kept in touch better."

"Where are you going? Just stay, for the night at least. Make yourself at home here. I get back from work around six."

"Thanks, but I've got some more thinking to do. I'll call you soon." I gave her a big hug and walked back to the car that I'd pretty much stolen from Scott. I called Brian when I got in the car but he didn't answer. I had more messages from Scott but didn't bother listening to them.

I sent Brian a text. *Please, if there's any hope or a possibility that we can work, please, call me back. I love you. I'm sorry. I need you and the kids. I want to fix this!*

Now, you're all caught up with my life. I'm in deep shit if you haven't already picked up on it. It doesn't look like Brian will take me back, and Scott isn't an option anymore. He's finally stopped calling, but he did send me a text saying he was reporting me as a missing person if I didn't call him back soon. I'm still ignoring him. He'll bounce back I'm sure. I'm just hoping he really isn't as crazy as Mia said.

I'm kind of at the end of the road here. As great advice as April gave me, I don't see that as a viable option for me. I want my old life back—all of it.

I've spent the past three days sleeping in my car like a homeless person, and I still haven't heard from Brian. My mother has called to see where I am but I haven't responded to her either. So, I guess there's only one thing left for me to do.

18

Reap What You Sow

I had hit rock bottom. After five days of driving around aimlessly, I ended up back home with my mom. That lasted a whopping two days before I wanted to rip my hair out from the incessant nagging and commotion my siblings brought in and out of the house.

When I finally left my mom's, I returned to San Antonio. I had to give Scott's car back before he reported it stolen. The last thing I needed was an arrest on my record for grand theft auto. I left it in the condo's parking garage and made sure the doorman sent the keys to Scott a small note.

Thanks for everything. I'm sorry, but I have to be on my own.

Not sure how he took it, but I never looked back. I'd heard from the few mutual friends we'd had that he was living the high life. So high in fact, he'd landed himself in a first-class rehab. He lost his job in San Antonio and had moved back home to help with his family's business.

Next stop was a visit to Brian. I took a taxi to the base and waited outside my old home for him, careful to avoid eye-contact with any of our neighbors.

Brian pulled up. It even sounded like the gravel hated me. He got out of the car, and I stood up.

"What are you doing here? The kids haven't seen you, have they?"

I shook timidly. "I've been waiting outside. Your mom doesn't even know I'm out here."

"Well, what do you want?"

"I signed the divorce papers. If that's really what you want," I said handing the envelope he'd given me a week ago.

He grabbed them slowly and sat on the step with his head down. "No. I've never wanted a divorce, but I feel like you haven't given me a choice. You left, and life has gone on without you. What about the parental rights?" The softness in his voice disappeared.

"Brian, I won't sign those. If you want your divorce, I won't fight it. I can't, and won't give up my kids again. I just can't," I said through tears.

He just sat there, staring at a lone beetle making its way across the sidewalk.

I broke the silence. "I am willing to do anything to make our marriage work. I meant what I said before. I will go to counseling alone, with you, with your parents even. I know they hate me. I'm not saying we'll be happy overnight but we can start over. We can rebuild us. Don't you think we're worth a shot? The kids deserve that."

He looked at me for the first time since he'd sat down. "They deserve everything. They deserve two parents who love them and would never just abandon them. I deserve a wife who loves and trusts me unconditionally. We took vows. I was supposed to be your best friend. I'm not saying I'm perfect and without fault, but you never gave me a chance to help you through your pain. I'm sorry, but I'm going to proceed with the divorce. We can discuss custody arrangements later," he said as he got up to go inside.

I stood there dumbfounded. I truly believed we had a small glimmer of hope. That we could piece together the shattered glass I'd created. I was wrong.

With no home, no money, and no idea how to fix my life, I walked to the on-base chapel and did what I hadn't done in years. I prayed.

Prayed for forgiveness. Prayed Brian's heart would soften and eventually forgive me. Prayed for my children's happiness. Prayed for healing. I desperately wanted a sign but nothing came.

I left disappointed. Scott hadn't cut my phone or credit cards off yet so I picked up my phone and texted April.

"Mind if I stay with you for a while???"

She replied immediately. "Door's always open. I'll make up the guest room."

I booked my bus ticket, let her know when to pick me up, and got on my way.

April picked me up right on time. I was grateful. 3 hours on a bus when you've had your life implode takes a toll on someone.

She greeted me with a big hug. "I'm so glad you came back. I've been really worried about you."

"Thanks. Listen, I just want to let you know how much this means to me. I don't plan on staying long. Just long enough to get my shit together. I swear."

"Don't even worry about it. Whatever you need, just say the word," she said smiling.

As we drove to her house, I closed my eyes, took a few deep breaths, and began nodding off to sleep. *Tomorrow was a new day. Tomorrow I'd begin the process of rebuilding. Tomorrow would bring hope in some way*, I thought.

EPILOGUE

Here I am! Alive, breathing, and fairly functional three years later. A lot has happened in those three years. I'd love to say Brian and I reconciled, but sadly, we haven't. I'm OK with that now. We are, however, successfully co-parenting.

I had saved enough money after staying with April for nearly six months for a small apartment and cheap car. She helped me get a job at her company in the human resources department. It wasn't anything I wanted to do, but it was a job and paid well, especially for someone with no work experience or degree.

I entered counseling at a non-denominational, contemporary church. I finally began to lean on God and those around me. Brian even attended some of the sessions with me. We needed to work together for the sake of our children. It also gave him the opportunity to see I was trying and making positive changes.

To say our first few sessions were rough is an understatement. Next to losing Joseph, having to face the gravity of what I had done and the pain I caused was the most difficult thing I had to endure. Brian had been shattered by my actions. Nina was cautiously happy about me being around more, although she still didn't understand why we couldn't all live together. Jacob barely knew who I was. It was a blessing in disguise. He hadn't known or understood the pain of his mother tearing his family apart. Re-building a friendship with Brian for the sake of our children, at the least, has been complex, tough and, at times, awkward, but it's a work in progress and gets better each day that passes.

Brian opted to get out of the Air Force and fly commercial instead as a way to make sure the kids would have consistency. I eventually relocated to San Antonio to be in the same city as Brian and the kids. While he still has primary custody, we do share a pretty equal amount of time with the kids.

Our situation is certainly not ideal, but it's working. I'm on stable ground again. I've made amends with my former in-laws. I have a great support system. April and I are closer than ever. Unfortunately, and understandably, Mia keeps her distance from me but has kept in touch with April. And, I even finished my degree. I found a job at a local non-profit geared at helping single-parents get back on their feet. My personal experience has helped me related to these parents more than I ever could have imagined, even though I wish I couldn't.

I'm hopeful for the future. I'm hopeful for my children. And, I'm hopeful that Brian and I both find happiness, even if it is with other people. I don't know what will happen, but I know everything will end up the way it's supposed to be.

Printed in the United States
By Bookmasters